Second Chance
SISTER

Mary —
The sisters are
back! Hope you enjoy.
Thank you so
much for your support.
Sue

SUE HORNER

Second Chance Sister
Copyright © 2018 by Sue Horner

ISBN 978-0-9912177-1-7

Library of Congress Control Number: 2018947507

Published by:

ROSU Publishing
Roswell, GA USA

Chapter 1

Alicia Lawrence, known by Ali to family and friends, laced up her yellow and orange athletic shoes, put her phone in her shorts pocket, and left her house on Plum Court in Willoughby, Georgia. Her faithful Miniature Schnauzer Roxie, looked out from the bay window of the kitchen, and whimpered as she watched her owner leave.

Ali jogged onto Willoughby Lane and accelerated her pace. This was a pleasant time of year—early May before humidity intruded later in the month. She waved to longtime neighbor Mr. Bigelow who was walking his rescued Great Dane Zoe, or rather Zoe was walking Mr. Bigelow. "How's my favorite redhead? Are you competing with your sister for the Miss Skinny title?" the elderly gentleman called out.

She acknowledged him with a wave and muttered, "If I don't kill myself first."

A variety of large and small dogs, with their owners, populated the street. A cycling club whizzed by and left a rainbow blur of their colorful shirts and helmets. Several coffee drinkers outside the Provision Company relaxed on benches as they read newspapers or talked on their phones.

Ali slowed her pace at the crosswalk and wiped her forehead with an already damp wristband. She stopped to search pockets for a tissue to wipe her nose and watery eyes. Without success, she improvised with the hem of her shirt. The dreaded spring invader, aka pollen, had arrived several weeks ago. This was the price Atlanta paid for the abundance of trees, foliage, and warm temperatures. Cars, decks, patios, and people were the recipients of the ubiquitous troublemaker.

Ali stopped in front of the shuttered Maggie's Tea Room and stared at the "for sale" sign. Her thoughts drifted to her deceased friend Maggie Stratford who had been Ali's stalwart cheerleader. She often told Ali to stop walking in her older sister Janelle's shadow. "You are the better person Alicia Maureen Lawrence. Stop whining and accept Janelle for who she is, warts and all."

Easier said than done.

Enticing aromas from the Sugar Shack, a previous favorite haunt of the former chubby Ali, distracted her, but she kept running. She had overcome her ham-biscuit-pimento cheese temptation. Most of the time.

She increased her pace and after a few blocks, reached Books in the Nook. The owner and friend, Diane, was trimming glistening golden forsythia branches lining the pathway to the store. She put the shears down and hollered, "Have you seen Janelle's Facebook page?"

Ali slowed to jogging in place. "Janelle doesn't do Facebook," she hollered.

"She does now, and you'd better check it out. You won't like it one bit." Diane resumed her gardening chore.

"Thanks. I guess." Ali continued her route for several blocks. Vibrant purple Eastern redbud trees canopied Willoughby Lane, which added to the street's picturesque charm.

Ali stopped in front of Kitchen Bliss, the store she and her husband Matt had purchased two years ago, to catch her breath. Ali didn't want to enter. She preferred to return home and work on story ideas

2

for the second novel she and her sister had agreed to write. Matt had complained Ali no longer showed interest in the store. Perhaps a quick visit would pacify him.

As she entered, the bell over the door jingled and a whiff of freshly brewed hazelnut coffee greeted her. "No coffee today, Bailey, I need water," she said to the teenage part-time employee who stood behind the counter.

Bailey claimed she ate like a horse, but her spaghetti-thin figure made Ali wonder. She was six-feet tall with dark hair flowing past her shoulders.

Ali filled a paper cup and took a swig. "Tastes good," she said.

"He's in the back, Mrs. Lawrence," Bailey said.

Ali entered Matt's tiny storeroom/office and squatted on a stool while he finished a phone call. "You seemed a little down this a.m. Everything okay?" she asked.

"I wish my wife wasn't always holed up writing. When we bought this store, we agreed to work together, a joint venture. Plus, you're a superb salesperson. You make sure everyone who enters leaves with a purchase. Or, at least a free cup of coffee and a favorable impression of Kitchen Bliss."

Ali raised her eyebrows. "You're doing what you want to do—own a business. I'm doing what I want—write another novel."

Matt said, "Don't forget about tonight. We have the event at Barrington Hall. A chance for you to show off your new body."

She stood when Matt complimented her.

Matt eyed her up and down and gave a wolfish whistle. No way would Ali forget tonight—a fundraiser sponsored by the Willoughby Merchants Association. She considered the event her coming out party to show off her weight loss. She had purchased a figure hugging Little Black Dress and black strappy stiletto heels. When she had made the purchases a month ago, the zipper on the back of the dress hesitated midway. With any luck, the hours she spent at the gym had reduced jiggling back fat, providing an easy ride for the zipper tonight.

Best friend Ellen had suggested she try shapewear. Ali balked at the idea at first, but she had made a trip to Macy's at North Point Mall and bought a bodysuit for insurance.

Ali returned home, slumped on the steps of the front porch, untied her shoes, and wiped her forehead with her wristband. She entered the house and picked up whining Roxie. "Let me run one race. To prove I can do it. You slow me down, little one." Ali had decided the goal of running the Peachtree Road Race was incentive to continue her exercise and weight loss plan.

Roxie did not seem appeased and trotted to her bed underneath the window in the kitchen.

"Now, let's see what trouble Janelle is brewing on Facebook." Ali sat at the kitchen table and opened her laptop. She searched for Janelle Jennings on Facebook.com. As Diane had warned, a glamorous picture of Janelle at a beachfront location confronted Ali. "What?" Ali's voice attracted Roxie's attention who ran to her side.

Ali's cell phone chirped. She took it out of her pocket and glanced at the caller i.d. "This is one call I don't want to take."

"I know you're there. Please pick up. We must talk," the voice on the other end said.

"You've done enough talking, Sis," Ali said to the phone without answering. She returned to reading Janelle's Facebook posts. Her jaw tightened as she read the announcement that Janelle's next novel would be without Ali.

"What a liar," Ali said aloud. Janelle had been pressuring Ali to write with her again since the success of their novel *Broken Bones-Broken Promises.* Ali agreed to the proposition if Janelle contributed to the partnership. Janelle had promised to deliver story ideas to Ali months ago, but none had materialized. For a few minutes, Ali thought about the prospect of writing solo. "Guess Janelle and I will go our separate ways, Roxie. No more Janelle. Yeah!"

Ali's euphoria was short-lived.

A novel. 80,000 words? By myself?

Ali took a deep breath and smiled at Roxie. "A daunting thought, but I can do it."

One of her mother's favorite sayings came to mind: Be careful what you wish for because it might come true.

Chapter 2

Janelle Jennings lounged in the living room of the Casa Ybel suite she had rented for a month on Sanibel Island, Florida. This trip would max out her credit cards, but she'd worry about that later. An advance from her publisher would ease her financial woes.

She gazed out the sliding glass door and observed the gentle waves of the Gulf of Mexico creep toward the white sand shimmering in the noon sun. She'd be contented to stay in this paradise for another month or two except the hot Florida weather was forcing her to leave. Her phone binged.

The caller avoided pleasantries. "Your publisher is nervous, Janelle. He wants to see the first hundred pages or some proof you and Ali are working on a novel. He won't send either one of you an advance until he sees your work to date."

No advance?

She took a sip of wine.

"Did you hear me, Janelle? Are you there?"

"I'm surprised at you, Kenny. Have I ever let you or my almighty publisher down? I'm working on it."

Ken Luzi had been Janelle's agent, publicist, and sounding board since she published her first book, *The Secret of High Mountain Love,* twenty years ago.

"I hate nagging you. I'll call Ali."

"No, no. Don't call Ali. You'll receive something soon."

"Keep in touch." He hung up.

Janelle had taken a chance by posting on Facebook, but she was desperate to attract her sister's attention. Emails, texts, and phone calls had gone unanswered. Janelle knew why. She never produced story ideas for their unnamed novel that she had promised Ali. Janelle felt brain dead, unfocused, nervous, stressed out. She wanted to explain her state of mind to Ali. Facebook seemed like a good idea. . .at the time.

Janelle decided to put her worries on hold for today and especially for tonight. She moved from the living room toward the partially opened sliding glass door facing the balcony. She attempted to open it fully with her foot and held her phone in one hand and the wine glass in the other. Inching forward, she lost her balance and jammed her toe into the track of the door. "Ow. Damn that hurt," she said as she sloshed wine on the terracotta floor.

She put the phone and the glass down and pushed the door aside with her hand. Janelle picked up the glass and her phone, stepped over the puddle, and stood at the railing of the balcony, which overlooked the lapis lazuli sea. The hem of her white chiffon tea dress floated with the warm balmy breeze. She took a deep breath of the cleansing saltwater air before moving to an adjacent chaise lounge.

Her phone rang. She looked at the caller i.d. before she answered. "Hey, my fave niece. Where are you?"

"Still at school. Finals this week," Kayla Lawrence said.

"Study hard. By the way, I'm coming to Willoughby soon."

"I need your help, Aunt Janelle."

"I'll do anything for you. You're my one and only niece." Despite Janelle's four marriages and four divorces, she had no children. Her niece was the closest she had to a daughter.

"Long story. I need a little money."

"Does your mother know you're asking me?"

Kayla's silence answered Janelle's question. "I made a promise to your mother—no interference or overriding her rules. She claims I'm a negative influence. Why she thinks that, I have no idea."

"Mom thinks I'm still a kid. She'd be shocked if she knew all the non-kid things I've been doing in college."

"We need to talk about those things. You don't want to grow up too fast."

"Janelle, *I am* grown up."

"What's with the 'Janelle'? I'm *Aunt* Janelle."

"Okay, Auntie."

"I prefer aunt."

"Aunt, Auntie, Janelle, what the hell! You're the only one who can help me."

"And what's with this language?"

"You've become just like Mom. Forget it."

"Now hold on. Why do you need money?" Janelle put her wine glass down and stood, leaning on the ledge of the balcony.

"Airfare to Italy. Sort of a public service project. Near Florence."

"When are you planning this trip?"

"As soon as I come up with the money."

"How much do you need?"

"About $4,000 should do it."

"Seems like planning would have been appropriate."

"You're my last resort. Gramps said no, and I didn't dare ask Nana because she would tell Mom and Dad and I'd be in trouble. They want me to work in the store all summer. All summer!"

"Sounds fishy. Why would your parents prevent you from a public service project? Your mother's the queen of volunteerism. What's the whole story? Is there a boy involved?"

"Sort of," Kayla mumbled.

"I said I would think about it. No guarantees. Our secret." She paused. "Has your mother said anything about me? About writing another book with me?"

"Dad says all she does is write or at least she spends a bunch of time sitting at her computer. Mom and I don't talk much anymore. She used to bug me constantly. Wait a second. What's Mom's writing have to do with your loaning me money?"

"I need a little information from you—quid pro quo."

"I guess Mom's right for once. You are a schemer."

"I meant…never mind. We'll talk when we're both in Will—"

Too late. Kayla disconnected.

Janelle returned to the chaise lounge and stared at her phone. She loved her niece as much as the characters in the eighteen novels she had written. . .nineteen. . .if she counted the one she wrote with Ali. Her books were her children.

Giving, or even loaning, Kayla money was not a good idea. Janelle didn't want to irritate her sister. Only Ali knew the secret that still gnawed at Janelle's stomach. Janelle's eighteen books were written under a cloak of secrecy, a secret she shared with her sister and Phoebe. Of course, Phoebe. Deceased Phoebe Patterson was Janelle's ghost-writer. Janelle never wished her old high school English teacher death, in fact, she liked Phoebe. They shared common traits. They were both determined and outspoken. With Phoebe gone, after a bad fall in the parking lot of the Willoughby Library, their secret remained safe. Faithful, loyal younger sister Ali vowed never to reveal the truth.

Money was another obstacle preventing Janelle to help her niece. Janelle's financial situation was on the shaky side. She needed the money another best seller would provide. Warnings from her financial advisor that she was spending too much money went unheeded and now she was suffering the consequences. If she sold some of her portfolio, she would pay a high tax penalty.

Janelle left the balcony and retreated to the bar in the luxurious living room to survey the assortment of liquor and wine she had requested from room service when she checked in. Gin, vodka, tequila, sparkling wine. She filled a shot glass with tequila, lifted it to her lips, and tossed it down. She filled another shot glass and returned to the balcony where she set it on the ledge. She changed her mind and returned the glass to the bar.

Janelle heard a knock on the door. She checked her lipstick in the mirror above the bar, fluffed her hair, and answered the door.

"I've been counting the hours," she said to the male visitor.

"I hope you won't be disappointed, Mia Bella," he said.

* * *

Janelle found a secluded spot at the Southwest Florida International airport terminal before her flight to ATL. She preferred waiting for a flight in an airline's members-only lounge rather than public spaces, but there was none here. She removed her oversized sunglasses and her Eugenia Kim floppy sunhat embroidered with "do not disturb." The hat had shielded her from fans who might have recognized her. Never a smart idea to have a hangover while meeting fans. They might acquire the wrong idea. Regrettably, she had consumed more than her share of margaritas and Miami Vices during her stay in Florida. Janelle unhooked the button on her pants, so she could breathe. Tortilla chips and guac were making themselves noticed.

Her phone binged. She didn't recognize the number and let the call go to voicemail. She listened to the message. "Hello, gorgeous. Remember me? We were seatmates on the flight to New York last month. I've wrapped up my business here and am heading to Atlanta tomorrow. Was hoping we could meet."

Janelle stared at the message deciding what action to take. She would have free time in boring Willoughby. But…a more fascinating and more handsome man was pursuing Janelle and he was waiting for her in Willoughby. She deleted the voicemail.

Chapter 3

Ali returned home from her daily morning jog and walked up the white and purple impatiens-lined pathway with her hands on her hips, trying to catch her breath. She let Roxie out of the house before she sat on the porch steps to remove her shoes. Her phone alerted her to a text. Matt sent her a message forwarded from Kayla.

> Kayla: i've got a great idea for my summer
> vacation. more later. be home soon

A call to Ali from Matt followed the text.

"Did you read Kayla's—?"

"She's supposed to work in Kitchen Bliss for the summer."

"Yeah, but what does this daughter of ours have in mind?" Matt asked.

Lately, Kayla was more Matt's daughter than Ali's. Kayla didn't reveal any information about her life at school to her mother. Ali attributed this as payback for the years Ali hovered. Matt delivered *Kayla Updates*, edited to prevent overreaction by Mom. "I know you're counting on her," Ali said.

"She promised. Kayla won't break a promise," Matt said. "I'm confident she'll work with me at the store."

"I hope you're right, becau—"

"I know. You don't have time to help because you want to write another novel with your sister. Beats me why you want to put yourself through that misery again."

"It's a moot point about writing with Janelle. She posted on Facebook she's going to write solo. Was news to me."

"That should make you happy. Right?"

"I suppose."

"I texted Kayla and asked what 'soon' meant. I'll let you know if she answers," Matt said.

After the success of her first novel, one she co-authored with her sister, Ali thought her writing career was completed, at least writing with her sister. She'd rather roll around naked in a colony of fire ants than spend one more hour with Janelle arguing over which four letter word a character should use or which sexual position Janelle wanted to detail. However, due to pleading and begging by Janelle, Ali had relented to writing another novel together.

Janelle's work ethic was non-existent. Despite Ali's requests that they Skype to share story ideas and work on the new novel, Janelle was hard to track down. She did pop into Willoughby on two occasions and that was the only time they accomplished meaningful work.

Ali's phone binged a text message.

Matt: She's home in five minutes

Before Ali removed her sneakers, the vroom of a motorcycle caught her attention. "Holy Moley! Somebody needs a muffler." Roxie left Ali's side and ran for shelter underneath a pink azalea bush.

As the sound intensified, Ali covered her ears with her hands. The telltale buzzing in her ears signaled trouble. Ali knew the noise in her ears had nothing to do with the motorcycle and everything to do with the sharp pain in her gut about who might be driving it or who was riding in the passenger seat. A motorcycle-riding boyfriend? Ali was deathly afraid of motorcycles and hoped her daughter was not on the back of this one.

The offending motorcycle stopped at the end of the driveway. The passenger got off the bike, removed the helmet, and shook loose dark brown tresses with rainbow highlights before she handed the helmet to the driver. Driver and passenger hugged then the bike zoomed away.

Roxie yelped a greeting and trotted to Kayla. "Hi, little one. Did you miss me? I missed you so much." Kayla set her backpack on the ground and picked up her canine sibling.

Ali stood as still as granite from nearby Stone Mountain. The plan had been to pick up Kayla and her belongings from her dorm at the University of Georgia in Athens. Evidently, the plan had changed.

Ali regained her composure and shouted Kayla's name as she ran with unlaced shoes to meet her daughter. She tripped and fell into Kayla's arms. "Whoops," they both said and giggled in unison. As mother and daughter embraced, smothered Roxie wriggled in the middle. They untangled Roxie in response to the dog's whining plea for mercy and placed her on the ground.

"What a wonderful surprise. Everything okay?"

"Mom. Why do you always think the worst?" Kayla said as she helped her mother stand. "Thought I'd save you the time and trouble, so I accepted my friend Taylor's offer to bring me home."

"Motorcycles are—"

"I know. Unsafe. But here I am. Not a scratch on me." Kayla twirled around in a circle.

"What about all your stuff?"

"Another friend will watch everything. For now." She picked up her backpack.

"But—"

Kayla kissed her mother on the cheek, diffusing a possible argument.

Ali touched pieces of Kayla's colored hair and said, "Cute. Rainbow. Let's go inside and you can tell me about your summer—besides working in Kitchen Bliss."

"Let's wait until Dad's home." She brushed her mother's arm away as they entered the house. Kayla set her backpack on the floor.

Ali stared at her daughter who had inherited her height, thin frame, and gorgeous straight hair from her aunt and her maternal grandmother. Not from Ali.

"I'm curious about your plans," Ali said.

Before Kayla had a chance to answer, Matt arrived. "I got here as fast as I could," he said, breathless from jogging the few blocks from Kitchen Bliss. He was still wearing the store's green apron. "I thought we were going to pick you up at school?"

"Who was on the motorcycle? Is that the big announcement? A new boyfriend? You should have introduced us, Kayla," Ali said.

"No boyfriend. Taylor's a girl."

"Give her a break, babe. She just got home," Matt said. "Your room is ready and waiting for you," he said with a bow. "I sure missed you, princess." He kissed the top of her head.

"Thanks, Dad. I missed you, too." She gave her dad a hug. "Going to take a quick shower. Be right back." Kayla took her backpack off the floor and jogged upstairs with Roxie trailing.

"Are you hungry? Thirsty?" Ali hollered. "Glad to see you, too," she said to an unresponsive Kayla. She looked at Matt. "She's different."

"Weren't you? After your freshman year?"

"I should go upstairs and find out what her great summer plan is."

Matt took Ali's elbow. "Leave her alone. You'll have the summer to interrogate her." He kissed her cheek. "I'm going to take a shower."

Chapter 4

The honking of a horn drew Ali to the front porch where she observed her father, Ed Withrow, as he arrived driving his SUV. He veered to the right of the house, slammed on the brakes, and stopped on the grass within inches of hitting the garage.

"Not the Jane Austin roses!" Virginia Withrow, a passenger in the vehicle and Ali's mother, said loud enough for the entire neighborhood to hear. Virginia, a Master Gardener, was protective of all flowers, even if they were in someone else's yard.

Richard Petty unhooked his seat belt and exited the vehicle. "Nothing wrong with my driving, Virginia. And, I didn't come near the blasted roses," he said. "Where's Kayla? Can't wait to see my only grandchild."

"That husband of mine. Someone should take away his driver's license. He scares me to death." A wide-brimmed Hampton hat served to shade Virginia's luminescent skin, which was rarely the recipient of Atlanta's unforgiving sun. She removed the hat and patted her salon-styled dark hair, which had no signs of incipient gray waiting to spring forth.

"Go inside, everyone. We need a cool drink."

"How about a manhattan?" Ed asked as he joined his wife and daughter in the kitchen.

"Too early. I swear, you start drinking earlier every day," Virginia said.

"How did you know Kayla was coming home?" Ali asked her parents.

"This texting thing is sure handy. Now that I learned how to use it," Ed said.

"Everyone received texts except the mother," Ali said.

Ed moved to the bar in the living room. "Who brought her here? I thought you were going to Athens next week to pack her up." He dropped a maraschino cherry into his cocktail. "Oops." Red cherry juice splattered onto his white T-shirt. "Sit down and relax, Gingersnap," Ed called out to Ali. "Quit pacing. She's easier to deal with than you and your sister were."

Virginia entered the living room carrying a tray with a pitcher of iced tea and glasses. "Janelle and Ali were fine while they lived at home. It's their adulthood that's rampant with tension." Virginia put the tray on the table in front of the sofa and sat.

"What about tension?" Kayla said. She had wrapped her wet hair in a white towel shaped like a turban. Her oversized red and black University of Georgia bulldog T-shirt hung over black yoga pants. "I've missed you, Nana and Gramps." She embraced her grandfather and took a seat on the sofa next to her grandmother. Ali sat across from the pair.

"Don't keep us in suspense. What's your plan for the summer? Don't forget that you promised to work at the store," Ali said.

"What plan?" Virginia chimed in.

"Let her talk," Ed said.

"Gramps, is that one of your manhattans? I'll have one, too."

"How about a beer instead? Bet you've had practice drinking beer in college," Ed said. "Ever tried watchamacallit, beer bong? Seen it on YouTube. Looks like fun."

"Don't encourage irresponsible underage alcohol consumption," Virginia said. "What's your tube? Whose tube?"

Kayla skipped to the kitchen and returned with a bottle of Sweet Water 420. She took a swig and placed the bottle on the coffee table.

Virginia picked up the cold bottle and placed it on a coaster. "You are so beautiful, Kayla. You could be Janelle's daughter."

Ali squirmed.

"My announcement is I'm leaving Willoughby for the summer. I've moved my things into an apartment off campus with some friends where I'll live next semester. The rent doesn't cost much split three ways and I thought you and Dad could pay my share while I'm away." She eyeballed her mother.

"Apartment? Away? Where?" Ali asked.

"I've decided to spend the summer doing something positive for the world. Something like the Peace Corps. I've lived a spoiled life and I want to repay society."

"Where?" Ali asked.

"Italy."

"The Peace Corps? I thought you were going to say Guatemala, Malaysia. . .but Italy?"

Kayla avoided eye contact with her mother and fiddled with her nails.

"Honey, we shouldn't pay rent on an apartment you won't use," Ali said.

"I promised my roommates."

"Let's talk about it later. I'm so glad you're home." Ali stood and moved to the sofa next to Kayla. She put her arm around her daughter who inched away.

"Aunt Janelle said she *might* help me," Kayla said. "*She* loves me."

"Janelle said she would help you with what? Rent for an apartment you won't be living in or a trip to Italy to help the impoverished, illiterate Italians?" Ali said.

"And your parents and your grandparents love you, too." Virginia said.

"Didn't we discuss your staying here this summer, so you could help your dad in Kitchen Bliss? He's counting on it. He didn't hire summer help except Bailey and she's part-time."

"*I* never committed to staying here. That was *your* idea."

"We never committed to paying your rent. Strike that. We never committed to paying rent for your friends," Ali said.

Kayla joined Ed who hadn't moved from his post at the bar. "Why is she so mean, Gramps?"

"She's not mean, sweet pea. She's a responsible parent."

"Her parenting sucks." She turned to face her mother. "Why can't *you* work at the store, Mom? You've nothing else to do except sit at your computer all day and all your volunteer stuff." She stomped upstairs.

"Oh, my," Virginia said. "This homecoming is not going well."

Ali grabbed her stomach and closed her eyes. "I need a Tums."

Ed moved toward Ali. "Kayla's growing up and wants to assert herself. Stay calm. She'll come around."

Ali met her dad's soft blue eyes and made a crooked smile. She knew if she spoke, the tears would fall in torrents. A loving and close relationship with her daughter wasn't going to happen today.

Ali checked her Fitbit for the time. "Guess I better dress for the fundraiser. I hate to leave Kayla alone the first night she's home."

"How about I volunteer to stay with her? I detest going to these things," Ed said. "Besides I want to hear more about the Peace Corps in Italy."

"You're coming with me," Virginia said. "Kayla might appreciate the time by herself. Let's go home and get dressed."

"I hope Kayla's attitude isn't a precursor to our summer," Ali said.

"If it is, it's going to be a hot one," Virginia said.

Chapter 5

"What do you think of this dress?" Ali asked as she met Matt in the kitchen. "Not too tight?"

"Wow! Hot mamma." Matt twirled his wife around, caught her, and planted a sloppy kiss on her red-stained lips. He dipped her so her recently straightened auburn hair grazed the floor. "Uh-oh. Guess I smeared your lipstick." He smacked his lips together. "Tastes good. You smell good, too."

"Don't blame me if we're late," Ali said. She sashayed to the bathroom. She took a quick glance over her shoulder to make sure Matt was viewing her newly sculpted butt.

"I sure like your new look," he called out.

"What look?" Kayla asked as she descended the stairway. She followed her mother into the bathroom. "Is that you, Mom? You must be kidding." Kayla eyed her mother's dress and shoes. "Your makeup's okay. You never wear enough. The dress? A little tight. Can you walk in those shoes?"

"I've been starving myself for months, squeezed into this straight-jacket, and you can't say anything complimentary. Gee, thanks a lot, girlfriend." She gave Kayla a playful nudge.

Kayla shook her head and joined Matt in the kitchen who was sitting at the counter drinking a glass of water. "She's trying to copy—"

"You can *think* whatever you want, Kayla, but don't *say* it. Your mother wouldn't like the comparison with her sister."

"True though."

"You have to admit she looks good," Matt said.

"Mom doesn't dress like that. I don't like it one bit." Kayla plodded to the refrigerator; she took out a glass container and removed the lid. "Guess this is my dinner. Leftover tuna salad." She took a fork from a drawer. She ate standing with her back against the sink facing her father.

"Mom can never be you know who. No matter how hard she tries," Kayla said.

"Let's give her a little slack. She's been dedicated to an exercise and diet regimen, which I guess I should follow, too." He patted his stomach. Matt approached his daughter and kissed the top of her head. "Hate to leave you on your first night home, princess."

"No worries, Dad. Have fun. Don't stay out past your curfew. I wouldn't want to ground you."

He gave her a thumbs-up, picked up his jacket from a bar stool, and left for the garage to turn the air on in his SUV.

While in the bathroom, Ali glanced in the mirror to approve the shopping decision she had made at Marshall's where she had found a designer dress at a reduced price. Black sling back Manolo Blahniks were no bargain but worth the expense. The shoes made her feel elegant and sexy. She'd never tell Matt how much the stilettos cost, even if it was her money earned from writing *Broken Promises*—her one and only novel, to date. She fixed her lipstick, took it and a small mirror, and met Matt in the driveway.

"Thanks for turning the air on." She handed him the lipstick and mirror, which he put in his jacket pocket.

"Wouldn't want my date to have sweat marks on her new dress."

"Appreciated."

Matt put the car in drive and they left the house.

"Kayla doesn't approve of your new appearance."

"I refrained from saying I don't like blue, green, and pink streaks in her hair. . .even though I told her they were cute."

Ali re-checked her makeup and lipstick in the visor mirror during the short ride to her parents' home.

"Don't worry. You look terrific," Matt said.

She turned to her husband and smiled.

Ed and Virginia were waiting on the front porch. Virginia wore a champagne beige sheath and jacket combo and Ed wore gray dress pants and a navy-blue blazer. His jacket was unbuttoned, and his necktie was loose.

At Barrington Hall, male and female servers dressed in white shirts and black pants met the attendees at the front door holding silver trays of sparkling wine flutes.

"Still off alcohol?" Matt asked.

"Guess a glass or two won't hurt." They took their glasses and circulated the room filled with other Willoughby merchants, the city council, and local government officials. Comments such as "you look fabulous, girl," greeted Ali.

Ed found a chair on the veranda not far from the hors d'oeuvre table and plunked down with a plate of food in his lap. Virginia joined her garden club friends.

Ali wasn't accustomed to an onslaught of compliments about her appearance. She was starting to become self-conscious. After a second glass of wine, it was time to visit the ladies' room.

Matt took her glass. "I'll be on the veranda. Trying to find your dad."

Once in the stall, she struggled to pull down her shapewear and made loud noises as she tried to remove it. "Oh, damn," she said.

"You okay in there, Ali? I was behind you when you walked in. You were in a hurry," friend Jill said. "Stomach problems?"

"No. Having trouble pulling down this blasted girdle. Why did I think I could squeeze myself into this ridiculous dress?"

"Girlfriend, we don't call them girdles anymore. You want some help?"

To maneuver herself out of the undergarment, Ali lost her balance, and landed on the floor on her butt with her legs spread. "Ow!"

"Open the door," Jill said.

Ali reached for the lock and let her friend squeeze in. Jill pulled her to a standing position and yanked on the offending garment.

Ali let out a huge sound of relief. "Just in time."

Jill closed the door. "Stop competing with your sister. Let's face it; you'll never be a size two."

Her friend's candid remark struck Ali like a slap in the face. She scrunched up her lips in a pout and was glad Jill couldn't see her childish expression.

"None of us can be a size two. Can't measure happiness by a dress size. Come out of there and join the party and show off your new body," Jill said.

Ali collected herself and searched for Matt on the veranda.

"Where have you been?"

"A little trouble in the underwear department."

"Anything I can help you with?" he said with a wicked smile.

"Not now. Later." She winked at her husband.

Several friends approached the couple. "When will we read another best seller from the sisters of Willoughby?" someone asked.

"Don't know," was Ali's curt answer.

Someone else asked if the sisters would be writing together. Ali said, "Hell, no," and finished her third glass of sparkling wine.

Chapter 6

Kayla peered through the front door window as her parents drove away. She returned to her bedroom with Roxie close behind and logged on to her laptop. She Googled "emeralds."

"What the?" she said as she scrolled through the various prices. $57,000, $48,000, $23,000.

Kayla continued her search and found some green jewels in the hundreds of dollars price range, which wouldn't come close to what she needed. She'd have to have the gem appraised before she sold it.

Kayla couldn't remember where she had stashed the jewel. She surveyed her room for possible hiding spots. Ali had wanted to put the item in the family's safe deposit box at the bank, but Kayla had balked. She wanted treatment as an adult who could keep track of her belongings and guard them from theft.

An obvious choice was the jewelry box on top of her dresser. No luck. A search of the closet and dresser drawers yielded no result.

She ran out of ideas, so she decided on another type of search and typed Travelocity.com. Depending on how many stops the flight made and because she was booking at the last minute, she might need as much as $4,000 for a flight to Florence. And, would have to add money for a place to stay. She searched "hostels in Italy" and "cheap hotels in Italy." She found many inexpensive options.

Now, to find the emerald. She rifled through the drawers in her nightstand. A photo of her and her family taken on a beach sat on the white antique desk Virginia had given her. "The beach!"

Kayla raced to the bathroom. On the countertop stood a glass jar filled with pieces of sea glass, which she had collected during family vacations to North Carolina beaches. The emerald blended with the blues and greens making it difficult to differentiate from the sea glass. She took the jar to her bedroom and dumped the contents on her bed. Roxie jumped on the bed to investigate. On top of the pile glistened the jewel.

Kayla ran her hands through her hair. "Whew!" She secured the emerald in her backpack and picked up her phone to send a text. She waited for an answer and when none came, she sent another text and waited. No answer either on FaceTime. "Darn that Luca. Why doesn't he answer?" she asked Roxie who was sitting next to her.

Kayla lay on her back staring at the ceiling fan. She thumbed her keyboard sending another text, this time to a different person.

Kayla: can we meet tomorrow?
Logan: why? u don't care romantically about me anymore
Kayla: true but I need your help
Logan: you think I'll come running to your aid
Kayla: meet me at the Sugar Shack in a.m. I'll buy coffee
Logan: BFD. want more than coffee
Kayla: what?
Logan: pimento ham biscuit. this better be important
Kayla: paramount. BFN

She searched the internet again, seeking advice on where to have a valuable object appraised.

* * *

Kayla asked her dad if she could sleep in this morning and he agreed. If she didn't come up with the money for the trip to Italy, she'd be stuck in Willoughby for weeks. Surrounded by pots and pans in Kitchen Bliss was not how she wanted to spend her precious summer vacation.

She waited until she was sure her dad had left for work. Her mother was in the backyard with Roxie and wouldn't notice if Kayla slipped out. She walked to the corner of Plum Court and waited for Logan to take her to the pawnshop.

He arrived in a metal gray Mustang convertible. "I borrowed my dad's car. Top down okay?"

"Whatever. Let's get this over."

"What about the ham and pimento cheese—"

"No time."

Logan drove to Jim's Gem on the outskirts of Willoughby.

They arrived before the pawnshop opened and waited in the parking lot with other potential customers hoping to buy, sell, or reclaim their possessions. Logan parked between a beat up red pickup and a white Lexus. The male driver of the pickup was smoking a cigarette. The female Lexus driver was sitting low. She wore a Braves baseball cap and aviator sunglasses.

"Diverse clientele," Logan, the amateur sociologist, noted.

"Everyone needs a little help sometimes," Kayla said.

A muscular man unlocked the door of the pawnshop and turned the closed sign to open. Kayla and Logan exited the Mustang and entered the store.

"Looks like the *Pawn Stars* show on TV," Logan said.

"Don't watch it."

"You should have."

The neat and clean store was crammed with an assortment of items including musical instruments, flat screen TVs, and cameras with huge lenses. Kayla moved toward the glass cases displaying jewelry and watches. She was trying to find something comparable to the emerald she had in her pocket.

A grandfatherly man with thinning gray hair wearing a black pocket T-shirt stretched over his beer belly approached the twosome. His name badge read, *Jim the Gem, owner.* "Where have I seen you? Been in here before, kids?" He stared at Kayla.

"No, sir," Kayla said as she glanced toward the floor avoiding eye contact.

"Buying or selling?" the Gem asked.

"We're selling. And, sir, I am old enough. I'm eighteen. Do you want to see my driver's license?" Logan said.

"Calm down, kid. Whatcha got?"

Kayla retrieved the emerald she had placed in a tiny white box and handed it to Jim. They moved to the glass cases where Jim pulled out a piece of black velvet and placed the emerald on it. He scrutinized it with a jeweler's loupe.

"Is this yours or hers?" Jim asked the pair.

Kayla and Logan answered "mine" and "hers."

"Do you have proof of ownership?"

"I didn't steal it," Kayla protested.

Logan shoved his elbow into Kayla's side. "I can swear her aunt gave her the jewel." He raised his right hand.

"Got it. How much do you want?"

"$4,000," Kayla said. "When do I receive the money?"

Jim examined the gem. "Hold your horses, missy. We have procedures. I must check this out. I don't want to cheat you. It could be worth more. It could be stolen. Come back tomorrow." He picked up the gem and closed his fingers around it.

Logan put his hand on top of Jim's fist. "We can't leave this valuable item with you, sir. I demand a receipt."

"I can see you're one smart kid."

Kayla and Logan exchanged a glance.

"Wait here." Jim returned with a piece of legal-sized yellow paper that read: "I hereby attest to the receipt of a large emerald from." He paused. "Put your name here." He gave a pen to Logan.

"Wait a minute. It's mine," Kayla protested.

"How old are you?" Jim said.

Kayla didn't answer.

"This piece of paper doesn't appear legal to me," Logan said.

"I'm not going to steal the damn thing. Leave. I have customers."

Jim watched them exit before he took his phone from his pocket.

"That was depressing," Logan said as they approached the Mustang.

"What do you mean?"

"Broken dreams. Someone had hoped to become a famous photographer or a saxophonist. Maybe someone else lost his job and sold a camera, which he had planned to take photos of his children with but needed the money to feed them."

Kayla turned to face Logan who was staring straight ahead. "You're pretty sensitive for a guy."

"Observant."

"You're a great person, Logan. Not many people our age would consider those things. I'm glad we're friends now instead of boyfriend-girlfriend. That was okay in high school, but we've both changed."

"Friends. Yeah." He turned the ignition on and they drove away from Jim's Gem.

Meanwhile back at the pawnshop, Jim was making a phone call.

"Hi, this is Jim from the Gem. Got a minute?"

Chapter 7

Ali was in the backyard recalling the previous night's event at Barrington Hall. She was pleased that her new physique was noticed by many of her friends and acquaintances. She did, however, regret her rude remarks about writing without her sister. *Too late now.*

Besides, what she said was the truth. No way would she write with her sister again.

Janelle still treated Ali like the little sister she could berate and criticize when they were young. If they were going to establish a partnership, it would have to be on Ali's terms meaning they were equal.

Ali went to the kitchen to prepare wontons stuffed with mango shrimp salad for a bridal shower for her friend Jill's niece when her cell phone binged. She glanced at the caller i.d. "Aw, no." She let voicemail do its work. She listened to Janelle's anguished plea.

"Ali, pick up, I know you're there. Please. I promise. Please, please, pretty please with sugar on it. My readers love me. Why can't you? Maybe I phrased the post incorrectly on Facebook?"

Ali hit the return call button. "You wear me down. I swear. What is it?"

"I'm on my way," Janelle said.

"To where?"

"Willoughby. Will arrive tomorrow. Twenty-four hours closer to my family and my dear sister, my co-author."

"Closer to your designer clothes and pricey shoes you left here," Ali muttered. "You should stay with Mother and Dad."

"I can't stay with them. Not with our parents. Mother suffocates me with attention. I'd rather be sentenced to solitary confinement like my misunderstood character Jessica Swanson in *Billionaire's Dilemma.*"

"What a terrible way to talk about our parents. They love you, Janelle, desp—"

"Despite my selfishness. Unconditional love is what you wanted to say. I'm going to make you love me. My long-term goal in life is to make you love me. Short term, not enough time. But wait. You'll see. I need a second chance. Frankly, I don't think I'm so bad. My fans adore me."

"I have fans, too."

"Of course, you have fans. Not as many as…okay, to prove to you I'm trying to change I'll stay with our parents. Anything to appease you."

Ali did a happy dance and hit the speaker button on the phone. She put the tray of empty wontons in the oven.

"I received a text from Brad Patterson. He wanted to confirm my arrival in Willoughby."

"Why?"

"He has a surprise for me. What could it be? Money? Do you think Phoebe left me money? I could use money now. What else could it be? You and Brad are close. Find out for me. Or, ask Matt to find out. They're friends." She paused and took a deep breath. "I mean will you *please* give Brad a call to pry out of him what the surprise is? I know you know."

"Take another deep breath after that rant."

"Not ranting. Curious. A trait that makes my books interesting."

"I don't know about any surprise. If I did, why would I tell you? It wouldn't be a surprise." Ali poured a glass of water. "*I* have something else, too. We need to keep our distance—you and me. Let's limit our contact to family dinners. Especially since you decided to write a book on your own without telling me."

"What?"

"Your Facebook page. Congratulations. You're writing a book without me. I thought we were still thinking about co-authorship. Too bad you didn't have the courage to tell me. I had to find out on social media."

"Let me expl—"

Ali hung up.

* * *

Ali placed a call to their mother informing Virginia she would soon have a visitor.

"Oh, no," Virginia shrieked.

"Mother, you don't understand. Janelle. Your firstborn. Your favorite daughter is honoring you with her presence."

"Alicia. She's not my favorite, but I can't have her here. I've been meaning to buy new towels and linens. She likes those 10,000 thread sheets."

Ali shook her head. "It's not 10,000."

"She's accustomed to the finest and I'm not ready. You'll have to tell her."

"Calm down, Mother." Ali walked to the microwave in the kitchen and paused to check her reflection in the glass door. At least her hair was acceptable. Janelle had convinced Ali to have her frizzy red hair straightened eliminating one less physical feature for Janelle to criticize.

After Ali's weight loss and hair improvement, there wasn't much to criticize, but Janelle would find something.

Your skin's too dry. Let me recommend the perfect moisturizer, which is a mere $225 an ounce. You can buy it online. Better buy two.

"Alicia, are you there?" her mother asked.

"Guess I can stand her for a couple of days. Is two days enough time for you to prepare for royalty, Mother?"

"Thank you, dear." Virginia sighed relief. "No sarcasm necessary."

Ali sent a text to Janelle telling her the change of plans. "You'll stay here for two nights."

Housework wasn't on Ali's to-do list today, nor had it been for a few weeks. The house could use vacuuming. She could write her name on the tops of the living room furniture. Janelle wouldn't care about the condition of the house, if the liquor cabinet was full. She grabbed the keys to her Green Monster Chevy pickup and headed out the door to Trader Joe's, but paused to send a text to Kayla:

Ali: Your aunt is arriving tomorrow. Should put you in a better mood.
Kayla: what? are you sure? why?
Ali: What's the matter with you? You're nuts about your aunt.
Kayla: sure. great. absolutely.

* * *

Janelle was tired of living out of hotel suites and planned to buy or rent a townhouse in Willoughby—maybe one on Webb Street or Goulding Place or in The Magnolias—strictly as a home base. Only problem was her financial situation, which would improve with another bestseller. Another enticing factor was that Bradley Patterson still lived in Willoughby. Why he chose to live in a small town was beyond Janelle. They had a wonderful time in Sanibel and he promised her more of the same. She knew she should return to Willoughby before some Georgia peach snagged him.

I'll play hard to get like my character Amanda Lilenthal in Harbormaster's Secret. Worked for her.

Janelle sent Brad her ETA. He answered with an apology for not meeting her due to an appointment with one of his business partners. He said he ordered a car service to pick her up.

When Janelle arrived at the top of the escalator at ATL, she searched for the limo service driver holding a sign with the code name: *Mia Bella.* The driver was one of those chatty ones, a retired automotive assembly line worker, when auto plants still existed in Atlanta. She explained how tired she was and requested silence.

"Whatever you want, ma'am."

"It's *miss,* if you please."

The driver nodded obedience.

Once settled in the back of the limo, Janelle read a text from Brad.

Brad: I told the driver to take you to Mimi's house.

Janelle had to think for a minute. Oh, yes, Mimi was Brad's nickname for Phoebe Patterson—his paternal grandmother who raised him after the death of his parents in a car accident.

Janelle texted **okay**. But it wasn't okay. Why would Brad want to meet at Phoebe's house? She was supposed to stay with Ali and connect with Brad later. She needed time to apply fresh makeup and change her clothes.

Due to a tractor-trailer crash on Interstate 75, Janelle had time to nod off for the hour-long drive to Willoughby.

"We're almost at your destination, ma'am, er miss," the polite driver said, as they approached Thompson Place.

"Look for a brick ranch style house with dilapidated bird houses swinging from the trees."

"Nice looking house, if you ask me," he said, as he pulled in front of deceased Phoebe Patterson's home.

The faded brownish brick house had been painted classic white. Black shutters and a new oak door gave the façade an inviting appearance.

"No. This couldn't be Phoebe Patterson's former home."

"Says right on the mailbox 'Mia Bella.'"

"My beauty? What's going on? Is this Brad's surprise for me?" Janelle paused and placed both her hands on her cheeks. "Oh, no. Phoebe didn't. She couldn't. She wouldn't leave this old house to me, did she? Would she? I'm going to sell it. I won't live in a house like this even if it was Phoebe's. I don't owe her a thing. I made bundles of money for her."

"Are you okay, ma'am?" the driver said as he turned around to assess his passenger. He didn't wait for a reply and hopped out of the vehicle. He removed her luggage from the front seat, the back seat, and left it curbside. "Shall I carry it inside?"

Brad stood in the doorway and began walking toward the car. "Leave the bags. I'll get them," he hollered.

Before the driver could make a getaway from Janelle, she yelled at him. "Put everything back in the car. Immediately! Hurry! Before he gets here. He's coming! Can't you move faster?" She grabbed two suitcases to hasten their departure and heaved them into the rear seat of the limo.

From the backseat, Janelle put the window down and waved to Brad. "I'll call you. Have to go to Ali's. An emergency." She pointed her finger to her phone. "See you soon. Ciao."

The confused driver shoved the bags into the back seat and threw the tote in the front on the floor. He slid behind the wheel, made a U-turn, and sped away.

Janelle pulled cash from her purse and tossed it on the front seat. "Here's another tip. Forget about your damn ma'am stuff. Ma'am or no ma'am we ma'ams don't like it."

"Yes, sir. I mean, yes, miss. Whatever. Thank you."

"Take me to 2323 Plum Court. Around the corner. A left turn. And make it snappy."

The driver sped away making a right turn.

"No, a left. Are you deaf? Plum Court. Do I have to repeat myself? Don't you have GPS?"

"Sorry, ma'am. I don't know this neck of the woods." He made a left turn.

Janelle said to the driver, "Am I making a mistake? Should I go back? How will I explain my departure to Brad? What do you think? I've got it. The house isn't for me. He wanted to show me the renovations he made. Do you think I'm right?"

"I think any minute I might dump you out at the corner, ma'am. You're making me nervous. Are you on drugs? I don't want any drugs or drug users in my limo."

"*You're* nervous. What about me? Drive around the block a couple of times until you calm down. You're driving too fast."

"You mean until *you* calm down." The perspiring driver wiped his forehead with the back of his hand and made another U-turn. "Hold on. I'll take you where you want to go." He accelerated toward Plum Court.

Take me where? I don't know where I want to go.

Chapter 8

Ali stood at the bay window of her kitchen and shielded her eyes from the late afternoon sun shining through the kitchen shutters. She watched Janelle exit the limo while the driver removed the familiar Louis Vuitton luggage Janelle traveled with and brought the pieces to the front porch.

"What? My goodness," Ali gasped when she saw Janelle step out of the limo. It was only six months ago since the sisters were together.

Ali's childhood nickname for Janelle fit today. "Big Sis" was indeed big. Now, her puffy body would match her ego. Same shiny black hair, same oversized glasses, same stepladder shoes, Ali observed.

Ah…I never envisioned the day I would be the thin sister. I like this picture.

Ali continued to observe Janelle and waited for her on the porch. *No need to be too eager.*

Ali stifled a laugh because she had a horrid thought. Could her sister be ill? Could she have newly diagnosed cancer and the chemo bloated her. Maybe she was on steroids for arthritis or gout. No. Most likely, she was eating and drinking too damn much.

With her long slender fingers, Janelle waved hello to Ali. At least her fingers didn't need a diet. Janelle met her sister on the porch.

"Before you say anything. Yes, I've put on a few pounds. All the wine-ing and dine-ing on the book tour. You know how it was in New York."

"No, I don't, Janelle. You gave me a signal to leave after you deliberately spilled Malbec on my white blouse."

"Merely an accident," petulant Janelle answered. "About New York. You didn't have to run off, you know. We were concerned when you fled."

"I had enough abuse and wanted to come home."

"St. Ali, the little homemaker and community volunteer. How would Willoughby manage without you?"

"You might want to add, co-author, with her former skinny sister, of a bestselling novel."

"And so it begins." Janelle glanced at her platinum Rolex with a bezel set with multiple baguette diamonds. "Not even five minutes and we're at it. We must stop our bickering. Starting today." Janelle and her sister had mended their fragile relationship, temporarily, but it was like putting Humpty Dumpty back together after the contentious book tour six months ago.

Janelle limped into the living room, plopped onto the sofa, and attempted to remove her metallic nude Jimmy Choo shoes. "Guess my feet are swollen from the flight. Excessive salt on the pretzels. A little help, please, Ali."

"Your wish is my command, your royal highness." Ali dropped to her knees and, with effort, attempted to pull off the platform shoes, which seemed glued to Janelle's feet. She yanked a little too hard and fell backward bumping her head on the floor. "Ow. That hurt." Roxie ran to Ali's side and gave her a sympathetic lick on her head.

Ali sat and studied the shoe size. "You'll need a larger size if you want to continue wearing these exquisite things." Ali examined the shoe as if it were Cinderella's glass slipper. She slipped off her sandal and tried one on. "A perfect fit, don't you think?"

"Keep them. A birthday gift."

"You already sent me a birthday gift."

"Make it Christmas." Janelle put her feet on the glass-topped coffee table. "Ah. Much better." She closed her eyes and rested the back of her head on the sofa. "A couple of days on a water and celery diet and I'll be as good as new."

"Did I hear 'royal highness'?" Matt asked, entering the room. "Must mean my sister-in-law's in town."

"Matt. Come give your favorite sister-in-law a kiss and while you're at it, how about one of your fabulous dirty martinis."

Matt opted for a pat on her head. He moved to the bar to comply with Janelle's cocktail request.

"No martini for Janelle," Ali said. "She's on a water and celery diet."

"Tomorrow will be soon enough," Janelle said.

"I thought tequila was your beverage of choice," Matt said. "And plenty of it," he muttered. He delivered the martini and said he'd move her luggage upstairs.

"Leave some of it where it is. She won't be staying long," Ali said.

Regardless, Matt made several trips up and down the stairs, groaning as he delivered the luggage to the spare bedroom.

"You need to soak your feet in Epsom salts. Your ankles are the size of tennis balls," Ali said. She sat next to her sister and stared at Janelle's sausage-like toes. "Consuming alcohol won't help the swelling."

"I appreciate your thoughtfulness. I'll be fine." She lifted her glass toward Matt when he returned. "Perfect."

Matt ignored her.

"Where's Kayla? I thought she'd be here to greet her favorite and only aunt."

"She's at the store," Ali said.

"And not pleased about being there," Janelle said.

"How would you know?" Ali asked.

"We had a little talk while I was in Sanibel. She told me she wanted to do public service. In Florence. I'm not sure about the 'public service' just the part about going to Italy."

"Why Italy?" Matt asked.

"She wants to meet her new boyfriend."

"Boyfriend?" Matt asked.

"Boyfriend!" exclaimed Ali.

"Not exactly a boyfriend. She met someone online. I think. Or somewhere else. I'm not sure where she met him. She wants to meet him in Florence. Florence, Italy. Not Florence, South Carolina. Or was it South Carolina? I don't know. Florence somewhere."

"Florence? Over my dead body," Matt shouted.

"I'm glad we made her commit to working at the store this summer. Guess we put a stop to any trip to Italy," Ali said.

"Barely," Janelle said.

"Don't you dare give her any money. Has Kayla asked?" Ali said.

"What did I ask?" Kayla joined the family and slumped into a chair. "When did you arrive?" Kayla asked her aunt. "Are you staying with us?"

"Arrived today. Staying at least for tonight." Janelle shot Ali a look. "Or a few nights."

"Don't I deserve a hug?" Janelle asked.

Kayla dragged to Janelle, kissed her on the cheek, and plunked down next to her aunt on the sofa. "I've missed you."

"Me, too, honey. Let's plan a shopping trip. Buy some attractive tops to show off the emerald I gave you."

Kayla bit her upper lip, and nodded agreement, as her hand went to her neckline.

"I see Aunt Janie's drinking a martini," Kayla said. "I'll have one, too."

Ali and Matt said, "No way."

"See what I mean, Aunt Janelle? Ask for anything around here and the answer is always no," Kayla said.

Ali stood and walked over to Kayla. "What's bothering you, woman? Your crabbiness meter is at an all-time high."

"Never mind. You'll get mad." Kayla stood, undid her ponytail, shook her rainbow-tinted dark locks, and headed for the stairs. "I'm going to bed." Roxie trotted after her.

"Who's watching the store?" Matt asked.

"I left Bailey in charge. She can call if there's a problem," Kayla said from the bottom of the stairway.

"At five o'clock you're going to bed?" Matt said.

Kayla ignored her dad's remark and raced up the stairs with Roxie close behind. She beat Roxie to her room and slammed the door. Roxie whimpered as she scratched the door forcing Kayla to admit her pal.

"See what you can do. She admires you," Ali said to Janelle. "She ignores me."

"She sure isn't showing admiration for me. Running off. How rude." Janelle took a sip of her martini. "I'll take her shopping. That will cheer her up."

"Let's talk about your Facebook post," Ali said. "When did you decide to write without me?"

"I needed to capture your attention. You wouldn't answer my texts or emails. Have your attention now, don't I?" Janelle said.

"Guess I'll break my no alcohol diet and have a glass of wine." Ali rose from the chair and left for the kitchen.

Matt met her at the refrigerator and said, "I'm going to the store. Open late tonight and I don't like leaving Bailey alone. Don't wait dinner for me." He kissed Ali on her cheek. "You know your personality changes when the beauty queen's around. Do us all a favor and try to ignore her."

Ali took a bottle of opened sauvignon blanc from the refrigerator, filled a glass, and returned to the living room.

"You want to hear something funny?" Ali asked her sister. "I told Mother and Dad you were arriving today—"

"But—"

"Calm down. The funny part is Mother didn't want you. Not now. She wanted to buy new sheets and towels and make everything top notch for her favorite daughter."

"Mother always did make me feel special. And, I'm not the favorite. The first born." Janelle paused. "One night or two here. I promise I'll move in with them. Won't be long with Mother and Dad because I want to find a place of my own. Nothing permanent. Maybe I'll rent. Cash flow problems."

"Promise?" Ali asked.

"Of course. Meanwhile—cheers," Janelle said. "Let's toast our successful partnership with more books in the future."

"Let's discuss this so-called partnership."

Janelle's phone rang. She let it go to voicemail. Her phone binged indicating a text.

"Someone's trying to reach you, Janelle."

Ali received a text. "It's from Brad. He wants to know what kind of emergency? What does he mean?"

"Tell him not to worry about me. Tell him. . .tell him. Tell him something. Say I have the stomach flu and I'll call him tomorrow. Tell him I'm contagious. Tell him anything."

"Why should I lie to Brad? He's our friend. What's going on?"

"Please. This one time. Be a good sister."

Ali sighed and texted Brad.

Ali: Janelle has a bad case of stomach flu. She doesn't want to infect anyone. She'll call you in the a.m.

Brad: Keep me posted.

"Tell me what's going on, Janelle. Why the lie? What's with you and Brad?"

"Nothing. Nothing at all. Or nothing for you to concern yourself with. Damn Phoebe Patterson. This is her fault."

"Phoebe?"

Janelle told Ali her suspicion that Phoebe left her house to Janelle to trap Janelle in Willoughby. "He put a Mia Bella sign on the mailbox."

"Why?"

"Sort of a nickname. The name of his restaurant."

"Would that be so bad? I think the house is going to be a showstopper. The whole town's been watching the progress of the renovations."

"Forget about the house. I have something to tell you, if you promise not to say anything to anyone."

Ali paused before she answered. She recalled the times when they were young, and Ali innocently confided in Janelle about a crush on a boy. Janelle betrayed the confidence and blabbed to everyone in Willoughby High. "Just like you promised not to reveal my high school crush on Benny Greenway."

"That was years ago. Please forget about that silliness. We're adults now and I need your advice."

"You never ask for my advice. Why now?"

"Brad and I have been seeing each other. New York. Mexico. Italy. Ahh, Tuscany. I even snuck into Atlanta last month. We met in Buckhead. I'm way in over my head. It's gone too far."

"What do you mean?"

"I think he wants to marry me."

Chapter 9

Kayla texted Logan before she reached the top of the stairs heading to her bedroom.

Kayla: she's home

Logan: who?

Kayla: my aunt

Logan: so?

Kayla: the emerald. she'll want to see it. gotta get it back from the pawnshop

Logan: what do you want me to do?

Kayla: help me

Logan: will take more than a pimento cheese ham biscuit

Kayla: whatever

Logan: you'll go to the Ed Sheeran concert with me

Kayla: i said whatever

Logan: say it like you mean it

Kayla: stop it! pick me up in the morning, 9:45 at the corner

* * *

The next morning Kayla left the house and jogged to the corner of Plum Court where Logan was waiting. She jumped into his dad's convertible. Kayla hoped her parents bought the lie she told about meeting a friend for coffee thus her late arrival at the store. They drove to Jim's Gems pawnshop hoping to be the first in line. No such luck. Three customers were ahead of her and three employees were ready to wait on them.

"Welcome to Jim's," said a young woman with tattooed arms and a nose ring. "Be with you soon."

While Kayla and Logan were waiting, she paced the jewelry case aisle like a store security guard watching for thieves.

"Sorry to keep you waiting," the nose-ringed clerk said when it was Kayla's turn. "I'm Destiny. Buying or selling? If I had to guess, I'd say selling. You seem nervous."

"I want an item returned to me that isn't in the cases."

"Where's the paperwork?" Destiny asked. "Will be easier to identify. Might be in the storeroom."

Kayla pulled from her pocket the yellow piece of paper, which Jim had given her and Logan during their previous visit. Destiny read the paper, front and back. "This doesn't mean anything to me. We don't have receipts. We have contracts. What else do you have?"

"This is legitimate. I'm a witness. I can attest to the legality," lawyer Logan said. "I'm eighteen."

"Mr. Jim gave me this," Kayla said raising her voice an octave. She took the paper from Destiny and rattled it in the air causing other employees and customers to stare. "He said he had to have the item checked out. I must have it. You don't understand." Her fierce shaking made the paper fall from her damp hand.

"I haven't seen a green pendant come in recently. Is that what you want? Hard to read the handwriting on this." She picked up the paper and flicked it with a long, pointy fingernail painted black.

"Yes, a green pendant. Expensive," Kayla said.

"Priceless," Logan added.

Destiny eyed Kayla up and down. "Wait here. Better calm down. You look like you're going to explode." She walked over to another employee and conversed with him. They both stared at Kayla and Logan.

"Do they think I'm a thief? A con artist? Why are they staring at us? This was a huge mistake," she said to Logan.

When Destiny returned she said, "You have to come when Jim is here. He's the one who can help you. Don't worry. He's an honest guy."

"Later today? Tomorrow?" Kayla asked.

"He's fishing in Idaho. He'll be back next week."

"What?!" screeched Kayla. "We were just in here and he said to come back the next day."

"Not so loud. Please."

Logan patted Kayla on her shoulder. "Take a breath."

One of the other employees, a man wearing a tight muscle-revealing black T-shirt and three gold chains around his oversized neck, approached Destiny. She waved him off. "We're okay here."

"Can't you contact him? Doesn't he have a phone? Text or email or something? I'm desperate." Kayla explained her story to the young woman.

"Have you considered a fake? A stand-in? A substitute until Grandpa returns."

"What do you have?"

Destiny signaled Mr. Big Neck and the two of them walked to the storeroom. They motioned for Kayla to join them. They told Logan not to come with them. Kayla was shown a box of green jewelry—rings, bracelets, necklaces. "If you see something similar, we'll let you borrow it, under the circumstances. Our guess is Grandpa didn't want to sell it. He does that sometimes."

Kayla's heavy breathing slowed. She sorted through the container of green items. "This one might work. From a distance." She held it up to Destiny's neckline.

Big Neck picked up a different pendant. "This one's better quality even though it's smaller," he said. His soft voice belied his menacing presence.

"I'll take the smaller one."

The employees led Kayla to the front of the store where they filled out paperwork and took her picture.

"You're saving my ass. Thanks so much."

"My grandpa wouldn't do you wrong. Besides, this piece we're giving you isn't worth a whole lot."

Kayla thanked Destiny and Big Neck before she and Logan left. Her breathing returned to normal, but she was hesitant about wearing the jewel in her aunt's presence. Since Janelle had begun to wear reading glasses, Kayla vowed not to let her aunt get too close to the substitute gem. Kayla glanced at her watch. She entered the car and sat in the passenger side.

"Your hands have stopped shaking. You okay now?"

"Let's get out of here," Kayla said. "I'll have to think of something to stall my aunt for a freaking week."

Chapter 10

Ali arose early the next morning after Janelle's arrival and reached her arm over to Matt's side of the bed searching for him. His spot was empty but still warm. The aroma of brewed coffee drew her to the kitchen. She was surprised to see Janelle dressed, full-on makeup applied, and reading the newspaper with glasses perched on her nose.

"You win. I'll stay with our parents. This is my way of telling you I'm a changed woman," Janelle said.

Ali filled her mug and joined Janelle at the table. She put on her reading glasses. "I want a pleasant relationship with you, Janelle, but you upset me during the book tour, and I'm still mad."

"That was months ago. Please forgive me. I don't like this prolonged animosity either."

"You thrive on it."

Janelle made no reply and picked up the newspaper to work on the crossword puzzle. The sisters sat at the table in silence until Kayla entered the kitchen.

"How many fights have you had since last night?" Kayla asked. She moved toward Janelle and gave her a hug. "I'm so glad you're here. Sorry I haven't been welcoming. I wish you would stay and not argue so much with Mom."

The sisters made eye contact. "We're not going to argue anymore. As of today," Ali said.

"We made a promise," Janelle said. "Sort of."

"Breakfast, honey?" Ali asked her daughter.

"I'll get it, Mom."

"Let me spoil you." Ali stood from the table, took a step, and tripped over Janelle's gargantuan tote. She put her hands out in front of her to brace the fall. She saved her wrists but twisted her ankle. "Oh, no. Please. Not my ankle. The race is coming up."

Janelle stood so quickly she knocked her coffee cup, spilling the contents over the newspaper. "Are you okay?" she asked.

Kayla tried to help her mother up.

"Wow, that hurts," Ali said when she failed to stand. "Damn you, Janelle. This is your fault."

"Now, you're really going to hate me," Janelle said.

Kayla inched closer to her mother. "Don't be mad at Aunt Janelle. You should have watched where you were going."

"Any minute I'm going to send you to your grandparents, too."

"Not a bad idea," Kayla mumbled.

Roxie came to Ali's side and licked her foot.

Kayla retrieved a plastic bag from a kitchen drawer and filled it with ice. She took a bottle of ibuprofen from a cabinet and returned to her mother's side. "Can you move to the couch in the den?"

"Let's try," Ali said.

Kayla helped her mother hobble to the den where Ali fell onto the couch. Kayla took a couch pillow and placed it under the ankle. "Does it hurt?"

"Not so much. Probably will tomorrow."

"I'm careless. I know how awful I am. I know how much you hate me," Janelle wailed.

"Calm down, Janelle. I'll be fine in the morning." Ali studied her now swollen ankle. "Or not."

"According to the internet, a sprain can last from five to fourteen days," Kayla said looking at her phone.

"I'm screwed. No Peachtree Road Race for me. Months of wasted time running my butt off."

"But there's a bright side. You lost sooo much weight," Janelle said.

"Thanks for the observation," Ali said with a glare toward her sister.

"Let me help." Janelle repositioned the bag of ice on Ali's ankle. The bag slipped, spilling the contents on the floor. "I'm useless. No wonder you hate me."

"I don't hate you."

"They'll understand why I have to stay here with you."

"Who? What?" Ali asked.

"I can't move in with our parents as we planned since I caused, accidentally, your injury."

"I have Kayla and Matt to help me."

"Not the same as a guilty and loving sister."

"Janelle the caretaker," Ali said.

"Chocolate. You need chocolate. Where's all the candy you brought from Italy? The vacation I paid for."

"That was over a year ago," Kayla said. "We ate it."

"Should I take you to the emergency room?" Janelle asked.

"It's sure swollen and it hurts," Ali said.

The doorbell interrupted the discussion of Ali's ankle.

Janelle approached the bay window in the kitchen and made a slight scream. "Crap! He's here. Tell him I'm throwing up in the bathroom. Tell him I have a fever and a sore throat. Toss in some diarrhea. Tell him anything." Janelle grabbed onto Kayla's arm. "You must help me. I can't see him. Please!"

"You are one needy person," Ali said from the den.

The doorbell rang again. Kayla waited until Janelle ran upstairs and was out of sight. She opened the door. "Hello, Mr. Brad."

Brad and Kayla embraced. "Glad to have you around this summer. Makes your parents happy, too."

"I guess."

"Was that your aunt I saw in the window?"

"She had to go to the bathroom, quick. Not feeling well. Welcome to the infirmary." Kayla led Brad to the den where Ali had her ankle elevated on a pillow.

"What happened?" he asked.

"I took a little tumble over one of Janelle's misplaced pieces of luggage. Clumsy on my part, I suppose."

He approached her and eyed the ankle. "What a shame. No Peachtree for you."

"Unfortunately," Ali said. Avoiding eye contact with him, "Janelle's still not feeling well." She repeated Kayla's report.

Kayla added, "Her stomach is still in turmoil and now she's upset because of this." She pointed to her mom's ankle.

"I'll go upstairs for a minute and check on her."

"No! No!" Ali and Kayla said.

"If she isn't perfectly dressed, she won't want to see anyone, especially a handsome man. She's been spending hours near the toilet. Smells awful up there," Kayla said.

"But—"

"She's probably contagious," Kayla said. "You don't want to take her germs to your restaurant. Bad for business. I'll tell her you came to see her. That will cheer her up."

"Sure, sure. I'll come by later."

"Better call first," Kayla said. She took Brad by the arm and led him to the front door.

"Ask her to at least answer my texts."

"Sure, Mr. Brad."

"And give her this."

"What?"

"A key to my Mercedes I'm not using."

She opened the door and watched him leave. "That was terrible, Mom. I don't like lying to him."

"What can I say? That's your aunt."

"And *your* sister," Kayla said. She found more pillows in her parents' bedroom closet and elevated her mother's foot higher. She put another ice bag around her ankle. "Can you put weight on it?" Kayla asked.

"I'm afraid to try, but here goes." She gingerly tried to stand. "Ah no. There's goes the Peachtree Race T-shirt."

"Is the coast clear?" Janelle whispered from the top of the staircase.

"Yes, we sent Brad on his way, but you made liars out of both of us. You don't deserve him. Bring me my phone and another cup of coffee. Please," Ali said.

"My mistake to make you lie, but now that I think about it, my stomach is upset."

"Here," Kayla said to her aunt as she tossed the car key to her. "His Mercedes."

Janelle smiled. "He's crazy about me."

"Whatever," Kayla said.

Ali retrieved her calendar in her phone and reviewed her plans for the week aloud. "Take Mother to estate sale; book club meeting; help plan Olivia's daughter's baby shower; write; write; write. What I need is another me. A chauffeur, cook, and housekeeper. If only wishes could come true."

After Kayla left for work, Ali and Janelle were alone in the den.

"Are you going to tell me more about Brad wanting to marry you? Seems sudden, don't you think?"

"Can't talk about Brad right now. Need to help you. What can I do?"

"I appreciate your helping me, but you're hovering a bit. Why don't you do something for yourself? A mani-pedi? You have your own transportation now thanks to Brad."

"Look at us. We're both showing consideration for each other. Similar to old times."

"Refresh my memory. The old times? When we were six?"

"You are so funny." Janelle stared out the window. "Now, let's talk about this book we're going to write. You have plenty of time since you can't walk, and all your volunteer activities are out of the question."

"You don't understand, Janelle. For once, you're not going to have your way. Our writing partnership is over. Finished. Never again."

"I'm lost without a ghostwriter...I mean a co-writer."

"Don't worry. No one knows Phoebe was your ghostwriter," Ali lied.

"I'm imploring, begging. Do I have to bow down on my knees? I've tried writing alone. I have no ideas. I'm stale. Phoebe gave me all my ideas and you did the same. And frankly, I need the money."

"I don't believe you."

"You would if you knew how much alimony I have to pay. I need one more book." Janelle glanced at her phone. "Why does Ken keep pestering me?"

Ali had long suspected roly-poly Ken Luzi had an unrequited crush on Janelle. Ali thought Janelle should treat him with more respect and at least take his phone calls.

When Janelle didn't answer Ken, he sent Ali a text.

"Ken has lined up an editor who wants to read our ideas," Ali said, reading the text from him with her cheaters sitting on the tip of her nose.

"I'm tired, Ali. After eighteen books, ah, nineteen counting ours, I don't think I have it in me anymore."

"Of course, you do. How about Mary Higgins Clark? She's ninety. Written over forty novels plus short stories. She never stops. James Patterson, Janet Evanovich, and Nora Roberts. They keep churning out books and you could, too, if you would focus on writing and not spend an inordinate amount of time worrying about your physical appearance and your clothes. Not to mention putting your love life in order."

"It's not only the writing. It's the marketing, the public appearances, the media interviews. Now, if you would share some of this burden with me. Our book tour was an anomaly. I promise next time will be different. If only you'll write with me."

"The key word is *if* I'll write with you. Not right to call it a 'burden.' Think about the writers who aren't as accomplished as you. They're struggling to have their books published. Begging readers to write reviews on Amazon. Selling one book at a time. Going to book signings where two people show up. You should be grateful."

"One more book? We'll write together, publish it, and I'll retire. Do you have any ideas about a plot?" Janelle asked.

"Nope. Not gonna do it."

"You know what will happen. I can't do it by myself and I need the advance from our publisher."

"I don't believe you need money and you don't need a ghostwriter. I've told you before. You must have learned something by now."

"Let me bring more ice for your ankle."

"Stop evading this discussion. Besides, anymore ice and you can throw me into a freezer."

"Freeze? Frozen? That gives me an idea. An ice princess will be our heroine."

"What's an ice princess?"

"We'll make it up. Fantasy. Sci fi. Might have been a Disney movie though."

"Sounds desperate to me," Ali said. "I don't read those genres so how can I write about them?"

"What do you have in mind? I'm open."

"How about a murder mystery?"

"Continue." Janelle grabbed paper and a pencil from Matt's desk. "I'm listening."

"Two sisters."

"Easy to write since we know everything about being sisters," Janelle said.

"One is beautiful and the other is plain."

Janelle made no comment about the appearances of the fictitious sisters and wrote what Ali dictated.

"Murder-suicide."

Janelle dropped the pencil to the floor. "You are so funny. Ha ha ha. Miss Comedian. You should go on SNL. A mani-pedi sounds good. You can get your own damn ice."

As Ali watched Janelle depart, she wasn't sure if they had reached a resolution about writing together. She knew one thing. She'd have to get her own damn ice.

Chapter 11

After Janelle left, Ali limped to the front porch and checked the thermometer sitting on a wicker table. The temperature was inching toward a predictable high of eighty degrees. A welcomed rainstorm the previous night washed away the yellow pollen invader. She was adjusting the ice pack on her ankle when her cell phone rang.

"Where are you?" she asked.

"Paradise," Ellen said.

"Which paradise? The Bahamas, Maui?"

"Better. And farther away."

"What time is it there? Should I find a world atlas and throw darts?"

"North Bali. At a divine resort called Lovina. I'm stretched out on a massage table underneath a star-filled sky, and palm trees with the warm breeze from the Bali Sea wafting over my tan body. A massage before bedtime—can't beat it. Thought I should check in. Where's Janelle? Still causing trouble?"

"Everything's okay except I sprained my ankle tripping over Janelle's tote bag and she appointed herself as my caretaker." She adjusted the makeshift ice bag Matt had put together tying it with lightweight rope.

"Hang tough and don't let her…here he comes. . .my handsome masseur who has the most amazing hands. And I mean *amazing*."

"When are you coming home?"

"Depends on Rio."

"Rio de Janerio? I thought you were in Bali?"

"No. His name is Rio. Later."

Ellen and Ali had been friends since their parents bought homes next to each other when the girls were in elementary school. Both families had moved from Ohio to be near aging parents, giving them an instant bond.

The two friends attended the same college and became sorority sisters. If anyone understood the dysfunctional dynamics between Janelle and Ali, it was Ellen. After Ellen's divorce, she sold the gourmet kitchen store she had inherited from her parents to Ali and Matt. Ellen had no interest in anything kitchen related. Ali and Matt renamed the store Kitchen Bliss.

"Come on, Roxie. Let's take a walk. Darn. I can't walk." Roxie jumped into her lap and licked her face. "But I can eat chocolate. Think we can make it to the pantry where I have a hidden stash of chocolate chips?"

Ali's phone rang. "We haven't seen much of you since your book tour with Janelle last year," Jill said. "You've been close mouthed about the tour. How about tonight? You must tell all. Diane wants us to meet at her store."

Ali's book club, the Book Babes, was a cadre of close friends who met monthly to discuss a book as well as their lives. The more wine consumed, the less book discussion.

"Could you come here? Sprained my ankle and I think I'd better stay off it."

"Sprained? How? What about the Peachtree?"

"An accident. No race this year."

"We'll bring the wine and the food."

"On second thought. Janelle will be here. She'll crash the meeting."

"Tell her she's not invited."

"Hmm. I'll try to persuade Matt to take her someplace."

"Alaska's pleasant this time of year," Jill said.

"See you at seven," Ali said.

* * *

"We're here," Diane and the other Book Babes shouted as they entered the unlocked front door of the Lawrence home. The group knew their way around the kitchen and found wine glasses and corkscrews.

"I'm in here," Ali said from the sunroom.

Jackie carried trays of food and placed them on several tables.

"Is Janelle still alive or did you use blunt force trauma with one of her books to knock her out?" Jill asked as she approached Ali for a hug.

"Working together and now *living* together," Diane said. "Sounds like a recipe for disaster."

"Janelle's moved in temporarily because she wants to take care of me until my ankle heals."

"Janelle taking care of anyone? What a picture." The Book Babes shared a laugh.

"Nurse Diesel comes to mind," Diane chimed in.

"Forget about the book. We are proud of you," Jill said.

Ali took a sip of chilled French sparkling rosé, which Diane handed to her. "What does a girl do without friends?" Ali asked.

"End up like Janelle," several of the Book Babes said.

Ali put the glass down on the table in front of her and attempted to stand. "Ow. That hurts. I wanted to give you all a hug." She extended her arms.

"I supplied the food tonight. Please eat because nothing's going home with me," Jackie said. She motioned to the trays of food.

"Spanakopita, garlic stuffed olives, dolmades with mint yogurt sauce, hunks of feta cheese, and grilled pita."

"Let's begin," Jill suggested. "Tell all. Every detail."

"Thanks for this wonderful food," Ali said as she observed the plate of food she was handed, mentally counting the calories.

"What? No ouzo? I arrived just in time. What's a Greek party without ouzo?"

Silence enveloped the room as the Book Babes heard Janelle enter through the front door and join them in the sunroom.

"Janelle, what are you doing here?" Ali asked. "I thought you were having dinner with Matt."

"I think I bored him. He's gone to Kitchen Bliss to check on something. No doubt a fictitious excuse to avoid me."

"You weren't invited," Jill said.

"Thought you'd enjoy hearing from me. My mistake." Ignoring Jill's comment, Janelle found a chair leaning up against the French doors and dragged it toward the group with one hand while clutching a brown paper bag in the other. "Here," Janelle said as she handed the bag to Ali.

"What's this?"

"Ouzo, of course. Follows the theme of my, er, Broken—"

"Yes, we know the title of your book, Janelle," Jackie said. "It's Ali's book, too."

"Thanks, Janelle, but this is a wine drinking group. I don't think anyone will drink this strong stuff," Ali said.

Tina, the quiet one in the group, countered Ali. "I've never had ooozoo. Ohzo? Is that how you pronounce it?"

"You rarely have a glass of wine," Jill said.

"Let the girl live a little." Janelle surveyed the table laden with food and wine glasses. She pulled the bottle from the bag. "No shot glasses handy? This will have to do." Janelle picked up a stemmed wine glass and filled it half way with the clear, potent aperitif.

"No way will I let Tina drink ouzo," Diane said. She grabbed the glass from Janelle, but it slipped from her hand and the contents spilled onto the feta and olive platter, which was now swimming in alcohol.

"Damn," Janelle said. "Guess we have drunken cheese and pickled olives. Even better." She leaned over and popped a piece of cheese and two olives into her mouth all at once. She resembled a squirrel with a mouthful of nuts.

Ali sat motionless. She didn't say a word.

The women stared at Ali waiting for her to do something—apologize for her sister's behavior, display mortification, show embarrassment, something. Ali was as rigid as the Corinthian column pictured on the cover of the sisters' book. The only time she moved was when she took a sip of wine.

"Now what?" Diane asked.

"Don't let me hinder your discussion. I'm sure you want to know the details of our book tour. The tour that, unfortunately, Ali had to quit early."

Ali took another sip of wine, well not a sip, a gulp. With ladylike aplomb and restraint, she said, "Janelle, I believe you have overstepped your welcome. Please leave my friends and me. Go upstairs to your room. I'll see you in the morning." She repeated, "I'll see you in the morning," as she glared into Janelle's eyes.

"Please pardon my sister for her bad manners, ladies," Janelle said. She stood and clicked her heels together like Dorothy and took the bottle of ouzo upstairs.

After Janelle had slammed the bedroom door, Diane said, "Congratulations, Ali. Glad you stood your ground."

"I was a little rough on her though. Wasn't I?"

Moans and groans from the group sounded like the reaction from tennis fans to a double-fault by Roger Federer.

"It's getting late. Let's move on and forget about our intruder with the fake eyelashes and the skyscraper shoes," Jill suggested.

The women formed a semi-circle and bombarded Ali with questions.

"Were you picked up in a limo?"

"Did you stay in an elegant suite?"

"Did you meet any famous people?"

Jill came to Ali's rescue. "One at a time."

"The accommodations were lovely, for the most part. If we weren't picked up in a limo someone escorted us to our hotels, book signings, and restaurants." Ali hesitated. "It was a memorable experience...it was tiring...hectic." Ali stopped speaking, put her wine glass down, and dropped her head into her hands. The room was silent except for the gurgle of wine filling glasses.

Ali lifted her head. "It was awful, terrible, embarrassing, humiliating. It was a freaking nightmare. I hated every freaking minute. I hated my freaking sister. I hated writing with her. I'm a lunatic. Why did I ever think writing with Janelle would work?"

The women sipped their wine and avoided eye contact with Ali who had put her face in her hands again and bent over her knees in a near state of meltdown.

"Ah...you did have second thoughts about writing with her. I was surprised you agreed to a partnership," Jill said.

Ali sat up. "Ellen tried to talk me out of writing with her. I didn't listen. We need to always listen to our friends."

"Water under the bridge. Tell us about the book tour," Jackie said.

"You haven't told us why it was horrid," Tina said.

"Janelle thought we should have been scheduled in more cities and she constantly complained."

"You sold lots of books though."

"Yes, but not as many as Janelle or our publisher projected." Ali explained to the group how the publisher hired "media escorts" in each city.

"What do you mean by an escort?"

"Usually women, or aspiring writers, who know the city backward and forward. They picked us up at the airport, took us to our hotel, met us in the morning, and delivered us to the radio or TV station or speaking engagement. Made sure we kept to the schedule. As you can imagine with Janelle along, that was a challenging task. Meeting these friendly and knowledgeable women was the best part of the tour. Mostly women. Sometimes a man."

Ali explained how Janelle sabotaged her. The only dressy shoes she packed mysteriously disappeared. Janelle spilled red wine on Ali's white blouse while they were having dinner with a local newspaper reporter. "Another time I waited for her in the lobby for one hour before I learned she had already left for the book signing. I had to take a cab and arrived two hours late. If the media escort hadn't given me a copy of the itinerary, I wouldn't have known where to go. Did I paint a picture for you?"

The Book Babes gave Ali sympathetic looks and nodded their heads.

Ali took a deep breath and continued. "You'll love this. At the book signing when I was late, I stood in the long line of Janelle fans. I purchased our book and gave it to her to sign."

"What did she do?" Jackie asked.

"She seemed flustered but regained her composure and signed a book. No one figured out the person on the back cover was little ole me."

"How did she sign the book?" Olivia asked.

"'To St. Ali – if they only knew.'"

The Book Babes questioned Ali about her next book. She was evasive and didn't have much to say. "I'm struggling with some ideas. I'd like to set it in Willoughby, which would be fun."

"You mean you'd put the Book Babes in your book?" Tina asked.

"Better change our names to protect the guilty," Diane said.

"You must have a few ideas you could tell us?" Jill asked.

"Promise me you won't share this information with anyone. Even your husbands or your families."

"You can trust us," Olivia said.

Ali hesitated. "You are my best friends, but one person here is loose with the emails."

"Please, Ali," Diane said.

"My unnamed novel is about two sisters. It's a murder mystery. One sister kills the other and she avoids prosecution," Ali said. She lowered her head and rubbed her hands together as though she were brushing away cracker crumbs.

"You're kidding us. You wouldn't write such a thing. What would happen if Janelle suffered an accident? The police would suspect you," Tina said.

"You watch too many *Law & Order* reruns," Jackie said.

"I'm kidding. But, it would make a good story. Don't you think?"

Chapter 12

The next morning Ali and Matt were sitting at their kitchen table. "Will you deposit this royalty check for me?" Ali asked, as she filled out the bank slip. "I received it yesterday, but I didn't make it to the bank." She pointed to her ankle.

"Why don't you have direct deposit?"

"Holding the piece of paper in my hand represents accomplishment. Touching it. Smelling it. Makes me happy." She paused to assess the amount and smiled. "Won't be long until we have enough for Kayla's undergrad tuition."

"These days an advanced degree is mandatory." Matt reached for a notepad and pencil across from him on the table and made some notes. "We need another book."

"We? Or me?" Ali was still holding the check. "Don't complain about me not working at the store. Can't work with you and write. You can't have it both ways."

"You know what I mean. Wish Kayla would make up her mind about a major." Matt was concentrating on his notes. "These days has to be something with computers. Or, cyber security."

"An MBA and law degree might be a lucrative combo," Ali said.

"Discussing my life?" Kayla said as she joined her parents.

"Reviewing your options, princess, and going to Italy this summer is not one of them."

"I want to do something to improve lives. Helping an old lady choose which Bundt pan to buy isn't fulfilling."

"It is to the old lady," Ali said. "She feels joyful baking a double chocolate fudge cake, which brings pleasure to others."

"Fulfilling and filling to the person who eats the cake," Matt added.

"Not funny, you two."

"What happened to your sense of humor, Kayla?" Matt asked. "Leave it in the dorm?"

"I'm an indentured servant. All you want me to do is work in the damn store. Why do I have to give up *my* time?"

"Let me count the ways," Matt said.

"Count. As in money. Is that all you think about, Dad?" She removed Roxie's pink leash, which was hanging on the back of the kitchen door, and attached it to the dog's collar. "Since I have no money in my account, guess you have to pay my share of the rent." She tossed a white envelope on the table between Matt and Ali. "It's due on the first. See you," she said as she left.

"Wait one second," Ali said. Not fast enough. Kayla was out the door.

Matt opened the envelope. "It's not much. I think we should pay it." He took out his phone. "Let's see how much money she has in her account." He paused, opened up an app, and said, "She's right. Not much."

"I say deduct the rent from her wages," Ali said.

"All summer. You and she bickering. You and Janelle arguing."

"I don't bicker with anyone."

"I didn't predict this would happen with Kayla. I envisioned walking to work in the morning swinging our hands. We'd return at night discussing the day's events. Kayla telling me about her life at school, her hopes, her dreams," Matt said.

"My friends with daughters tell me not to give up on Kayla because she'll come around. They predict we'll become best friends. Eventually." Ali took a sip of coffee. "Let's give her some control in the store."

"She could hire someone. One of her friends. Or, let her arrange a display of Le Creuset or Emile Henry."

"Pots and pans?" Ali said.

"Colorful pots and pans."

"How about a food tasting?"

"I'll talk to her about that today. Need to figure out something to make her happy."

"More like making *us* happy," Ali said.

They kissed goodbye. Ali opened her laptop.

"Where's Dad?" Kayla said when she and Roxie returned from their walk.

"He had an early meeting of the merchants' association. Said he'd meet you at the store in time to open."

"Shh. Be quiet. Aunt Janelle is still sleeping. In fact, she's snoring. She must be super tired."

"Gee, I wouldn't want to wake up any of our guests at the Lawrence B&B," Ali said.

"So, what can I do to help you before I leave?"

"Thanks for asking, but I'm okay. You could do laundry for me after work. A pleasant attitude would be appreciated, too."

Kayla took a banana from the countertop. "See you, Mom. Off to the mines."

"No kiss?"

Kayla walked to her mother's side and kissed her cheek.

"If I didn't know better, I'd think you were ignoring your aunt."

"If I didn't have to work so much, I'd have time to spend with her. Ciao."

* * *

Ali suspected Janelle was embarrassed by the way she presented herself last night with the Book Babes. Ali smiled hoping her sister was stewing over her outlandish behavior. A text answered Ali's question:

Janelle: I'm soooo sorry about last night with the
Book Babes. I was out of line. Will you
forgive me? Guess I had a little too much to
drink.

Ali hesitated before she answered. Janelle rarely apologized for anything because she never thought she did anything wrong. Maybe she *was* trying to change.

Ali: Forgiven.

* * *

"Where's Kayla?" Janelle asked when she joined her sister in the kitchen. "Thought we needed to schedule our shopping trip."

"Off to work," Ali said without looking at Janelle.

Janelle poured a cup of coffee and sat at the table across from her sister. "Does Kayla wear the emerald pendant I gave her? I haven't seen it since I've been here. She keeps it in a secure place, I suppose."

"I had suggested she put it in our safe deposit box at the bank, but she declined. Probably in her room somewhere."

"Probably," Janelle said as she pinched her eyebrows together.

"No, no, no," Ali said. "Frowning causes wrinkles. Isn't that what you've been telling me for years?"

Janelle unfurled her brow and took a sip of coffee. "Has Kayla been avoiding me?"

"Why would she do that?"

"Just wondering."

* * *

When Kayla arrived at Kitchen Bliss, the door was locked, and the lights were off. She sat on the bench in front of the store wearing earbuds and tapping her foot to the music of Fitz and the Tantrums.

"Sorry I'm late," Matt said. "The meeting was longer than anticipated." He unlocked the door and ushered her in.

"You don't trust me enough to give me a key even though I'm giving up my entire summer vacation for you. And, I'm your daughter. Remember? A trusted family member."

He pulled a key chain with a tiny whisk on it from his khaki pants. "If we have a slow period today, go to the hardware store and have one made."

"And how am I supposed to get there? I can't walk that far. Remember, I don't have a car. I think Mom should let me drive the Green Monster until her ankle heals."

"Your mother is protective of that truck. You can use my car for now." Matt handed Kayla another key, which she grabbed from his hand. She walked to the back of the store and put on a Kitchen Bliss apron. She shuffled to the front glass door to clean it. She put out the blackboard announcing specials. Kayla positioned herself at the checkout area, crossed her arms, and leaned her back against the counter.

Matt brought the cash box to the front of the store. "If you want to make any changes to the store, feel free. Who knows? It might be yours someday. Just check with me first."

"Like what changes?"

"Rearrange merchandise, choose the food for tastings."

"Trying to give me more responsibility to make me want to come here? It won't work."

"We can afford to hire one more person, part-time, of course. How about one of your friends?"

Kayla moved to the coffee grinder and ground beans, decaf and regular. When the machine stopped whirring, she said, "My friends from high school have real jobs. No one would want to work here anyway."

Before they could continue the discussion, the first customer of the day arrived. "Welcome to Kitchen Bliss," a sullen Kayla said in a monotone without making eye contact with the customer.

"Good morning, Miss Lydia. Glad you recovered from that nasty bout of pneumonia," Matt said.

"I'll help myself to a cup of your enticing coffee before I start shopping."

Matt accompanied Miss Lydia to the coffee station and poured a cup. "Service with a smile." Matt glared at Kayla and opened his hands as if to say this is how we treat customers at Kitchen Bliss.

Miss Lydia wandered around the store, returned to the coffee pot, and made a few inexpensive purchases—a tiny wooden spoon, a dishcloth, and a small box of tea bags.

"What a waste of time," Kayla said after Miss Lydia left. "She drank more coffee than her measly purchases were worth."

"She lives on a fixed income. All her friends have died. I'm glad she chooses to come here."

"Whatever." Kayla returned to crossing her arms and scowling her face.

Late in the afternoon, Matt approached Kayla. "We're having a slow day. You can leave now. I'm sure your mother could use some help with the laundry. I can't imagine your aunt is much of a caretaker. I'll walk home."

"Sorry I'm such a pain in the butt. Thanks for the use of the car."

"Given any more thought about what we talked about this morning?"

"I liked the idea that I could hire someone, but I don't know anyone. You're on your own, Dad."

The bell announcing a customer interrupted the father-daughter conversation.

"Saved by the bell," Kayla muttered. She took off her apron and hung it in the storeroom.

Before she left, Matt said, "Come here, princess, and give me a hug. I hate to see your pretty face with a miserable expression."

Kayla hugged her dad in return.

Chapter 13

The caller i.d. on Ali's landline indicated her mother was calling. Bad enough Janelle was trying her hand at caretaking, now her mother probably wanted to jump on the Red Cross wagon.

"We're all coming to my house for dinner. A family reunion. Won't it be wonderful?"

"Sure, Mom. What can I bring? Forget that. Hard to cook on one foot."

"You don't need to bring a thing. We're going to have our family's favorites. Especially your sister's favorites—oven-fried chicken, potato salad, coleslaw, corn on the cob, and baked beans."

"I don't remember Janelle liking any of those foods. Are you sure?" Ali stopped before she reminded her mother her second daughter hated the sight of baked beans, as well as the favorite daughter.

"I know my own daughter don't I, dear? Now don't be cranky. Be here at seven."

"Okie dokie."

Kayla entered the house dangling the keys to the store and the car. "Hey, Mom. Freedom. Dad gave me the key to his car since you don't trust me with your old pickup."

"What's he supposed to use?"

"The Green Monster. You aren't driving anywhere."

Ali shrugged her shoulders. "We're going to your grandparents' for dinner," Ali said.

"Gramps texted me. I'll meet you there. I need some exercise," Kayla said, as she took Roxie's leash from the back of the kitchen door.

"Guess the laundry can wait until tomorrow," Ali said.

At the sight and sound of Kayla taking the leash off the door, Roxie barked and jumped around in circles. The twosome left the house and headed to the Withrow home. Straight ahead, a young man was walking toward her. He had two dogs in tow. As they moved closer, Kayla crossed the street, hoping to bypass the dog walker.

"Kayla. Kayla. Stop. Don't you want to talk to me?" Logan said.

Caught in the act of trying to avoid Logan, Kayla returned to her side of the street. She bent down toward Logan's dogs and scratched their ears. "Hi there, Jake and Elwood. Come say hi to Roxie." The three dogs sniffed each other.

"Any news from the pawnshop?" Logan asked.

"No. And no time to talk. Family dinner. You know how my grandmother is about family dinners. Can't be late."

"Would it be rude if I came? Your grandparents like me."

"Not this time. Sort of a reunion since my aunt's home. Strictly a family thing."

"Yeah, sure. You used me to take you to the pawnshop because I had a car and I'm eighteen."

"I'll call you."

"Sure you will. Don't forget you said you'd go to the Ed Sheeran concert with me."

"Whatever."

"I'll let you know when I buy the tickets."

Kayla flipped her hair.

They went their separate ways. "He's another reason why I don't want to be in Willoughby all summer. What did I ever see in that loser?" Kayla said to Roxie.

When Kayla and Roxie arrived at Virginia and Ed's home, Alva, Ed's canine companion and Roxie look-alike, was waiting at the screen door wagging his tail. Kayla entered the house and unleashed Roxie who greeted her pal and the two dogs ran to the doggie door off the sunroom to romp in the backyard.

"Smells yummy, Nana."

"Home cooking makes everyone happy." Virginia wore a denim apron trimmed in white lace. "Give your Nana a hug."

"Can I do anything?" Kayla asked. "Set the table?"

"There's my college girl."

"Regular or fancy?"

"Fancy. This is a homecoming to celebrate your aunt's arrival in Willoughby. Let's hope it's permanent."

Kayla walked to the wooden box where the sterling silver was confined and released for special occasions or holidays.

Matt heard Kayla and joined her in the dining room. "See you're doing the traditional work of the grandchild."

"Do I have a choice?"

"I don't suppose you do." Matt walked over to Kayla and kissed the top of her head. "Misery won't make being stuck in Willoughby all summer any better."

"Thanks for the advice, Pop." She placed a fork on the table with a thump, a spoon with another thump, and let a knife slide from her hand. "Why six placemats? Who else is coming tonight?"

Virginia overheard Kayla. "Shh. I have a surprise for Janelle."

"We're out here," Ali hollered from the sunroom. "Janelle too."

"All drinking cocktails. What do I drink? A Coke?" Kayla directed her comments to her dad.

"Take a beer. Your mother can't criticize you for that. She put away a few when she was in college." He gave her a conspiratorial wink.

Virginia had prepared the family's traditional hors d'oeuvres: celery stuffed with cream cheese and chives, cheese straws, pimento cheese and crackers, and sliced red apples. A cheesy family. She placed the food on platters and carried the appetizers to the porch with Kayla's help.

Ali was sitting in a club chair covered in yellow and blue flowered chintz. Her ankle was elevated on an ottoman covered in material matching the chair.

"Everyone's watching calories, so you can put the pimento cheese on apples," Virginia said. "You think my food is old-fashioned compared with Ali's fancy food, but you always eat everything I prepare."

"Under penalty of waterboarding," Ed said.

"If I thought you were serious, I would be offended. You and Ali both have an odd sense of humor. Not from my side of the family."

Ali and Ed shared a smile.

The family continued eating their "favorite" albeit old-fashioned appetizers. Ed served Virginia a gimlet and made manhattans for Matt and himself. He poured Ali and Janelle glasses of Edna Valley pinot grigio.

"I'm overjoyed to have everyone I love together," Virginia said as she sipped her cocktail.

After everyone had his or her favorite beverage, the conversation centered on Janelle. Virginia peppered Janelle with questions regarding her life. Where did she buy the beautiful piece of jewelry hanging around her neck or did a special someone buy it for her?

"This is costume. Not expensive. Speaking of jewelry, Kayla, I see you decided to wear the emerald. It seems different. The chain perhaps?"

Kayla put her hand to her throat. "Ah, sure. Cheese straws anyone?"

The sound of the kitchen timer alerted Virginia dinner was ready. She placed her drink on the table next to the pimento cheese.

"I'll help you, Nana." Kayla took her grandmother's cocktail, snuck a sip, and followed her into the kitchen.

Virginia removed the chicken from the oven. A black crust had formed on the bottom and sides of the pan. "Oh dear, the chicken is a tiny bit overcooked, but we don't care, do we, darling?"

"Doesn't matter, Nana. What counts is you made it with love." Kayla turned on the ceiling fan.

Back on the porch, Ali said to Janelle, "You might want to lend a hand in the kitchen."

"I have no talent in the kitchen."

"Make an effort," Ali said.

Janelle entered the kitchen, removed the salads from the refrigerator, and took them to the dining room where she positioned herself at the head of the table.

Matt put his arm around Ali's waist and helped her hobble to the dining room.

"Don't forget the beans, Kayla," Virginia said. "Your aunt's favorite."

"Baked beans? Have I ever eaten a baked bean in my adult life? Ghastly," Janelle said, loud enough for Virginia to hear.

"Are the beans Alicia's favorites? My, my. Someone likes them," Virginia said.

"Me," Kayla said. She took the beans to the table and set the bowl in front of Janelle. They stared each other down.

Janelle blinked. "I'll try one little bite." She took a spoonful. "I was mistaken, Mother. The beans are tasty. When I have my own place, you'll have to share the recipe."

Kayla snickered.

Ali motioned for Matt to go to the kitchen where he rescued the corn on the cob from a pot of boiling water, drained it, and brought it to the table.

The doorbell rang. "Oh, goodie. Our surprise guest has arrived."

Chapter 14

"For crying out loud! Why is he here?" Janelle asked when she approached the bay window in the dining room.

"I'm glad you could join us tonight, Bradley," Virginia said as she greeted their dinner guest at the door.

"I'm grateful for the invitation, Virginia." He held a bouquet of yellow and red tulips and handed them to her.

"How thoughtful," she said, as she accepted the flowers.

"Can't compare with your spectacular garden," Brad said. When he entered the dining room, everyone but Janelle greeted him. She sat straight as a ruler and twirled the stem of her wine glass.

"Too bad you've been under the weather, Janelle. The airline food?" Brad asked.

"Have you been sick, dear?" Virginia asked.

"Let's put the flowers in water," Janelle said as she stood and took the flowers from her mother. She indicated Brad should follow her. Janelle searched for a vase and dumped the flowers in it. She set the vase on the kitchen table with a bang, rocking a wicker basket of fruit.

"I suppose I blindsided you, but I don't know how to get your attention. You don't answer my texts, my phone calls. You're hiding out at Ali's. What are you afraid of? I'm not one of your loser ex-husbands."

"This is not the place nor the time. How could you barge in on our family's dinner?"

"Excuse me. Your mother invited me. What was I supposed to do? Ask for your permission? Do you want me to leave? Because if I leave now, we're over before we gave ourselves a chance to start."

Janelle tried to rearrange the drooping tulips.

"What's the answer? Leave or stay?" Brad asked.

"If you leave, they'll all interrogate me. Please don't leave," she whispered as she gripped his arm and locked her eyes on his.

Brad turned his back on Janelle and returned to the table taking a seat next to Virginia. He put his napkin in his lap. All eyes were on him. "Everything's fine. Let's enjoy this excellent meal our delightful and attractive hostess has taken the time to prepare."

Virginia blushed. "Oh, Brad," she said.

After an obligatory blessing by Kayla, she added a p.s. "I'm so happy Aunt Janelle is here, and she and my mom are friends."

A few "cheers" and the family passed the food around the table.

"The chicken's overcooked, but you make the best potato salad in Willoughby," Ed said as he piled the food on his plate. "The beans aren't bad either."

"The food is terrific, Virginia. Thank you so much for inviting me," Brad said. He sent daggers Janelle's way.

Everyone ate, but conversation was limited. Ed broke the silence. "How're you girls getting along with the new book? Going to give us a little hint about the story?"

Janelle glared at her sister. "Ali refuses to write with me."

"Write alone. In fact, you two should write separate novels," Ed suggested. "Why do you need a co-writer, Janelle? Or Ali either? All you do is argue."

"Writing can be such a solitary occupation, but Ali and I shared such a pleasant time. Didn't we?"

"It was grand," Ali said. She took a sip of wine. "Once was enough."

"Girls, you can't write alone. I was proud to have two daughters who have such a wonderful friendship that they wrote a book together. I've told all my friends you're going to repeat your success—together."

Ali and Janelle remained quiet.

"Let's have dessert and talk about this later," Virginia said.

Brad declined dessert. He thanked Virginia and Ed and left the house.

Janelle followed him to his car. "Let's talk tomorrow," she said. "I've been out of line." She grasped the sleeve of his shirt. "I panicked when I thought Phoebe left me her house. That's not true is it?"

"You can try to call me and let's see how fast I return *your* calls."

Janelle watched his car leave the driveway.

Will I ever see him again?

When Janelle returned to the dining room she said, "Mother, whatever gave you the idea to invite him? Your timing is awful. I wasn't ready."

Virginia curled her lower lip and put her hands on her face. "What have I done? Some of my garden club friends have been watching the changes to Phoebe's house and they overheard Brad say something to one of the workers that the house was for you, so I thought there must be something going on with you that you didn't want anyone to know and you know how much we love Brad and now I've caused trouble—"

"For Pete's sake, Virginia. Control yourself. I don't think having Brad here was so bad. I like the guy."

Kayla stood and moved to her grandmother's side. "Don't cry, Nana."

Ali and Matt glowered at Janelle and shook their heads.

"Now what are you going to do?" Ali asked her sister.

Chapter 15

J anelle tossed and turned throughout the night. She regretted her rude and cruel treatment toward Brad at her parents' house. She didn't know how to gauge his reaction. He was either hurt or angry. She hoped the email she had sent to Brad would remedy her disrespectful attitude toward him.

Plus, her outrage at her mother was unacceptable. Janelle decided an apology to her mother was needed, too. She would agree to meet with her mother's garden club, as Virginia suggested. One time.

When she knew sleep was unattainable, she put on a robe, crept down the stairs, and entered the Lawrence kitchen. Although Matt was not there, she was grateful he had made the coffee before he left for his morning run. After pouring herself a cup, she sat at the table with her phone and searched for messages. The message she was hoping for didn't appear.

With nothing else to do, Janelle opened the *Atlanta Journal Constitution*, which Matt had placed on the table. She turned to the obituaries, a routine she had copied from Ali. She scanned the names of the departed but didn't recognize anyone. After she finished one pot of coffee, she prepared another.

At least there's one thing I can do in the kitchen.

"Morning, Big Sis," Ali said as she limped into the kitchen rubbing her eyes. "Hope the coffee's ready."

"Good morning, Li'l Sis," Janelle said as she raised her cup in the direction of the coffeemaker. "Fill mine up, too. Please." She hesitated. "Stop! I'm supposed to wait on you." Janelle brought the coffee carafe to the table and filled two mugs.

The bright morning sun snuck through the bay window shutters.

"That sun is irritating," Janelle said.

"Put on your sunglasses," Ali said as she reached for the *Metro* section of the paper.

"I won't bug you about writing together. I accept your decision to write alone, but don't be disappointed when my book does better than yours," Janelle said.

"I'll be heartbroken," Ali said as she flipped a page in the paper.

"Your decision is firm?"

"You betcha," Ali said. "Case closed."

Janelle flinched when her phone pinged indicating a text message.

"This is it. I knew he'd come around," Janelle said. "I have nothing to wear. I've gained so much weight. Not that much. A few pounds. Where will I shop in Willoughby? Nowhere. I need more time. What about my hair? Are my roots showing? Do I need color?"

"A retail explosion has taken place on Willoughby Lane. You'll find upscale shops. And, your hair is fine."

Janelle handed Ali her phone. "Read the text from Brad."

Ali read the short message. "He's asking you out for dinner. So what?"

"I thought he was gone from me forever after he showed up unannounced at Mother's for dinner. I was rude. I admit it. Not too rude?"

"Mother invited him. Yes, you were unpleasant. Made everyone uncomfortable. What's going on with you and Brad?"

"Mother should have told me he was coming. I don't like surprises."

"You seemed pretty excited when he told you *he* had a surprise."

"He didn't say anything about a surprise when we were in Sani—"

"When you were where? You've hardly seen him since you've been back. In fact, you've been ignoring him and asking me to help you with your subterfuge. Brad's our friend and I won't lie to him anymore."

Janelle disregarded Ali's question. "This must be it. He'll give it to me tonight."

"Whatever." Ali returned to the obituaries. "This is a shock. I saw Mr. Bigelow a week ago. Lived to be ninety-five. The casserole brigade will be out in full force. Hope I have one in the freezer." She paused. "Here's an idea. How would you like to make a chicken casserole?"

"You are so funny. Anyway, I asked you to try to find out what Brad has for me but evidently you didn't."

"Guess not."

"Aren't you the least bit curious?"

"You're curious enough for both of us. It's probably some knick-knack Phoebe left for you. Or some books."

"What am I supposed to do with old books?"

"You're an author. No personal collection of your favorite books?"

"Besides the eighteen I wrote? Ahh. Nineteen. I always forget to count the one we wrote together. Can't say I have a book collection." She took the *Living* section from the paper. "By the way. What would you think if I lived here?"

"Where?"

"Where do you think? Here. Willoughby. Not *here* in your house, of course."

Ali choked on her coffee. "Why?" she sputtered.

"Who, what, where, why? Are you becoming a journalist? I want to live near my family. I want a burial plot in Willoughby to make it convenient for my family to visit my gravesite. Even though everyone asks how I maintain my appearance. Some people think I'm the younger sister."

"Is that right?"

"Don't misunderstand. Willoughby would be a home base. You can take care of the house or townhome or whatever I decide to buy or rent. Yes, rent is the better option. That way I won't be tied down."

Ali took a sip of coffee. "I suspect you won't find anything up to your standards. What's your budget?"

"No budget. I'll buy what I want." And then she whispered to herself, "Have to finish the book first."

"Excuse me?"

"Nothing," Janelle said. She glanced at her Rolex and stood to leave. "I'd better get dressed for lunch."

"Who are you having lunch with?"

"No one important. After lunch, shopping for my date tonight. I wonder where he'll take me."

"Probably Mia Bella." Ali lied to her. She had promised Brad not to tell Janelle the surprise was a generous gift from Phoebe—a house. A newly renovated house. Brad had been secretive about the house saying it was all Phoebe's idea and he had nothing to do with it. Before Ali's ankle injury, she would jog by the house and marvel at the changes Brad was overseeing. The front yard had been torn up and replaced with lush sod. A pile of attractive stones was waiting to replace the worn walkway.

Ali thought about the loyalty Brad had shown toward his grandmother. Despite his feelings or lack of feelings for Janelle, he was going all out to respect his grandmother's wishes.

"I thought we would go into Buckhead. He didn't say in his text. Oh well, food is food. See you later." She approached the staircase, stopped, and returned to Ali's side.

"Here's the deal. You're right. I don't want to live year-round in Willoughby. I would suffocate, but if you help me write the book, I promise to leave. Return for holidays and birthdays. Special occasions."

"What about marrying Brad?"

"That was his idea, not mine." After she retreated upstairs to her bedroom to dress for lunch, she left the house without saying a word to Ali.

"She's tenacious. I'll give her that," Ali said to Roxie. "But I'm not giving in."

Chapter 16

"Thank you for the lunch invitation," Monica Livingston said to Janelle after they took their seats at The Big Ketch on Willoughby Lane. "I must say I am curious. We haven't seen much of each other since high school."

Janelle observed Monica's smooth skin and unwrinkled neck. She'd been under the knife, no doubt. She wore a two-tone striped black dress with a crew neck and cap sleeves. Janelle recognized it as a Hugo Boss design. Monica carried an oversized yellow clutch purse. Her only jewelry was a pair of sparkling diamond stud earrings. Janelle surmised they were several carats.

"I want to become part of the Willoughby community now that I'm going to live here semi-permanently and thought you could help me. Your list of accomplishments is impressive. Are you going to run for mayor someday?" Janelle asked.

"I love Willoughby and want to ensure this town doesn't lose its charm," Monica said. She glanced over her shoulder to where a group of smartly dressed women entered the restaurant. "Why Willoughby? Aren't you more of an urbanite? I'm surprised at your choice of suburban Willoughby as a permanent residence."

"Semi-permanent."

"Why lunch today? You said you want my help?"

"I know how influential you are in the community. Some might say you are the doyenne of everything Willoughby."

"I wouldn't go that far. You always were one to exaggerate."

"Could you recommend a worthy volunteer opportunity that might suit me and, of course, aid unfortunate people in need?"

"Hmm." Monica tapped her French-manicured fingernails like a woodpecker on the white tablecloth. "The humane society always needs volunteers."

"Dogs?"

"Pretty much."

"Allergic," Janelle lied. The thought of dog hair and drool made her nauseous. She faked a cough.

"The homeless shelter always needs people—"

Janelle wrinkled her nose. "Germs? My skin is sensitive."

A young male server approached their table with glasses of water. He presented menus and recited the specials for the day. Janelle was grateful for the interruption. She took a sip of water to quench her dry mouth. "Perhaps we should order now," she said, hoping to move this lunch along.

After the women placed their orders, Monica said, "Why not discuss your altruistic epiphany with your sister? Ali's involvement in the community is well known. She did a fabulous job chairing the Willoughby Book Banquet, for example. Now that she's a full-time author, she had to curtail her volunteerism. Why not ask her for advice?"

Janelle took another sip of water. She was craving a glass of wine but was reluctant to order one since Mrs. Upstanding Citizen of Willoughby was her luncheon companion. Janelle had heard she was straight-laced and perhaps a liquor-abstaining Baptist. "I want this to be a surprise." Janelle took a tissue from her purse and dabbed at non-existent tears. "You'll find this hard to believe, but I have been somewhat self-centered. I want to change my ways and make Ali proud of me. She must never know what I'm planning. Until I'm a success at whatever I choose to do, of course."

"May I be frank, Janelle? I have known you and of you for many years. I can't think of a single organization suited for you so cut the bullshit."

Janelle's eyes widened.

"Those are the phoniest tears I've ever seen." She paused and motioned to their server. "Two glasses of your house Chardonnay. Alcohol is required at this table. Now. Please."

While they were waiting for the wine to be served, Monica said, "I'm only trying to be helpful, Janelle. I admire your successful writing career. Ten books you've authored?"

"Actually, eighteen. Nineteen counting the one with Ali."

Another reason why no one should ever discover Phoebe was my ghostwriter.

"I want to protect Ali who is a dear friend. You have never had her best interests in mind. Remember how unkind you were to her and many other girls when we were in high school."

"I've changed. Ali and I are fabulous friends. After all, we wrote a book together. And, we rarely disagreed during the entire process." Janelle hoped Ali had never confided in Monica because what she said was a fat whopper of a lie.

"You don't say. If that's true I promise to suggest some organization, which could use your skills. Whatever those skills are."

"You're outspoken," Janelle said above a whisper.

"Now, now. Don't be sensitive." She placed her napkin on the table. "I see a few friends I must say hello to. Excuse me." While Monica was talking with her friends, she glanced over at Janelle several times. Her friends giggled and stared at Janelle.

Janelle had purposely reserved a table in the center of the restaurant so other diners would see her with influential Monica. She regretted her decision, as she checked her watch. Her throat tightened, and she was grateful the server refilled her water glass.

When Monica returned, Janelle was sipping the glass of Chardonnay Monica had ordered.

"Glad you didn't wait for me," Monica said observing Janelle's half-empty glass. "Perhaps you'd like another."

Janelle shook her head. *That's all I need. Drink too much and have Monica spread it all around town that I'm a wino, even though I seem to be headed in that direction.*

"Tell me about your latest book you and Ali are writing. Your fans are waiting."

"We might try writing separately. Nothing definite."

"What a mistake. The book you co-wrote was far superior to those other books. At least the few I read."

This time Janelle's tears were sincere. The woman wouldn't stop berating and demeaning her. Janelle wasn't sure what she had done to Monica to deserve such animosity thrown at her like confetti on New Year's Eve. Must have been something to do with a boyfriend. Janelle recalled that was the reason she didn't have many girlfriends in high school. All the girls were jealous of Janelle and claimed she stole their boyfriends.

The server delivered their seafood salads and both women inhaled their food. Janelle paid the bill and they said curt goodbyes.

Before they left, Monica said to Janelle, "The Drake Closet. On Mimosa. Check it out. Don't tell them I recommended you."

Chapter 17

Janelle opened the blinds to let the morning sunshine fill the spare bedroom. With effort, she pulled one of her suitcases from the closet and dumped the contents on the floor. Shoes scattered everywhere. She examined a pair of yellow and green ballet flats.

What was I thinking? I must have been tequila-influenced to buy these. Looks like something Ali would wear.

She tossed them aside and continued throwing shoes haphazardly into a pile. One shoe hit the wall causing a picture on the wall to fall to the floor.

Ali shouted from downstairs, "What happened?"

Janelle opened the bedroom door and shouted, "I'm fine. Organizing shoes." She selected a pair of open toe wedgies, not as high as her usual stilettos, but still high.

She showered and applied makeup. She hesitated before she left the bathroom. Should she clean up the mess she and Kayla had made—makeup scattered around the countertop, towels on the floor, wastebasket overflowing?

I'm a guest. This is Kayla's job.

A few minutes later Janelle met Ali in the kitchen. "Think I'll take a walk around the neighborhood for inspiration for my book."

"So, you *are* writing a book."

"I'll try."

"Are those shoes comfortable for a walk? I saved your tennis shoes from last time you were here. They're in the back of my closet."

"Never mind. These will do just fine."

"Suit yourself, Janelle. If you break your ankle, *I'd* have to take care of *you*."

"I'm supposed to help you, but you are too independent."

"Have a nice walk."

Janelle waved goodbye to Ali and left the house. She walked toward Willoughby Lane. She had no destination in mind but wanted to clear her mind and try to figure out a way to find some money.

She found herself on charming Mimosa Street where Ali and Matt were married thirty years ago. The tree-lined street was the home to three Protestant churches built circa 1800: First Baptist, United Methodist, and First Presbyterian. The Doric columned First Presbyterian served as a hospital during the Civil War or as some Southerners said, "The War of Northern Aggression." Janelle paused at the white picket fence, which surrounded the entrance to Primrose Cottage event facility, where Ali and Matt held their wedding.

When it was time for Ali to choose a maid or matron of honor, Ellen was Ali's first choice. Virginia overruled Ali's decision saying it would be inappropriate not to choose her sister. "What would people think?" Virginia claimed. Janelle declined citing an unspecified previous engagement.

If Janelle closed her eyes, she could visualize the shock on Ali's face when Janelle made a grand entrance at the wedding. At the last minute, she surprised everyone when she crashed the party. Janelle could picture every detail about Ali's special day. The flowers, the music, Ali's elegant dress.

I wouldn't mind having a real wedding someday, reminiscent of Ali's.

She reached the end of Mimosa and headed back toward Willoughby Lane when she passed a small one-story brick house painted white with a white columned porch. *The Drake House Closet,* the sign on the front lawn read.

This was the place Monica mentioned. Did she mean for me to volunteer or to shop?

Ali was right. The shoes Janelle chose to wear were not comfortable for walking. Maybe she could find a pair in this store.

When she entered through the front door, a woman with reading glasses on the tip of her nose greeted Janelle. She wore her salt and pepper hair pulled into a ponytail. Long thin silver earrings dangled and swayed. "How may I help you? Do you have clothes to drop off or are you in a buying mood?" the pleasant woman said.

"Shoes?"

"To buy?"

Janelle ignored the woman's question. She picked up a pair of Feragamo flats and examined the soles. "What is this place? These shoes aren't new."

"Gently used. You'll see original price tags on some of the items."

"Consignment?"

"No. Everything's donated. Proceeds go to a women's shelter." The woman paused and tilted her head. "Have we met?"

"Ah, don't think so."

Janelle picked up and read a white and purple card at the checkout counter. "The Drake Closet is a ladies' resale shop of new and gently used ladies' clothing, shoes, and accessories. All sales proceeds go to support The Drake House."

Janelle returned her attention toward the designer shoes.

Not bad. Anne Klein. Ralph Lauren. She glanced toward the woman who greeted her. *I bet she's trying to figure out how she knows me. Of course, she does. Everyone in Willoughby knows the author Janelle Jennings.*

Janelle walked toward a glittering display of costume jewelry and picked up a turquoise cuff bracelet. She replaced it, stood back, and admired the small but well stocked store. She would be hard-pressed to make one change to enhance the surroundings—except carrying more designer clothes and shoes, names like Manolo Blahnik and Jimmy Choo. Brands she had in her closet.

When Monica mentioned this place, I thought she meant a place to shop, not volunteer.

"Our designer merchandise goes right out the door," the affable woman said.

Her cheery personality was starting to grate on Janelle. "You're a happy one."

"Why not? When I think of the women and their children whom we support, I have nothing to complain about."

"What is this Drake place?"

"The Drake House provides short term crisis housing. . .this and many other programs for homeless single women and their children."

"Do you need volunteers?"

"Always. You'll find an application at our website. An orientation meeting for new volunteers is coming up. Whatever you need to know is online. Check it out. We love to have volunteers with a sense of style and fashion sense." She aimed her pointed finger at Janelle. "I can see you're a fashionista." She handed her card to Janelle.

"Thank you." She turned to leave. "Who are these women who need help? Not from around here."

"You'd be surprised."

Janelle took the woman's card and left the store. If it hadn't been for Phoebe's help writing her novels, perhaps she'd be one of the women in need, she mused. If she didn't come up with a large amount of money soon, she'd have to move in with Ali or her parents on a permanent basis.

When she returned to the Lawrence home, a FedEx delivery sat on the table in the foyer.

Ali called out to Janelle. "You received mail. The return address is from New York City. I had to sign for it."

Janelle stood in the hallway and opened the envelope, which she set on the table. Inside was another envelope. She read the contents, clutched both envelopes, and ran upstairs.

After a few minutes, Janelle returned downstairs. "Taking a walk," she said to Ali.

"You're sure in a walking mood," Ali said to her sister who closed the front door without responding. "Better change your shoes."

Chapter 18

Ali was in the kitchen when Roxie ran to the front door barking like crazy.

"I'm glad to see you, too, little one." Ellen picked up Roxie and joined Ali in the kitchen. "I'm back. Brought you some lo-cal snacks. You can't sit all day on your butt and eat chocolate."

"Come here and let me give you a great big hug. I sure missed you. Was the trip great?"

"Better than great. But always good to be home."

Ali scrutinized the container Ellen brought. "No sugar, no fat, tastes like seaweed?"

"About right." Ellen pointed to Ali's ankle. "Making progress?"

"Well...I am improving. It's only been a week." She hopped to the kitchen table.

"You should make an appointment with the physical therapist at my gym. Seems like you should have healed by now. Unless it's more than a simple sprain." Ellen filled her water bottle at the sink. "Where's Queen Bee?"

"Out. Taking a walk."

"In stilettos?"

"Wedgies. She received something in the mail that upset her and took the envelope upstairs. I heard her crying, I think. She came downstairs and left."

"What was in the envelope?"

"I sure would like to know."

"What are you waiting for?"

"I shouldn't. She might have taken it with her. In her purse."

"You shouldn't, but you know you will. Gotta run. Keep me posted."

"Thanks for the gift. I guess," Ali said. She stared out the window for a few minutes. If her sister had been crying, no, sobbing, the contents of the letter must be of consequence.

Ali made an imprudent hop up the stairs using the banister as a crutch. She opened the door to Janelle's bedroom. "As I imagined, it's a mess up here," she said to Roxie who had followed her. Ali sat on the unmade bed and surveyed the multiple pairs of shoes and boxes strewn around the room like a BOGO sale at DSW.

Ali decided if the FedEx envelope was in plain sight, no search warrant was needed. At least that's what happens on *Law & Order*. However, the law might apply to law enforcement and not nosy sisters. "What's your opinion, Roxie?"

While still sitting, she glanced around the room. If the envelope was confidential, Janelle might have secured it in her purse. Ali saw her sister's purse on the floor near the closet. Ali bent over to rub her now throbbing ankle. She'd better make this quick before Janelle returned. She rested for a few minutes on the side of the bed. When she stood on one foot, she saw the FedEx envelope peeking out from under a corner of the bedspread. Ali seized it.

She held the envelope up to the light but couldn't see anything. She shook it, hoping something would fall out. Nothing. The seal was broken on the envelope. Would be easy to slip out the contents, read it, and put it back without Janelle ever knowing.

This was reminiscent of the sisters reading each other's youthful diaries despite hiding them in a covert location every day. Regardless, they always found each other's diary. The difference was Ali kept secret what she had read in Janelle's diary, unlike Janelle who blabbed everything she read in Ali's. When Ali was thirteen, she wised up and put the diary under lock and key.

She placed the envelope under the bedspread hoping it was in the exact place where Janelle left it. "Oh, why not," she said. She pulled the FedEx envelope out and searched inside for its content. Another letter addressed to Janelle was marked personal and confidential. Ali sat to read it.

Dear Ms. Jennings: My heart is heavy as I tell you that my stepfather Howard Jennings passed away last week. He died peacefully in his sleep while I was holding his hand.

He loved my mother and me, but after my mother died ten years ago, he told me he alone knew the real Janelle, the Janelle he loved. The sweet, vulnerable, beautiful woman he had married.

Howard bequeathed to you a generous financial gift. He was an immensely wealthy man.

Howard stipulated, before you receive the money, you must write another novel with your sister. Broken Bones-Broken Promises seemed more authentic and soft, the way he remembered you. Your heroine wasn't as cold-hearted and manipulative as heroines in your previous books. (He read all your books.) Howard credited your sister for the change in tone.

Subsequent to the publication of your next novel, with your sister Alicia Lawrence, Howard's lawyer will contact Mr. Kenneth Luzi and arrange for the disposition of assets.

Howard thought you might procrastinate, thus he has given you and your sister a deadline of one year.

I hope I will have the pleasure to meet you sometime.

I read your books, too.

Best regards, Alexandra Ryane

Ali clutched her stomach. She needed a Tums.

I should not have read this.

She waited a few minutes to recover and limped downstairs to hunt for her phone.

"Dad. Can you come over? I've done something terrible and I need your advice."

"I'm on my way, Gingersnap. Alva needs a walk."

Ali was waiting for her dad on the front porch.

When Ed arrived, he unleashed his dog to let Roxie and her canine cousin chase butterflies in the yard. He knelt and strapped his version of an ice pack to Ali's ankle. "I whipped this up in my workshop. Better than that contraption Matt made for you."

"Thanks, Dad."

"So, what's going on?"

She confessed to her dad what she had done. "The letter is upstairs under Janelle's bedspread. The seal on the envelope was already broken. Go upstairs before she returns and—"

"I don't read other people's mail. Including my children's."

"Dad, please."

"What if you *tell* me about the contents? Not the same as *reading* it."

After Ali told Ed about Howard's bequeath and the stipulation, he said, "You must never tell Janelle you read it. What you did was wrong. And now I'm your accomplice."

Ali bowed her head.

Ed remained silent.

"What do I do now?"

"Make the decision I know you will. The right decision." He patted her on her head. "By the way, I miss your curls. Don't know about this straightening look." He stood and said to Alva, "Let's go."

Ali knew she now had a responsibility to write with Janelle. Sure, she could blow her off, but Janelle's recent complaints about needing money had escalated. Writing with her sister wasn't altruistic. Ali was a slow, methodical writer and the sooner she finished the novel with Janelle, the sooner she would see her name on the cover of the book.

She reached in her pocket for a Tums and threw it into her mouth. The old resentment was percolating in her stomach. She wasn't sure if she could handle Janelle for the duration of writing a book. Now, she had no choice. Since she shared the contents of the letter with her dad, she didn't want to let him down. He would lose respect for her and she couldn't bear that.

Ali sent a text to Ellen asking her to stop by on her way home from running.

Ellen joined Ali on the front porch steps. "What did you find out?"

"I read it. Felt sneaky though." Ali detailed the contents of the letter from Howard's stepdaughter.

"How much money are we talking about?"

"I don't have a clue, but Howard was a wealthy man, according to his stepdaughter. Janelle seems to be in a money crunch. She cites cash flow problems. I should help her."

"What?! You're going to write another novel with her? Go ahead and pull out your eyebrows and eyelashes and your fingernails, so you'll remember how pain feels."

"The result surpassed the process. My problem is that I made a huge deal about not writing with Janelle and now I have to reverse my decision."

"Wait a few days and tell her you've had an epiphany. Say Phoebe came to you in a dream. No, make it a nightmare. Say she demanded you write with Janelle."

"If I can't think of anything better, I'll use that." She clutched her stomach. "Let's change the topic," Ali said.

Chapter 19

J anelle was in a funk after the unsettling lunch with Monica. And, Janelle was desperate for the return of the emerald. She still hadn't figured out how to persuade Kayla to "loan" her the item so she could sell it. Time was running out. She had sold her other pieces of expensive jewelry. Her Rolex was still a possibility. Would he take it as a payoff and leave her alone forever?

Ali's blasé comment about the jewel "being somewhere in Kayla's room" sent up a red flag. Plus, Janelle was convinced the emerald Kayla wore at dinner was a fake.

Janelle decided to confront Kayla at Kitchen Bliss. If the conversation between aunt and niece escalated to an argument, perhaps a customer strolling in would defuse the situation. Matt was attending a gift and housewares show at the Mart and today was Bailey's day off. Ali, complaining of cabin fever, had been rescued by Ellen for brunch with friends.

Janelle knew firsthand that a trail of deception leads to unhappiness and she wanted to protect the niece she loved so much. . .and retrieve the gem, of course.

Except for Kayla, the store was empty when Janelle arrived. *So far, so good.*

Kayla's monotone "Welcome to Kitchen Bliss" greeted her. Janelle noticed Kayla's hand immediately touched the base of her throat. A revealing clue. A sign of guilt. "Time to confess, missy. I could spot that phony emerald you wore the other night a mile away."

"No one else did," Kayla said. "I thought your eyesight was getting bad. You know, at your age. Mom's is." She offered a crooked smile. "By the way, good morning, Aunt Janelle."

"Never mind the chitchat. I'm not mad, Kayla. I am curious. The gem was a gift. A rather expensive gift."

"Which means you didn't pay for it."

"And why would that devalue the jewel?"

"It was a gift to you and then it was a gift to me, so I guess it's mine to worry about," Kayla snickered.

Janelle hit her fist on the counter. "You admit you lost it? Damn! I was counting on it."

"What?"

"None of your concern, sweetie. I'm not angry. Disappointed." Janelle walked toward the coffee station. "Don't you have any real cups? I don't like paper."

"Gee, Aunt Janie. Every time I think you're becoming a different person, you revert to being bitchy."

"Show some respect."

"Ha! You should talk." Kayla took a mug off a shelf that read: "Never Underestimate a Well-Read Woman." She filled it for her aunt and resumed her post at the checkout counter.

Janelle followed her niece and perched herself on a stool next to Kayla. The doorbell jingled announcing a visitor. "A very good morning to our dear customer. Welcome to Kitchen Bliss," Janelle said to the stranger. "That's how it's done," she whispered to Kayla who smirked.

Kayla slid off the stool. "A little over the top, if you ask me." Kayla offered to assist the customer who said she was browsing.

"Excellent customer service is essential in the retail business," Janelle said. "I should know. I've spent enough money shopping. Too much."

"Here's what happened," Kayla said when she rejoined her aunt. She creased her forehead and blurted, "I wanted money for Italy, but no one would help me so I tried to sell the gem but Luca came here so I didn't need to sacrifice the gem so I returned to the pawnshop but—"

"Slow down! Take a deep breath."

At a slower pace, Kayla continued the saga about her inability to recover the jewel.

"Don't worry. Did you sign anything?"

"Logan did. It wasn't an official document. Just a piece of paper."

"Where did you go? Jim's Gems?"

Kayla nodded. "I'm sorry. Really sorry. It was probably worth a lot more than the pawnshop would have given me. I was desperate. Foolish."

Janelle kissed her niece on the top of her head and headed toward the door. "This is all going to work out fine. Your aunt is in charge. Besides, what's a gem? Only a material object. I'm trying to change my ways. I'm not the materialistic aunt you think I am."

"Aren't you forgetting the emerald is mine? It was a gift." She winked at her aunt.

"Minor detail. You have plenty of time in your young life to acquire expensive jewelry."

* * *

When Janelle arrived at Jim's, a beefy man wearing a black T-shirt opened the door. Janelle strained her neck to meet his eyes and said, "Who's in charge?"

A young woman with purple hair and a nose ring, standing nearby, said, "My grandpa is out right now, but I'm sure I can help you." Her name badge read *Destiny*.

Janelle pulled out her phone and showed the woman a photo of herself wearing a low cut, full-length carmine gown with the shiny stone hanging from a silver chain around her neck. "I demand you return this."

"Wow! A beautiful dress."

"Forget about the dress. What about the emerald?"

"Why do you think *we* might have it?"

"I don't *think*. I *know* because my niece Kayla Lawrence brought it here."

Several customers were entering the store. "Let's move to the back where we have more privacy," Destiny said.

"You okay? Need help?" the beefy man asked Destiny.

"I can handle this one," she said as she rolled her eyes. Once they were in the stuffy, dark room, the clerk said, "I'm sworn to secrecy but don't worry. Your precious jewel is safe."

"I suppose you're the one who gave my niece the phony one," Janelle yelled.

"She has that one on a temporary basis. Listen, lady, I'm not the bad one here."

"Where is it? I demand to see it."

"Lower your voice. The walls in here are thin. We can't upset our customers. Most of 'em are already nervous or sad when they come in here. Sometimes desperate. Like you."

"I'm not a desperate customer. You took advantage of my poor naïve niece and I want the item returned. Now where is it?" Like a mad woman, Janelle opened a drawer, took a box off a shelf, and threw up her hands in despair. She shook her finger at the nose-ringed girl who took several steps away from Janelle. "Where is it?"

"Sit down and take a deep breath or I'm calling the cops." She handed Janelle a bottle of water. Janelle waved it away.

Janelle didn't relish the idea of the Willoughby police paying a visit, so she acquiesced and sat on a wobbly white plastic chair. An arrest record would mar the new reputation she was trying to develop in Willoughby.

"Some old man came in and talked to my grandpa about it. They knew each other. The old guy left with the emerald, but I swore to both my grandfather and his friend that I wouldn't say a word to anyone. But you scare me, lady."

Janelle took out her phone again and showed Destiny a picture of Ed. "Is this him?"

"Yep. Cute old guy. I overheard him talking to my grandpa. He was complaining about his family. You part of that gang?"

Janelle rubbed her hands together as if she had lotion on them. "Damn it!"

"What?"

"I apologize for becoming hysterical."

"I understand, ma'am. We have many customers who come in here frantic. In fact, yesterday a man came in with his wedding ring—"

"No doubt you've heard lots of sad stories. I must go. Thank you for the information."

Destiny pointed to Janelle's wrist. "If you need money, fancy Rolex. You should talk to my grandpa."

Janelle ignored Destiny and hurried out of the store paying no attention to the stares of curious customers and employees who had heard her hysterics. Janelle sat in the Mercedes that Brad had loaned her reviewing all possibilities of raising enough money to squash her latest dilemma: blackmailing threats from slimy Philip, Ex Number Three.

She was foolish to agree to an outrageous alimony payment to Ex Number Four. Fortunately, Ex Number Two died in a yachting accident, which lowered her expenses. When she had agreed to one lump sum for Philip during the divorce settlement, she thought he was gone forever. She'd have to write more books, if she'd have any hope of regaining firm financial ground.

Howard's money would solve the blackmail problem. But. . .a published book takes months, even years. There's the editing process and meetings to decide the cover, and marketing strategies. It could be another year before the book appeared on bookshelves and on Amazon. *Talk about putting the cart before the horse. I need a manuscript. That's the only solution.*

She sat in the car watching people entering and exiting the pawnshop and wondered what brought them to Jim's Gems. Buying or selling? Returning to retrieve items? They were all trying to solve a problem.

"That's it!" she said. *I'll go to Howard's attorney and prove we have a manuscript. He'll trust us to produce the finished product and maybe he'll give us an advance.* "More of an advance than my stingy publisher will give us."

One slight hitch remained. She needed a manuscript.

Her mind wandered as she assessed her solutions to her problem. She turned on the ignition, stepped on the accelerator, and plowed into the cement stanchion, which supported the parking lot lights in front of her. "Damn!"

She exited the car to observe the damage when another visitor to the pawnshop approached her. "You okay, lady? You sure rammed into that pole." He surveyed the stanchion and her bumper. "Didn't do much damage to the light, but your car don't look so hot."

"Who cares about the damn light? It's the car I'm worried about." She hopped back into the Mercedes and accelerated out of the parking lot. "Aw shit," she said as she sailed over the speed bumps knocking her head repeatedly on the roof of the car.

Chapter 20

"What's that noise?" Ali said to Matt as she shook him awake.

"What noise?"

"A car door slamming and people talking. Shh."

They both listened for more activity.

"Two men, I think," Ali said.

"Better not be Kayla. What time is it?"

Matt checked the time on the bedside clock. "It's three a.m. Nothing good happens after midnight."

Barefoot and wearing only p.j. bottoms, Matt sprinted upstairs to Kayla's room. He opened the door without knocking. She was sound asleep with Roxie at the foot of her bed. Ali and Matt had struggled throughout Kayla's high school years to devise methods to wake her in the morning. Not much had changed.

He returned downstairs, approached the front door, and peered out the frosted glass sidelight.

A slumped body was leaning against one of the white columns on the front porch. Matt turned the porch light on and watched the male figure jump to attention. He towered over Matt, needed a shave, wore jeans, and a white T-shirt. His dark, wavy hair fell into his eyes. A black leather jacket sat on top of an oversized, well-used duffle bag.

"Who the hell are you and what the hell are you doing here at three in the morning?" Matt yelled through the sidelights. "I'm calling the cops."

"No, no! Forgive me. I wanted to surprise Kayla," the mystery visitor said.

When the stranger mentioned Kayla, Matt opened the door, but not wide.

"Why didn't you call or ring the doorbell?"

"I didn't want to wake everyone."

"Well you have. How do you know Kayla?"

Before the early morning visitor had time to answer, Kayla bounded down the stairs. "Luca, Luca, you're here. I gave up hope. You didn't answer my texts." She pulled the door open, but Matt stopped her.

"At least you have a name," Matt said.

"Dad, go put on some clothes."

"Close the door, Kayla. He's not entering this house."

When Kayla didn't comply, Matt shut the door in Luca's face.

"What are you doing, Dad? He's my friend."

Roxie danced in circles yapping and barking.

Ali stood in the background leaning next to the wall on her good ankle. She was wearing an oversized T-shirt and holding a stainless-steel soup ladle. "This could do some damage, or I can call the police," she said waving the ladle in the air.

Luca yelled through the glass. "Mr. and Mrs. Lawrence, I failed to introduce myself. My emotions were so elevated I forgot my manners."

"Open the door," Ali said. "A little." She hopped closer to the door.

Luca extended his hand through the small opening in the door. "Luca Cioni, from Italy. But I was born here. Not in Georgia. In New Jersey."

"New Jersey? Okay, you can drop the phony accent," Matt said. He opened the door.

"Dad. Luca is American and Italian. He goes back and forth from Italy to the states." She jumped into Luca's arms and wrapped her legs around his waist.

"To the kitchen. Everyone. Now," Matt said as he raised his hand and aimed a finger toward the kitchen looking like a tour guide in a museum.

Kayla dropped to Luca's side. He retrieved his duffle bag from the porch and joined the family in the foyer. Roxie sniffed the duffle bag before she trotted upstairs to bed in Kayla's room. A girl needs her beauty sleep.

"Roxie's the only smart one around here. Can't this wait till morning?" Ali said as she stifled a yawn.

"It is morning. Why aren't you more concerned about a strange man visiting Kayla," Matt asked.

Ali stretched her arms over her head. "I'm sure there's a reasonable explanation."

Kayla was staring at the tall Italian with the strong jaw and bloodshot eyes. She took both his hands into hers. "I'm as surprised as you are, Mom and Dad. This will be the best summer of my life. Then Luca and I will go to UGA together in the fall."

"If this conversation is going to continue, we need coffee," Ali said still waving the ladle. She pointed the utensil to Matt and said, "You need some clothes."

"Forget the coffee," Matt announced. "What are your plans, Louis?"

"Luca, Dad. L U C A?"

"Don't be insolent. Do I have to repeat myself, *Luca?*"

"Kayla and I have been communicating since we met in Italy. Last month she invited me here for the summer before we both begin school."

"Do you have money? Have you told your parents you're here? How will you support yourself? Why didn't you check into a hotel until the morning?"

"I think we decided it is morning," Ali said.

"Dad, Mom, please."

"How did you meet Luca?" Ali asked Kayla.

"At the chocolate festival in Perugia last year. The trip Aunt Janelle paid for."

"You were with your grandmother and me," Ali said.

"Not all the time. Sometimes I walked around by myself when you and Nana were napping."

"You walked around Italy by yourself?" Matt asked.

"Not around the country. Around a small city," Kayla said.

"Perugia is safe, Mr. Lawrence. You didn't have to worry."

"Of course, I didn't have to worry because I didn't know I had something to worry about."

"You should have told us you were out alone," Ali said.

"You don't have much of an accent," Matt noted.

"We moved to Italy when I was young, so my parents could help my grandparents with a restaurant in Perugia. I return to the states often. Still have relatives in Jersey."

"Kayla, find some sheets and pillows in the linen closet in the hallway and make up the sofa bed in the den for Luca. Tomorrow we'll figure out sleeping arrangements," Ali said.

"Aunt Janelle should go to Gramps and Nana's. Luca can move into her room," Kayla offered.

Janelle appeared sans robe with her eye mask pushed on top of her head. "Don't I have something to say about that? What's the commotion? I could hear you even with earplugs."

"Janelle," Ali said. "Go upstairs. You're practically naked."

"Aren't you going to introduce me to this handsome visitor?"

Ali put her hands on Janelle's shoulders and turned her around facing the stairway. She gave her a nudge. "We don't need you."

"Okie dokie," Janelle said as she walked toward the stairs.

"To bed, everyone," Ali said. "Luca's in the den for now." She turned off the light in the foyer blanketing everyone in darkness. They took the hint.

Matt stood at the bottom of the staircase expecting Kayla to walk upstairs to her bedroom. Instead, Kayla and Luca entered the den, arm in arm. Kayla glanced over her shoulder to her watchful father. She dropped her arm. "Night, Dad. Don't worry. We're just friends."

"Friends keep the door open," Matt said. He and Ali watched as Kayla closed the door.

"This is a losing proposition. Give up," Ali said.

Matt retreated to his and Ali's first floor bedroom not far from the den. "I can hear them talking," he said to Ali.

"Talking is better than moaning and groaning." Ali climbed into bed and switched off the lamp on her side of the bed. "Close our door."

"But I can't hear what's going on in the den."

"That's the point."

Matt joined her and kept the light on his bedside table lit. He stared at the ceiling. "She's growing up, isn't she? She says they're just friends."

"What we told our parents. She's already grown up and we have to stop hovering."

"Boy, have you changed. What happened to the helicopter mom I was married to?"

"I'm a realist. Come here, big boy." She gave him a sloppy kiss on the lips, turned her back to him, and fell asleep.

Chapter 21

Ali checked her bedside clock at four a.m. It was just an hour ago when their visitor arrived. She heard muffled noises from the den—Luca's assigned room. At five a.m., muted laughter. At six a.m. her body surrendered to sleep. The bright morning sun filtered through the shutters and awoke her an hour later. Matt was sound asleep on his back, gently snoring.

Ali pulled on yoga pants and a T-shirt from the chair next to their bed. She left the crutches behind and limped to the kitchen enticed by the aroma of freshly brewed coffee. The *AJC* was on the kitchen table. Luca was engrossed in looking at his phone.

"Good morning and thanks for making the coffee," Ali said.

Luca stood and greeted his hostess. "Good morning, ma'am. I took the liberty of retrieving your newspaper and hope I was quiet."

"What about you? How come you're up so early?"

"Jet lag, I suppose."

Ali's ritual of morning coffee and newspaper rarely deviated. "Thank you for the coffee and the paper."

He pointed to her ankle. "Please sit. Kayla said you had an accident." He brought her a mug filled with hot java.

"We got off to a bad start last night. I apologize for Mr. Lawrence and me. I'd never use a soup ladle on anyone. Especially my Rosle."

Luca smiled. "Yes, I know the brand." He made a nervous laugh. "No apology. I made the mistake of arriving at such a late. . .early hour." He took a sip of coffee. "I was so excited to see Kayla, I was on Italian time."

Ali took the *Metro* section of the paper and turned to the obituaries. She glanced up to observe Luca staring at her. "Something you want to say?"

"Ahh, no, ma'am." After a few more minutes of silence, except for the swishing sound of pages in the newspaper turning, Luca spoke. "I didn't give Kayla any notice about my arrival, so she was surprised, and you were surprised, too. I see now I made an error in judgment."

"Yep. About right," Ali said, concentrating on the newspaper.

"I'm not welcome. I should move on."

"Absolutely not!" Ali pushed the paper aside. "We'd never hear the end of it from Kayla. One word of caution. Please reassure Mr. Lawrence you can support yourself."

"Not to worry. I have enough money to last through the summer. My parents will help me when school starts."

Ali observed Luca's movie star looks—strong jaw, long eyelashes, dark eyes, and thick hair. Ali approved of her daughter's taste.

Kayla interrupted Ali's thoughts when she bounded out of the den and skipped into the kitchen. "Buongiorno."

"Good morning," Luca said as he rose. He stood still with his hands by his side. Kayla kissed him on his lips and threw her arms around him.

Just friends.

Ali smiled and returned to the newspaper.

"Morning, Mom. You're up early," Kayla said.

Matt joined the party, rubbing his eyes with a scowled expression.

"Coffee, Mr. Lawrence?" Luca asked.

"I'll get my own coffee," Matt said. He went to the coffeemaker and filled a mug.

"Hope you fell back to sleep, Dad."

Matt grunted.

Luca moved to the cupboard and filled one cup with coffee. "Latte?" he asked Kayla. She retrieved milk from the refrigerator and added it to her coffee.

"Mr. Lawrence, I apologize about this morning."

"We'll talk later." Matt picked up the *Sports* section of the paper.

A sleepy Roxie meandered into the kitchen and licked Kayla's ankle. "Let's go, little one." She took her coffee and motioned to Luca with her shoulder. "We'll be in the backyard."

"He's polite," Ali said, after they left.

"I don't want them sleeping together. I don't care how polite he is or isn't. Not sleeping together in our house. Under our roof."

"She's going to do whatever she wants."

"Is it serious with Luca and Kayla?" Matt asked.

"I have no idea. He could be gay as far as I know. Kayla doesn't confide in me anymore. You should do the detective work. Or I could ask Janelle to interrogate Kayla. At least she'd be helpful for something."

Matt put his head down on the kitchen table.

"Why don't you go to bed? Make Kayla open the store. She knows the routine. It's her fault we didn't sleep."

"I'm okay. Nothing a cold shower and an i.v. of caffeine won't fix." He took a sip of coffee. "What do you think about this Luca dude? Had Kayla told you anything about him?"

"Never heard his name. I predict we'll have a guest in our house for the summer."

"We'll see about that." He left for their bedroom.

Ali sat at the table drinking coffee and reading the obituaries. She noted that some of the deceased were the same age or younger than her parents. Ali vowed to have more patience with Virginia and Ed.

Janelle shuffled into the kitchen wearing a tiny piece of black lacy silk posing as a nightgown—lingerie meant for a youthful Victoria Secret model.

"We now have two males living in this house and I don't appreciate your wearing those revealing nightgowns."

Janelle shrugged her shoulders, left to change her clothes, and returned wearing leggings and a loose-fitting tunic. "Where is everyone?"

"Kayla and her handsome friend are in the backyard. Matt's getting ready for work."

"I believe Kayla joined Luca in the den last night. I could spy on them tonight, if you are concerned."

"Leave them alone, Janelle."

"Don't you care?"

"After a child moves away, parental control evaporates."

When Kayla returned to the kitchen, Ali said, "Your dad is exhausted. Lack of sleep." She peered over her reading glasses and stared at Kayla. "I hope you plan to work at the store today. He might need to come home to take a nap."

"I can't leave Luca. It's his first day here. What will he do?"

"Does it matter?"

"Why are you so mean? You've changed, and I don't like it one bit. I'm not leaving Luca alone. Dad will say it's okay."

"Ask him."

"I have to get ready first," she said as she stormed up the stairs.

A few minutes later, Ali heard Kayla and Janelle arguing. "I need the shower, Aunt Janie. Why are you up so early anyway?" Ali heard Kayla banging on the bathroom door. She came running downstairs. "Where's Dad?"

"Someone looking for me?"

"Mom says I have to work today because you might want to come home early to sleep—"

"Thanks for the great idea, Ali. Yes, hurry up and get dressed and we'll go together," Matt said.

"Aunt Janelle never wakes up early and she's monopolizing the bathroom. I have to wait till she gets out."

Luca entered the kitchen. "Kayla, go to work with your dad. I'll be fine. I've caused enough commotion."

"Thanks for your support, Luca. Now everyone's against me." She trudged to her parents' bathroom and slammed the door.

Luca, Ali, and Matt stared at each other.

"Welcome to our happy little family," Ali said.

Chapter 22

The next morning, after Luca's arrival, Matt and Ali were sitting at the kitchen table conducting their morning rituals of newspaper and coffee.

"What's that noise upstairs?" Matt asked.

"The consequence of having three people, two of whom are women, sharing a bathroom."

"What about Luca?"

"What about him?"

"He can't sleep in the den until he leaves for school. I want my den back."

Ali ignored her husband's petulant demand and continued reading about the pollen count. She pulled a tissue from her shorts pocket.

Matt left the table and walked into the den aka Luca's bedroom. The bed had been returned to a sofa with the sheets neatly folded and placed on a table. Luca's duffle bag was sitting on the floor next to the computer.

"I'm going to speak to our young interloper."

"Who are you going to speak to, Dad?" Kayla met Matt in the den and gave him a hug. She gently tugged him toward the kitchen.

"You're awfully chipper. What happened to the lousy mood you were in yesterday?" Ali asked her daughter.

"Once you get to know Luca, you'll love him as much as I do. I've decided not to argue. Take Mom and Aunt Janelle. Fighting forever." She made eye contact with her mother. "Whatcha going to make for breakfast?" she asked her dad. "Mickey Mouse pancakes?"

"If that's what my princess wants, that's what she'll receive." He pulled out a griddle from the pantry.

"Count me in," Janelle said as she entered the kitchen. "Can't remember the last time I ate a pancake. Especially a Mickey Mouse pancake." She was dressed modestly, albeit flamboyantly, in a gauzy black caftan and slippers trimmed in faux fur.

"*One* pancake for me," Ali said.

"Pancakes for four. What about lover boy?" Matt said.

"Dad. Please. He might hear you."

"Where the hell is he anyway?"

"Shh. Don't wake him," Kayla said.

"Everyone else is up. Why can't he get with the program? What does he plan to do all day?" Matt said. "And, how long is he going to be here?"

"Give him a few more days to adjust. Please. He just arrived."

"How long will this so-called adjustment take?" Matt asked.

"Good morning. Did someone say pancakes?" Luca stood in the doorway with a grin on his face. He was wearing the same clothes he had worn yesterday: jeans and a white T-shirt. He had a stubble on his chin and his hair glistened from a morning shower.

"Wonderful. Pancakes for five," the cook said. "Have a seat. Maybe I should invite the whole neighborhood."

Kayla and Luca embraced. Luca sat at the table. Kayla gathered plates and utensils.

Janelle seated herself at the table next to Luca.

"This reminds me of my home in Italy. Madre and my sisters making breakfast for my brothers and me—"

"And what would your father be doing? Slaving over a sizzling griddle?" Matt said as he adjusted the flame on the stovetop.

"Ah, my padre. I mean dad. He cooks in the restaurant but never at home."

"But your mother and siblings work at the restaurant," Janelle said.

"They like…they enjoy…they want to please the men in my family."

"Fine for the men. Not so much for the women," feminist Janelle said.

"In this house everyone pitches in," Matt said.

Ali added, "Enough about the sociological differences in Luca's home compared with ours. What's everyone doing today?"

Matt said, "Work. Kayla and I to Kitchen Bliss." He aimed a scowl at Luca. "What about you?"

"I don't have any plans. Maybe Kayla could take some time off from work and show me around Willoughby."

"Not going to happen, young man," Matt said. "Kayla has a job and you need to find one, too."

"Yes, sir. Do you have any suggestions?"

"Let's not talk about a job until Luca has time to settle in," Ali said.

"We have to move him out of the den," Matt said.

"Dad, he's sitting right here. You don't have to talk to him in the third person."

Pointing a pancake turner toward Janelle, Matt said, "You move into Kayla's room and Luca you move into Janelle's room. The den is not a bedroom." He flipped some pancakes and tossed them onto plates. "Please have this completed before I return home from work. Another thing. Listen up! Limit your showers to three minutes. I want hot water in the morning."

"How in the world am I supposed to share a bedroom with Kayla and a bathroom with her and Luca? An unreasonable arrangement," Janelle said.

"You have options, Janelle. Go to your parents' home, go to the Willoughby Inn, go to Timbuktu as far as I'm concerned." Matt continued pouring batter onto the griddle, flipping the pancakes, and tossing them toward the table. Some landed on plates, some missed their mark, and some were missing an ear or two.

"What's the matter with everyone? No one is behaving normally." Kayla took one more bite of a pancake, rose from the table, kissed Luca on the cheek, and stomped upstairs.

When the rest of the family asked for seconds, Matt complied. When their plates were clean, and the batter bowl emptied, Ali said, "You're the pancake king, Matt."

"What happened to being king of my house?" Matt asked Roxie who was in search of a piece of Mickey Mouse.

Chapter 23

Ali received a text from Brad inviting her to lunch. She had several reasons to decline his invitation. Matt's Mickey Mouse pancakes, while delicious, bloated her and she didn't think she could eat another morsel. She didn't want to take time away from thinking about story ideas. And, she was trying to figure out what to do with their new houseguest to keep Matt calm.

Ali's intrigue antennae soared when Brad asked her not to bring Matt. "I'll be there," she replied.

She found Luca in the kitchen looking forlorn and bored. Ali handed him the keys to the Green Monster. "Will you please drive me to Brad's restaurant."

"But Kayla won't like me driving it when you won't let—"

"Ask her about her driving record."

Luca took the keys and tossed them in the air. "Thanks," he said as he caught the keys, smiling.

Luca dropped Ali in front of Mia Bella.

"I'll text you when we're finished."

Brad greeted her at the entrance. "What's the doctor say about your ankle?" he asked.

"I'm healing. Don't need a doctor. Hardly using the crutches. Don't tell anyone." She smiled at Brad.

The two longtime friends hugged. "Follow me." He took her arm and helped her to a table in the rear near the kitchen. He pulled the chair out for her. "Glad you had time to meet."

"Your text said you are either apprehensive or unbelievably happy. Have you won the lottery?" Ali asked.

"No lottery. Hope you don't mind a table near the kitchen?" A bottle of uncorked white wine sat on the table in an ice bucket next to a bottle of sparkling water.

"The outstanding food here would make up for any distraction. Why didn't you want Matt here?"

"I know what he would tell me—what he's been telling me all along. I needed to hear your point of view."

"Welcome, Mrs. Lawrence," a young dark haired female server said. She took the black starched napkin from the table, shook it, and handed it to Ali. "I see you have selected a top-notch Australian wine, Mr. Patterson," she said as she picked up the bottle and faced the label toward Ali and Brad. "Oyster Bay sauvignon blanc is our most popular summer wine. It is zesty, aromatic, crisp, and elegant. A perfect accompaniment to the salad Chef is preparing for you."

"Excellent, Naomi. Obviously, you were listening to my wine lecture. We might need a wine sommelier during the dinner hours."

"I'm up for the job, boss. Sold two bottles already and this is only lunchtime. I'm trying to perfect my spiel. May I describe the Chardonnays for you?"

"You've done enough. Excellent job. Thank you."

Naomi poured a small amount of the zesty wine into Ali's glass and waited for her approval.

"Nice," Ali said when she finished a sip.

Naomi tilted her head and scrunched her eyebrows together as she made eye contact with Ali.

"A critique? Just as you described. Crisp and elegant. Is that better?"

Naomi smiled, filled both wine glasses, took a few steps backward, and walked away,

"I ordered our meal, but let's enjoy the wine first." He swirled the light-colored wine in a long-stemmed crystal glass.

"Here's to friendship," Brad said.

"Good legs," Ali said. "Is that a wine term?"

"Speaking of legs."

Ali searched the dining room. "Who?"

"No, not here." He stared at Ali without speaking.

"You want to tell me something. I've known you for a long time and I recognize that look."

"Don't know what's wrong with me, but she's always in my thoughts. She's like a persistent rash."

"Who? Aren't we talking about legs?"

"Janelle."

"Holy shit! Janelle?"

An elderly couple dining at a nearby table stopped eating and stared at Ali.

"She has her faults. But, she has *something* I find extremely attractive, magnetic."

"What about the uncomfortable scene at my parents? Don't forget the royal brush off she gave you when she came to town."

"She apologized. Wrote me a sincere and poignant note. I've forgiven her. However, she must make up her mind soon or I'm moving on. It will break my heart, but I can't stand this state of limbo she's put me in."

"I love my sister. Can't say I like her much, but I think you're setting yourself up for a crushing failure unless you give her a deadline. She'll string you along for years."

"Can't help myself."

"You may be a successful businessman and restaurateur, but you've lost your mind if you pursue her."

"Don't you think Phoebe's house will entice her to stay?"

"Hate to rain on your parade, but simply put—no. And I promise I *will* say I told you so." She dipped a piece of crunchy bread into a shallow white bowl of olive oil and balsamic vinegar.

"You will be at Phoebe's. . .er, Janelle's new home tomorrow night?"

"I'll be there for the fireworks. You're sure you want my parents?"

"Yes, a family gathering. Plus, Virginia can tell her friends she received a private tour."

Ali took a sip of wine. "You know my mother."

"Something else," Brad said. "Janelle wasn't alone when she was in Florida."

"How do you know? You're stalking her! Tell me you're kidding. Who was she with?" Ali shot the questions at Brad as fast as ping-pong balls at an Olympic competition.

"Janelle and I were together in Sanibel."

"Why?"

"I wanted to know if we were compatible under normal day-to-day circumstances. Our usual rendezvous were in New York City or somewhere in Mexico. Even Italy."

Their server interrupted their conversation when she delivered plates of colorful radicchio and arugula salad topped with grilled chicken and slices of ricotta salata. Bright green vinaigrette was offered on the side in a small glass pitcher.

"I know you're watching calories, so I requested from Chef a simple salad topped with grilled chicken."

"I suppose you rented a normal luxurious villa, overlooking the beautiful Gulf of Mexico, ordered buckets of normal Champagne, and dined in elegant, normal restaurants in between gallivanting around Sanibel."

"Janelle rented the villa. I thought those things were her definition of normal living, but I was wrong. She can be down to earth. We rented bikes and rode around the island. Stopped for leisurely lunches. Went to the Dairy Queen. Collected shells on the beach. She never put on makeup. No high heels. She wore sandals or tennis shoes. I'm telling you she was a different person from the one you know."

Ali smiled at the thought of Janelle eating soft serve at a DQ. "If you and Janelle are a couple, why keep it a secret?" Ali asked between bites of lettuce, which tasted freshly picked.

"Janelle doesn't want *you* to know."

"Me?"

"She thinks you'll interfere. Try to talk *me* out of a relationship with *her*."

Ali took a piece of chicken and chewed it slowly. "She might be right."

"Janelle wants a simple life. She hasn't been happy in years. She's different from—"

"No, she isn't. Janelle's the twin of your ex-wife—gorgeous, self-centered, fake. Rachael robbed you of your confidence and self-esteem. You were lucky to catch her in bed with—"

"Please don't remind me."

"Sorry."

"When we were in Sanibel, Janelle was an attentive listener and smart. The love making was out—"

"Stop. I don't want to hear about your sex life."

"Believe it or not, she's lacking self-confidence and questions her ability to write. Hard to believe after all the books she's written."

Or not written.

"She knows she's been a diva most of her life. She wants another chance *with you* to write a second book. And as corny as it sounds, she wants a happy romantic relationship, even marriage."

"Do you believe in regifting?" Ali asked.

"Not usually."

"Matt gave me a doormat to remind me not to become Janelle's doormat. I'm regifting it to you."

"I'm that bad?"

"Gee, Brad. Find someone else to give her the prospect of a happy life. She'll make you unhappy."

"But never bored. Now here's my plan for tomorrow night."

* * *

Later that night, Ali and Matt were in bed, each reading. Matt was on his Kindle. Ali was reading Elin Hilderbrand's novel about twin sisters.

"I had lunch with Brad today."

"Yeah. He told me. I saw him at the gym." Matt was engrossed in Michael Connelly's latest crime novel. "What did he have to say?"

"He told me how he feels about Janelle."

"I wish he would jump off that runaway train."

"The train is picking up steam."

Matt put the Kindle aside. "Brad still has the hots for Janelle? Has he lost his mind?"

"Probably."

"Has the hots or lost his mind?

"Both," Ali said.

"What are we going to do?"

"Can you talk to him? I would hate to see him hurt."

"Might be the other way around."

"You could try," Ali said.

"Speaking of the hots. Put your book down, mamma. I've got something for you."

Ali turned off the bedside lamp and dropped her book to the floor. The sisters would have to wait.

Chapter 24

The next afternoon Janelle sat on the front porch waiting for Brad.

"Where are we going?" she cooed to Brad.

"You knew I was renovating Mimi's house. I want to show it off." Brad helped Janelle into his Porsche convertible.

"I have to clear the air. I apologize for everything. The way I avoided you when I came to town, my rudeness at Mother and Dad's house. Everything. Thanks for giving me another chance and—"

"The note you wrote to me was the only apology needed. Your writing is impressive. No wonder you're a bestselling author. And, about the car. It's only a dent. Besides, I know some ways you can atone for your sins." He leaned down, put his hand on the nape of her neck, and pulled her close, aiming for her lips.

"Not here. Someone might see us," she said. "Lots of nosy neighbors around here."

"Who cares?"

"We have an agreement."

"For now, anyway."

They drove two blocks to where Brad stopped in front of deceased Phoebe Patterson's former home. He exited the car and offered his hand to Janelle who was checking her lipstick, Chanel La Sensuelle, in the visor mirror.

"I see the *Mia Bella* sign is gone."

"It was for the construction workers to i.d. the house."

Thank goodness. I thought Mia Bella was me.

Janelle hadn't noticed the changes the day she arrived. The stunning oak front door with glass sidelights gave the house an updated and fresh appearance. White Adirondacks rocking chairs beckoned to visitors.

"Let's go inside." Brad used a key to open the door. He put his hand on the small of her back and urged Janelle forward.

Janelle turned to face Brad. "Let's stop for a minute. Why did you want me to come here when I first arrived in Willoughby?"

"Will discuss that when the others arrive."

"Others?" Janelle scrutinized the formerly dowdy house. A vase of fresh flowers sat on one of two tables in the sparsely furnished living room. The sweetness of the flowers overcame her, and she began a sneezing litany.

"Sorry." He moved the vase of stargazer lilies to confinement in the laundry room.

Brad led Janelle to the kitchen where he opened the stainless-steel French door Sub-Zero refrigerator, selected a bottle of Dom Perignon, and expertly popped the cork. He filled two flutes and handed a glass to Janelle who immediately took a sip. "So, what do you think?" He waved his hand around the kitchen.

"Excellent Champagne. Reminds me of Sanibel."

Brad smiled. "I wasn't referring to the Champagne. I meant the house. The changes I've made?"

"I don't spend much time in a kitchen—anyone's kitchen. This is more Ali's style."

"Let's take a tour." Brad took the flute from Janelle and placed it on the obsidian granite countertop. "But before." He took Janelle into his arms and kissed her long and hard on her lips as he pulled her into his body. "I've been reminiscing about Sanibel and I hope you have, too." He ran his hands along the sides of her body and upward toward her breasts. "I've missed these babies."

Janelle smiled and didn't remove his hands. "You're trying to distract me, Bradley Patterson. Remember our promise. We can't tell Ali or anyone about our relationship, if we decide to have one."

"I agreed to honor your request. For now. Although I don't understand why."

I know how people in Willoughby regard me. And, I know what they think of Bradley. Until I can turn around my reputation, our relationship must be a secret.

"Glad you understand. Now show me around," Janelle said. When Brad was a few steps ahead of her, Janelle reached back and grabbed the glass of bubbly.

Knocked out walls gave the house an open floor plan. Newly installed oak plank hardwood floors added warmth and character.

"Is this a spec house? Not much furniture. Are you moving into it? You've been spending lots of time and money on this old house, I'm guessing."

Brad took Janelle by her arm, the one without the flute, and guided her through the French doors to the patio.

"I'll explain. Let's go outside. I need to tell you something."

Janelle followed Brad who was standing underneath the newly constructed pergola. Janelle took a seat on one of the cushioned outdoor chairs. Brad said, "I don't know why. Ah, Phoebe, my grandmother."

"What on earth are you trying to say? You're rambling."

What about Phoebe? Did she tell Brad she was my ghostwriter? Oh no. What will he think of me?

Janelle's heart pounded as she waited for Brad to finish his sentence.

"Phoebe left the house to you. She didn't want it known until the remodeling met your standards. She was afraid you would reject this old place."

"What am I missing? Phoebe Patterson left her house to me. Why? When?" Janelle took a slug of the fizzy beverage and followed up with a chaser sip.

"I have no idea."

"I'm confused. You didn't mention a thing about this to me while we were in Sanibel." She took another fast swallow of her drink followed by an unladylike burp.

"Neither do I understand nor her lawyer. Mimi made deliberate decisions. She was not reckless or hasty. She made the arrangements months before her sudden death. She often talked about you."

"Phoebe and I had more of a bus. . .relationship. . .more of a busy relationship."

"Busy?"

"Bizzy, buzzy, I meant buzzy. Like two honeybees. Buzz, buzz whenever we saw each other."

They returned to the living room. "Not much furniture," Janelle observed again. She walked around the room, glanced out the French doors, and plopped down in a black leather loveseat sofa. She set her flute on a small table on the side of the sofa.

"Why in the world would Phoebe leave me a house? It makes no sense. Was she losing it toward the end? Did she have dementia? Why didn't she leave it to you, Bradley Patterson? I don't want this old house."

The doorbell rang.

"Wonderful. Visitors already. No doubt the neighborhood welcome committee with a basket of homemade chocolate chip cookies," Janelle said.

Chapter 25

B rad opened the front door and greeted his visitors. "Glad you could make it, but it's not much of a celebration," he said to Ali, Matt, Virginia, and Ed. "She's not happy. She doesn't want this 'old' house. That's a direct quote." He put his hands in his pockets. "C'est la vie."

The family joined Janelle who was sitting on the leather loveseat with her arms crossed and her lips pressed in a tight line. "Why are *you* here?" she asked her family.

"Supposed to be a celebration," Ali said. "And you shouldn't criticize Phoebe's house. Brad grew up here after his parents died."

"Doesn't bother me, Ali." Brad turned to face Janelle. "If the house is too small, we can add a second floor."

Janelle shrugged her shoulders.

"What the devil's going on?" Ed said. "Why are we here?"

"Brad contracted major design renos and invited us here to see the fabulous results," Ali explained.

"There's more. My grandmother left the house to Janelle."

"Goodness gracious," Virginia said. "Phoebe did that?"

"Wow!" said Ed. "Nice house, but where's the furniture?"

"You can sell it, Janelle. It's yours. Do whatever you want." Brad walked to a built-in bookcase on the far side of the room and picked up a manila envelope. "The deed to the house is here. It's in your name." He handed the envelope to Janelle who continued to sit on the loveseat with her arms folded. "No hard feelings," he said. He pulled a key from his pocket and handed it to Janelle who remained stoic.

Ali took the envelope and the key. She leaned her crutches against the small sofa and sat opposite Janelle, glaring at her sister.

Virginia and Ed wandered from room to room. "If Janelle doesn't want it, we'll take it. Right, Virginia?" Ed said. "You could make it a Christmas present to your aging parents, Janelle," he hollered out to the living room.

"Nothing wrong with our house, Ed, but I love the landscaping. What a lovely pergola. My garden club would be impressed. Instead of always working on your unsuccessful inventions, you should build a pergola for me."

"I'll take that under consideration," he said.

Brad moved to where Janelle was sitting and stood behind her.

"I hadn't planned to stay in Willoughby permanently. A few months here and there when I could stay with Ali or my parents. Nothing permanent. Six months out of the year." Janelle flicked a ruby red nail on her now empty glass. "Ali. Refill. Please."

Ali glared at Janelle.

"You stay, Ali," Brad said.

When Brad was out of earshot Ali said, "Janelle, you told me you wanted to buy or rent in Willoughby."

"I didn't mean what I said to Brad. Didn't want to get his hopes up. I meant what I said to you that I'd live here semi-permanently."

"What? Don't blather. You sound deranged."

After Brad placed the bottle in the ice bucket and a tray of flutes on the table in front of the sisters, he led Virginia, Ed, and Matt to the backyard where landscapers were finishing for the day and loading their equipment.

"You've done a terrific job, Brad," Matt said. "I bet she'll come around." He patted his friend on the shoulder.

"I tried too hard," Brad said. "You warned me. She makes me appear wimpy."

"When it comes to Janelle, you *are* wimpy," Matt said.

Meanwhile in the living room, Janelle pleaded with Ali. "If I never ask another thing from you please get me out of here. I can't stand being here one more minute let alone *living* here. Don't you feel her presence?"

Ali evaluated the spacious, open living room. "I agree, sort of. I can still smell Phoebe's rose water." She filled the flutes. "What else is going on? What is it?"

"What do you mean? Nothing's going on except I feel stuck, suffocated. Help me."

"What do you want me to do?"

"We're sisters. We're family. You must help me." Janelle stood and squeezed next to Ali on the loveseat and clutched Ali's arm. "Please. Please."

"First of all, you're stopping the circulation in my arm."

Janelle put her hand in her lap.

Ali took a sip of Champagne. "This is terrific. French?"

"Stop it. Stop it right now," Janelle whispered. "You're changing the subject."

"Learned that from you." Ali waved her hand around the room. "Beautiful house. I'm amazed at the transformation. Would save you lots of money."

"I don't care about money."

"Since when?"

"Ali, please, please, please, with sugar on it."

"The lack of furniture could buy you some time. Come home with me and we'll figure out the next move. We'll have to think of something to assuage Brad. We can't and won't hurt his feelings."

"I knew I could count on St. Ali." Janelle leaned toward her sister to give her hug, but she lost her balance and spilled the contents of the flute onto Ali's feet.

"You did that on purpose," Ali said.

"No, I didn't."

"Not the first time you've spilled alcohol on me. Now find something to dry my feet."

"I'm clumsy."

"It was an accident, I guess." The sisters shared a slight smile.

When Janelle returned with a towel, she said, "I have something else to talk to you about. But not tonight."

"I have something to tell you, too," Ali said.

Brad and his guests rejoined the sisters in the living room.

"What about dinner? I'm starved," Ed said.

"My restaurant is expecting us," Brad said.

"Can we please have a meal without arguing or unpleasantness? Is that possible?" Virginia pleaded.

"I doubt it," Ali said.

"Probably not," Janelle said.

"But we will try, won't we, girls?" Virginia said.

Chapter 26

The next day, Janelle waited until Matt and Kayla had left the house for Kitchen Bliss. She needed Ali's full attention. No distractions. Howard's gift was the answer to Janelle's financial nightmare, if Ali would cooperate.

She tightened the belt on her ankle-length ebony robe and joined Ali, the modesty enforcer, who was sitting at the kitchen table. "Is this what you consider appropriate attire for living in a house with two men?" Janelle spun around in a 360-degree twirl before she sat across from Ali.

"Improvement," Ali said. "By the way, the bags underneath your eyes match the color of your robe. No sleep last night?"

"Thanks for the observation, kind sister. Nothing a little concealer can't fix." She tapped the guilty bags with her fingers. "You're right. I didn't sleep because I need to talk to you about—"

"Let me speak first before I change my mind," Ali blurted.

"Me first. I received something—"

"Let's write together," Ali said. "One more time. The last time."

Janelle picked up the neighborhood Willoughby newspaper, which was sitting on the table, and flipped through it.

Thank you, thank you. Don't act too relieved. Be cool.

"Why the change of heart?"

Ali fiddled with salt and pepper shakers on the table. "We need each other. I think we're better writers as a team than apart."

"I'm hungry. Bagel and cream cheese?" Janelle asked as she stood.

"Damn it! Sit down. Yes or no?"

Janelle obeyed, folded her hands, and placed them on the table. "I'll do whatever it takes to make my little sister happy."

"You are so full of it. What happened to begging and pleading?"

Janelle patted her chest. "Janelle Jennings never begs."

"The third person? Really?"

"How about a hug to confirm our partnership?" Janelle asked.

Ali remained seated.

Janelle came around the table and embraced her sister. "Glad we have settled our writing partnership and we can move on."

Ali took a sip of coffee. "Your turn. What did *you* want to tell *me* that's making you look like crap?" Ali asked.

Janelle returned to her side of the table, sat, and removed ads for Kohl's and Publix from the paper and set them aside. "This whole house thing." She paused and gazed out the window. "Is Brad guilting me into accepting Phoebe's gift of her house to trap me in Willoughby? Is this controlling and manipulative attitude no different from my exes who always wanted something from me? Remember what happened to Brooks Barrington in. . .the title has slipped my mind. Odd I can't remember."

Ali slapped her palm on the table. Her coffee cup trembled on its coaster. "What's the matter with you? Your characters are fiction. Either you love Brad, or you don't. If you love him, marry him. Move into the gorgeous home he renovated for you. Or sell the damn house and leave town."

"You make it sound so easy."

"Brad didn't use guilt. Phoebe's to blame." Ali pointed a finger upward. "Thank *her*. Brad fulfilled his grandmother's request."

Janelle dropped her head. "Why do you hate me?" she mumbled.

"I'm trying to help you." Ali reached across the table and patted her sister's arm. "What would your fans think if they knew you had a desirable man at your doorstep, panting like a dog, and you wouldn't let him in? You write steamy novels filled with sex and romance. Your characters have no trouble making a commitment to the men they love. But you can't?"

Janelle rubbed her hands through her hair and down her neck. "Where's the aspirin?"

Ali pointed to the cabinet above the telephone nook. "You are the queen of changing the subject."

"A favor, please. Let's postpone the Brad discussion for now," Janelle said.

"Okay. For now. But you're going to have to decide soon. Anything else we need to discuss?" Ali asked. "As if this weren't enough."

"Yes, but it can wait." Janelle's embarrassment prevented her from sharing with Ali the blackmailing threats from ex-husband Philip. She'd have to figure this problem out on her own. At least now, she was assured of receiving money from Howard's estate, if the sisters could write another book together. That was a big if. And time was running out.

"By the way," Ali said. "The title of your Brooks Barrington book was *Lost and Found Love*."

* * *

The next afternoon, the sisters were enjoying gin and tonics on Ali's sunroom.

"Any ideas you want to share for the book?" Ali asked.

Janelle handed Ali a piece of legal-sized paper. "What do you think?"

Ali read the paper. "Great minds think alike. My novel is set near Lake Tahoe, too." She continued to review what Janelle had written.

"The water is indescribable. The bluest of blues, as blue as my cobalt ring, as blue as—"

"Shh, I'm concentrating," Ali said. She ignored Janelle's colorful travelogue description and continued reading Janelle's paper. "Coincidentally, my heroine is a forest ranger and helps a handsome widower find his missing child. My child is autistic and yours is deaf." Ali paused. She took the paper and tore it into tiny pieces, which she threw at Janelle. "You stole my notes."

"What?"

"You knew I would catch you, but you took my ideas anyway. What's the matter with you?"

"Evidently, great minds *do* think alike, I suppose." Janelle sat still with her hands folded like a young child in church obeying warnings to behave. "It was meant to be a joke," Janelle said with her head lowered. "I'm blocked. Can't think of anything new. Brad's on my mind and other things...you have no idea. Your life is perfect and mine is complicated."

Ali pointed to the tiny pieces of white paper sprinkled across the floor. "Where did you find them?"

"On top of your printer and it wasn't cheating because we're collaborators."

"What you did was dishonest. I can't trust you. Maybe I should rethink this writing together plan."

"I apologize. I know I was wrong, but don't abandon me." Janelle crouched down on her knees and took Ali's hands into her own. "Please, please."

"Get up! Your histrionics belong in a book not in my sunroom." Ali picked up her empty cocktail glass. "Make me another drink. A strong one. Then we better start work, collaborator. We must meet on a regular basis. Monday through Friday. Right after lunch. No cocktails until 5 p.m."

"Anything your little heart desires." She picked up Ali's glass. "Something else. I have a problem, but I've been reluctant to share. I'm being blac—"

"Excuse me?"

"Never mind. Never mind."

When Janelle returned with two cocktails, Ali was on the floor picking up the pieces of paper littered around the room.

"No, no. Let me do that. You sit down."

"I can do it." As Ali stood, she bumped her hip into Janelle, knocking the drinks to the floor.

The sisters stared at the mess on the floor. Broken glasses, gin, limes, and ice cubes melded together with the shredded paper.

"I think it was my fault," Ali said.

"No, it was *my* fault."

"We can't agree on anything."

"Yes, we can," Janelle said. "We can agree to write a best seller."

Chapter 27

Ali walked, without crutches or a fake limp, to the sunroom earlier in the morning than she normally arose and sat on the cushy sofa covered in a magnolia-themed material, a pattern Virginia chose. Flowers, of course. Roxie had followed her and hopped up next to her mistress.

Ali had had a rough night tossing and turning while she second-guessed her decision to write another novel with her sister. It was the correct sisterly action to take and not entirely altruistic. Ali thought her ideas were stale and outmoded. She needed Janelle for a modern, sophisticated style, at least for this novel.

She reminded herself of her dad's advice after Ali told him about Howard's bequeath: "You know what to do." Once the book was published, the money from Howard's estate would solve Janelle's financial woes. . .until she was hoodwinked by another unscrupulous man.

The activity at the bird feeder outside the sunroom caught her attention. Nuthatches, turned upside down, were pecking for breakfast, then darted away seeking another meal. A ruby-red cardinal took their place. Ali opened her laptop to check for email. Since she didn't see anything urgent she switched to a document named: *new novel.*

Matt, carrying a coffee carafe, joined his wife. "Coffee before I leave for work?" He rubbed her arm and kissed her neck.

Ali nodded her thanks.

"Getting an early start?"

"Thought I better get ahead of Nurse Ratched before she descends on me."

"Since Janelle insists on helping you, I could use Kayla at the store. You don't need two caretakers and I'm expecting a shipment of merchandise we need to price."

"I'll try to help you pry Kayla from Luca and send her to the store. She hasn't been much help anyway."

He kissed her cheek and left for Kitchen Bliss. He turned around and returned to her side. "Here's another kiss...for last night. Glad your ankle hasn't slowed you down in the bedroom department."

"My pleasure. Entirely my pleasure."

* * *

Janelle joined Ali in the sunroom. Janelle was dressed in white ankle-length linen pants and a Moroccan-inspired kurta tunic in pale shades of blue and turquoise. In lieu of her signature stepladder shoes, she wore open-toed bone wedges. Her impeccably applied makeup reminded Ali of Estée Lauder magazine models.

"What are you doing up? I hope you aren't putting weight on your ankle. What do you need? I'll get my coffee first. Remember, I'm here to serve you."

"I'm—"

"Hold that thought." She whisked away to the kitchen and flew to Ali's side carrying a mug. "What do you need? What are you doing?" She pointed to the carafe. "I see you have plenty of coffee."

Janelle sat and took a sip of coffee. "So, what are you doing with those cards?"

Ali had a stack of multi-colored index cards in front of her. "Preparing for our time to write together. Afternoons. Remember?"

"Refresh my memory. What are the cards for?"

"Each card will be a plot point. We'll add cards for characters and eventually put everything into an Excel spreadsheet."

"Sounds complicated."

"Don't worry. We'll figure it out." Ali lined the cards in horizontal rows. "Where are you going so early? Nice colors."

"Not too fat?" Janelle turned her back to Ali. "I mean, I've gained a few pounds. Do these white pants make my butt look huge?" She pointed to her derrière. "And look at my eyes. Bags all gone."

"No, you look terrific." If Ali valued her life, she would never tell any woman she was fat, even if she was. Janelle belonged in the *even if she* did category. "Where are you going?" Ali repeated.

"A few errands to run. I'll return in time to write with you. Promise." Janelle turned and left.

"On second thought, I could use—"

The front door shut.

"The 'I'm here to serve' you statement just left the building," Ali said to Roxie. Why was Janelle running errands? She wasn't a running errands kind of gal. Other people ran Janelle's errands. Something was going on with Janelle. Ali thought of how her sister had changed, somewhat. She seemed to be genuinely regretful for causing Ali to sprain her ankle. She was trying to help Ali around the house, although her attempts were feeble and usually resulted in a disaster—breaking dishes, spilling food, over soaping the washing machine.

Ali reviewed the stack of index cards, reading what she had written the previous day and chuckled.

Janelle will be unhappy when she reads about two sisters feuding and how one ends up sans designer shoes, jewelry, and makeup in a smelly landfill. In a hot and sandy desert. Miles from civilization. Attacked by scorpions. Narcissistic Janelle will think she's the stranded, desperate heroine because it's always about her.

"Might have to put Ellen to work to find out what Janelle's up to," she said to Roxie.

Chapter 28

After Janelle left for her errands, Ali sat on the front porch reading emails when Ellen jogged by. Ali motioned for Ellen to join her. She turned her laptop to face her friend.

"Emails from fans," Ali said.

"You should keep track of how many you receive and have a competition with your sister."

"I'm not competitive with her. Besides, a reader doesn't know what I've written or what Janelle's written."

"Sure." Ellen wiped her forehead on her wristband. "You've been talking about hiring someone at Kitchen Bliss."

Ali had missed her best friend. Some women claimed their husband as their BFF, but a girl needs another girl. Ali was glad Ellen had returned home after a long vacation in Indonesia.

"Matt's been complaining he needs more help. Kayla's been a disappointment and is distracted by Luca. If I could hire someone right away, he'd stopped nagging me to help in the store."

"I might could suggest someone."

"I'm listening."

"This person has no retail experience, but she loves to cook so she can navigate around all that stuff you sell. That I used to sell."

"How do you know her?"

"You know her, too. From high school. Remember Celeste Flores? Short, bad skin, overweight, frumpy, and awful hair. Crooked teeth. Sweet. Pleasant personality though."

Ali barely remembered Celeste. She hoped she had been nice to her.

"She's in my spin class and mentioned she's looking for a part-time job."

"Tell her to give me a call," Ali said.

* * *

The next day, Ali was waiting on the front porch for Ellen who agreed to drive her to the Sugar Shack for the interview with Celeste. She carried the crutches to Ellen's car as she limped.

"I'm thinking the crutches are for show? You are healing, aren't you?"

"I'm taking the fifth," Ali said.

When they arrived at the Sugar Shack, Ellen said, "How long do you need?"

"Thirty minutes should be fine."

Ali smacked her lips and breathed in the heavenly smells wafting from the ovens as she entered the store. Her stomach grumbled as she eyed the chocolate croissants in the glass display case. "I'll have a mocha latte," she said to the clerk. "Better skip the whipped cream."

Pointing to Ali's crutches, the clerk said, "I'll bring it to you."

While looking for a table, Ali surveyed the yoga pants-wearing women seated in the patio shaded by oak trees. No one matched Ali's memory of Celeste. Ali made eye contact with an attractive brunette sitting alone at a table. The woman, about Ali's age, was wearing white leggings and an ocean blue and white print pin-tuck tunic. Her shiny hair was shoulder-length and rapier straight.

"Ali, Ali Lawrence. Over here," the dark-haired woman said as she waved her hand in the air.

"Celeste. Ah, Celeste. I didn't recognize you." Ellen forgot to mention the radical transformation from dumpy to glamorous.

I'll have to thank Ellen for giving me such an accurate description. Why did I wear tight cropped jeans and a tie-dyed T-shirt? I didn't want to make Celeste uncomfortable because I overdressed and now I'm dressed for dumpster diving.

Ali ran her hand through her hair, thankful she had had her hair straightened three weeks ago. Her hair stylist assured her the process would last through the summer.

"Most people don't recognize me. Happens when a fatty drops fifty pounds and has a few nips and tucks. More than a few, which my former husband insisted I endure." She patted under her chin. "New teeth, too." She grinned at Ali. "And no more adolescent skin."

Ali took a seat opposite Celeste.

"Crutches. Serious?"

"Minor. I should be able to toss these soon." Ali leaned the crutches on the side of the table. "Is this former husband still around?"

"Widowhood is my dream. Divorced for a couple of years."

"You look amazing, Celeste. Better than amazing," Ali said. "Not that you didn't—"

"Photos don't lie, and I have plenty from high school."

"How did you lose so much weight? I struggle to shed five pounds."

"After trying every weight loss program advertised on TV, I decided the only way for me to lose weight was to stop eating anything that tasted good. Plus, I exercised like I was competing for a triathlon. All to please my rotten scoundrel cosmetic surgeon husband. Get this! He molded me to suit his taste and then casted me aside for a newer model. Have to admit I like the new me, but not sure I have the willpower to maintain this." She waved her hands up and down her body.

"Maintenance is a bitch," Ali agreed as she stared at her favorite drink calculating the calorie count.

"Now I watch what I eat and go to the gym."

"Whatever you're doing is working."

The women paused to sip their drinks. Ali noted Celeste was drinking black iced coffee.

"Why weren't we friends in high school?" Ali asked Celeste.

Celeste stared at her coffee. "Lots of reasons, I suppose."

"You were too smart for me. Chess Club, Latin Club."

"I always admired you and your sister," Celeste said.

"Janelle the beauty queen. I can understand that. But me?"

"You were popular and had so many friends. I was shy. I joined the debate team, which forced me to conquer my shyness. Resulted in a scholarship to Clemson."

"I wasn't as popular as my sister who had a slew of boyfriends."

"I always wanted a sister and I envied your relationship. But, sometimes I thought you might be living in Janelle's shadow."

"Hard to compete with a beauty queen."

"You should write a book by yourself."

"Something to consider for the next one. For now, we're writing together." Ali paused to sip her coffee. "How long did you say you've been back in Willoughby?"

"Ten months. Have been playing catch up with lots of people. Social media helps. I love your Facebook posts, especially the ones about food."

"Guess I have food on my mind too much," Ali said. "The consequence of depriving myself."

They continued the usual Q&A session, which occurs when former acquaintances meet after a time lapse. Celeste had one married daughter and one granddog, no grandchildren. She moved to Willoughby from California to live near her daughter.

Perhaps reading Ali's mind, Celeste said, "Don't worry. I won't show you pictures of my perfect granddog Daisy."

Ali laughed. "Let's talk about Kitchen Bliss. We have thousands of items in the store. Will you be intimidated by customers asking for different types of baking pans, or knives or—"

Celeste leaned forward. "I was married to a wealthy narcissistic louche of a man and I had the guts to divorce him. Nothing intimidates me. And I mean nothing or no one."

Ali regretted conducting an interview rather than enjoying pleasant conversation with this delightful woman.

They discussed hours and pay. Ali reassured Celeste her lack of retail experience would not be a problem. "We pride ourselves on excellent customer service. A pleasant demeanor and willingness to learn is all we ask."

"I'll love working with you."

"You'll work with my husband Matt. You might remember him from high school. And, our daughter Kayla." Ali paused. "I must warn you. Kayla has a bit of an attitude. She doesn't want to spend her summer in the store."

"Must be a boy involved. No matter what the age. Always about the boy. Thanks for the heads up. When do I start?"

"I'll tell Matt to expect you later in the week."

The two former classmates shook hands and went their separate ways. Ali was excited to tell Matt about their new hire and hoped he would share her enthusiasm. On her way home, Ali texted Matt that she had good news.

"I thought you'd be relieved, at least," Ali said after she gave Matt the news about hiring Celeste when he came home from the store.

"Shouldn't I do the hiring since you don't come near the store? I have to work with this woman."

"What woman?" Janelle said as she joined Ali and Matt on the front porch. She took a seat on the swing underneath the whirling fan.

"You're still here, I see," Matt said.

"Don't worry. Not much longer. As soon as my patient is healed. She does rely on me quite a bit."

Ali glared at Janelle.

"So, who's this woman you're talking about?"

"Ali hired a woman to work part-time and I don't know anything about her and I'll be the one working with her."

"What's her name? How did you find her?" Janelle, the inquisitor, shot out questions like microwaved popcorn.

"She was Celeste Fontana in high school." Ali paused. "Her mother was a brainiac at the Center for Disease Control. Celeste's grandmother came to our home ec class and taught us how to make pineapple tamales. Her father was smart. I think he worked at the CDC, too."

Janelle narrowed her eyes and rubbed her chin. "Hmm. Maybe I remember her. Pleasant personality but not much in the looks department?" Janelle rose from the swing to leave. She whispered in Ali's ear. "Nothing to worry about."

"What does she look like?" Matt asked.

"Why does that matter? She likes to cook so that's a plus."

"She's fat?"

"Because she likes to cook doesn't mean she's fat."

"She needs to be able to lift boxes is what I meant." He picked up a leaf falling from a nearby dogwood and tossed it into the mulch. "I had someone in mind to hire."

"Who?"

"Kayla claimed she didn't know anyone but Logan's father's girlfriend—"

"You hired her?"

"Not exactly. I thought I'd have her drop by the store."

"What does she look like?" Ali asked.

"Now it matters?"

"Matt, I can't tell Celeste you hired someone. We shook hands."

"I'll tell my potential employee the truth. You hired someone without discussing it with me. Matt the spineless. Better retrieve that doormat from Brad."

"Here's the deal. If Celeste doesn't work out, we'll hire your person. Agreed?"

"Sounds like I'm letting you push me around."

Ali decided she would make it up to Matt, one way or the other.

Chapter 29

The next morning Ali was typing on her laptop in bed. Matt delivered coffee to her. He sat on the side of the bed and pushed her bangs off her face.

She stopped typing. "Janelle said something curious yesterday."

"Do you think I'm interested in anything Janelle says?"

Ali ignored Matt's question. "She said I might be jealous of Celeste."

"But you hired her. That doesn't make any sense."

"So, do I act jealous?"

"Maybe a little. But forget about Celeste. Let's talk about the Italian movie star who has been here for four days," Matt said.

"We can't count the first forty-eight hours because he needed time to adjust."

"What does he do when Kayla and I are at the store?"

"He sleeps late. Wanders around the kitchen as if he's a health inspector. Looks in the pantry. Asks me if I have certain ingredients. Drove me to meet Brad." She set her laptop aside and took a sip of coffee. "How's Kayla doing at the store? You haven't mentioned."

"She's putting in her time in body but not in mind. She's constantly texting, ignores customers. Frankly, Kayla's one lousy employee, but how do I fire my own child?"

"I thought you were going to talk to Kayla about giving her more responsibility."

"Nothing piques her interest," Matt said.

"Let's give Luca, what, about two or three more days before we lay down the law?"

"Too much time. Things have to change starting today." Matt stood to adjust the shutters to block the bright morning sun from Ali's eyes. "You like having him around."

"I've never had a chauffeur. Except if we count Kayla when she had a learner's permit. She claimed I was overbearing when she was behind the wheel. And, Luca will be an enormous help in the kitchen."

"He must find a job. Has to do more than cooking and driving you around town."

"More?"

"How's he with dogs? He could find dog walking jobs from some of our elderly neighbors."

"I'll find out today."

Matt kissed Ali goodbye and left for work.

Ali returned to her laptop typing possible plotlines she would transfer to index cards. She wanted to be prepared when the sisters met.

Her rumbling stomach reminded her she didn't eat breakfast and it was almost lunchtime. She tried standing on her ankle, but it still ached. On a scale of 1-10, a 5. Regardless, she limped to the kitchen and opened the refrigerator door.

"Sit down. My job is to help you," Janelle shouted as she entered the front door and saw Ali in the kitchen.

"That's what you and I thought you were here for, but you're never here when I need you. Where do you disappear to?" Ali noted that Janelle was dressed more casually today—capri pants and a magenta and white sleeveless cotton shirt. She chose to wear flip-flops.

"How about a sandwich?" Janelle asked.

"Can you make a sandwich?"

"Funny. Now you sit down. Where's the mayo and mustard?" Janelle opened the refrigerator. "Where's the turkey? Do you want lettuce? I don't see any lettuce in the fridge. How about a piece of fruit? Do you eat cheese? I don't eat cheese. Love it though. Here's a nice piece of white cheddar." She tried to break off a hunk with her hand. With no success, she found a paring knife and cut a piece, which she tossed into her mouth.

Ali directed Janelle to the necessary accoutrements for a sandwich. "You might want to take your purse off your shoulder."

Janelle dropped her suitcase-size tote on the floor. Ali pushed it under the table.

"I'm a little slow, but I can learn. I'm a fast learner. My character in *Hot Night in NOLA* was a trained chef, which required loads of research. I, er, I mean, Phoebe did the research for me."

"Good morning, ladies," Luca said as he joined Ali and Janelle in the kitchen. He stretched his long arms and yawned.

Ali pointed to the wall clock. "More like afternoon," she said. "Hope you slept well."

"Much more comfortable upstairs than in the den. Not that I'm complaining."

Janelle frowned at him. "Glad you're comfortable."

"Are you making lunch, Miss Jennings? I'll make the sandwich for both of you." He tried to nudge Janelle away from the countertop.

"No, no. I'm here to help poor Ali until she recovers from her dreadful accident."

"I tripped on your tote. Not a major catastrophe."

"I'm supposed to be of assistance, too. Mr. Lawrence won't be pleased if he knows you're helping. You're family. I'm hired help," Luca said.

"You are receiving a salary?" Janelle said.

"No money has been discussed. I'm lucky to have a free place to stay." He tugged at the bread Janelle was holding. She re-tugged. A bread tug of war ensued.

"Damn," Janelle said as the bread tore in half and one piece drifted to the floor as she clenched the other. The two competing executive chefs stared at the wasted food. One person was soon to become the sous chef or the fired chef.

Roxie didn't waste a second. She gobbled the rye bread in a nanosecond.

"Can dogs eat bread? Will she choke? What have you done? That was the last piece of bread," Janelle said to Luca.

Roxie pranced over to her water bowl.

"Ladies, please go to the porch and I promise to bring you an appetizing lunch." He pushed Janelle on her arm and pointed to the sunroom.

"You are one impudent young man, but you are a better cook. Make it snappy. Poor Ali needs nourishment."

Ali shot her sister a scowl.

"I mean, please, make it fast because injured Ali is hungry."

Ali sighed.

The sisters left Luca in the kitchen and moved to the sunroom. Janelle turned on the ceiling fan. "It was my idea, Ali. I had planned to make lunch for you, but Luca is pushy. You saw firsthand. He's merely finishing what I started. All the way home from the…all the way home I was deciding what to make you for lunch."

Ali smiled. "I appreciate your thoughtfulness. Let the kid do something for us. Matt's ready to kick him out if he doesn't start pulling his own weight around here. Matt maintains he's a freeloader and he does not approve of the relationship Luca has with Kayla."

"He certainly is handsome. No wonder Kayla is crazy about him."

Before long, Luca appeared carrying lunch on one of Ali's rock-flowerpaper trays with a starfish motif. "I made a note we're out of bread, Mrs. Lawrence, but you had a few tortillas."

The sisters eyed the attractive plates of rollups speared with cherry tomatoes on the top and carrot discs on the side.

"I made cucumber cream cheese turkey rollups with basil from your herb garden in the front of the house. Of course, lunch was Miss Jennings idea."

Janelle nodded to Luca.

"May I take your drink orders?"

"Water for me, but Janelle will have a glass of wine."

"White, please. You'll find a bottle in the fridge."

After Luca had brought the drinks, Janelle said, "Join us, Luca."

"No, thank you, Miss Jennings. I ate while I was making your lunch. What should I do now, Mrs. Lawrence?"

"How are you with dogs?"

"I love dogs," Luca said.

"Please take Roxie for a walk."

"Where to?"

"Around the block. Over to the park. Anywhere."

"We could stop by Kitchen Bliss and say hello to Kayla."

"No! Definitely not. Don't go near the store. She has a job. The leash is on the back of the kitchen door."

"How long?"

"How long is the leash? Don't tell me you're afraid of dogs?"

"No, Mrs. Lawrence. How long should I walk Roxie?"

"Until you or Roxie can't walk anymore."

Two hours later, Ali texted Kayla to ask if she had seen Luca.

Kayla: no. why?
Ali: He took Roxie for a walk two hours ago.
Kayla: maybe he's lost.

Ali: In Willoughby?

Kayla: don't worry. I'll text him.

Luca rushed through the unlocked front door as Ali put the phone down. "What have I done? I've screwed up. Kayla will be pissed. Mr. Lawrence will kick me out now."

"What's the matter, Luca? Calm down," Ali said.

"Roxie ran away from me."

"How? She doesn't weigh twenty pounds."

"I think I'm allergic to pollen. Roxie and I took a break while I had a sneezing fit and I must have dropped the leash because she disappeared."

"Janelle. Take off those flip flops and put on shoes and help Luca find Roxie."

Ali called Matt. "I took your advice and gave Luca a job—walking Roxie and now she's gone. Let Kayla leave the store and tell her to come over here. We'll retrace Luca's steps."

The dog search task force, commandeered by Ali, was out in full force. Ali told Janelle and Luca to split up and scour the neighborhood.

Matt and Kayla joined the group leaving Celeste in charge at the store. After about thirty minutes, they regrouped on the front porch of the Lawrence home.

"She's hit by a car," Kayla cried. "How could you do this, Luca? She's my little sister."

Luca, who was as white as his T-shirt, said nothing. He sat on the steps of the porch with his head in his hands, perspiration dripping from his olive skin. He resembled an escapee from a sauna. "I'm going to continue searching and I won't return until I have the little dog in my arms." He jogged down the driveway, glanced right and left, and took off headed east. Everyone watched him until he was out of sight.

"Anyone missing a cute little dog?"

The group eyed Logan who was walking up the driveway. He was leading Roxie by her pink leash and held leashes for Jake and Elwood in his other hand.

"Where was she?" Kayla demanded.

"Don't kill the messenger," Matt said.

"She was playing with your grandfather's dog in his front yard. How'd she run off?"

No one answered.

"You'd better text Luca," Matt said.

"Let him sweat it out," Kayla said. She took Roxie from her rescuer and cradled her in her arms.

"Want to hang out tonight?" Logan asked Kayla.

"No." She put Roxie down and walked toward the front door passing her mother who was on the porch.

Ali spoke to Kayla. "Logan doesn't deserve that kind of treatment. He's a family friend even if you don't have romantic feelings for him anymore."

"I have enough friends. If he's so great, you can have him as your friend."

Matt shook his head and followed Logan down the street. "Wait up. I apologize for my rude daughter. Thanks so much for finding Roxie."

"I get the picture. She's been talking about going to Italy to see some guy named Louie or Larry, but he came here instead. He must be the one who lost Roxie. I haven't had the pleasure of meeting him and don't care to."

"Luca?"

"Yeah. That's the name. Suppose it won't be the last time I have my heart broken. See you around, Mr. Lawrence."

"You're welcome at our house anytime. I mean it." Matt walked back to the house. "Your daughter is beginning to act more like her aunt," Matt said to Ali.

"She's *my* daughter when her behavior doesn't meet your expectations," Ali said.

"Guess I'll try to find the dog loser," Matt said. As he was leaving the house, Luca returned from his futile search for Roxie. "Mrs. Lawrence texted me. Sorry for the trouble I've caused."

"Let's limit your duties to chauffeuring and housework," Matt said.

Ali pointed to her ankle, "Plus, he can help with the cooking. Who knows how much longer I'll be incapacitated."

Chapter 30

The morning after the missing dog episode, a sleepy-eyed Luca entered the kitchen. "Is Mr. Lawrence gone?" he asked Ali who was sitting at the table.

"Coast is clear. He's out running. Help yourself to coffee."

"Mr. Lawrence doesn't want me here."

"He'll adjust. Meanwhile, we have to keep you busy." She stared at him and then reviewed her to-do list. A lightbulb went off.

"How about if I hire you? You could be my personal assistant."

"Excuse me, ma'am?"

Ali pointed to her ankle. "You could help me with many of my responsibilities until my ankle heals. I need more time to write with my sister. I'm overcommitted right now."

"I want to be of help, Mrs. Lawrence, but what do you have in mind?"

Ali put a piece of yellow-lined legal paper in front of Luca. "This is my to-do list. Read it to me."

"Make mini lemon blueberry scones, caprese bites, chocolate hazelnut tartlets," he read. "A lot of food to make. When's your deadline?"

"I like how you think. I need to deliver these items tomorrow afternoon and I haven't even bought the ingredients. Matt's too busy to help and I don't dare ask him to take Kayla away from the store. Mother and Janelle…ah, cooking isn't exactly their fortes."

"They have other skills though. Isn't that right?"

"Luca, the politician," Ali said.

He continued reading the list. "Let's review. I could drive you to the grocery store, help you prepare the food, and deliver the finished product. Yes, I can do these things for you. This might make Mr. Lawrence happy…and help you, too. Is this what a personal assistant does?"

"Want the job?"

"Absolutely."

"You are now officially my personal assistant." Ali and her new employee shook hands. "Let's drop by Kitchen Bliss first. I need to put in an appearance. Matt says I ignore the store."

"What happens when your ankle heals? You won't need me anymore."

"We'll deal with that when it happens." Ali paused. "Pay won't be much."

"Room and board is pay enough and driving your pickup will be cool." He sat still staring at Ali.

"Do you have something you want to say?"

"May I have breakfast, please."

"Ah, yes, you may eat breakfast. Help yourself," Ali said.

Luca continued to sit at the table staring at Ali.

"We prepare our own breakfasts around here."

"Mammomi."

"Excuse me?"

"I'm spoiled. My mother has always taken care of me. Or, my grandmother or my aunts. My sisters say I'm spoiled. They tell me to learn how to take care of myself. I'm a mama's boy, a mammomi."

"You've come to the right place, Mr. Mammomi, and your education begins today at the University of Lawrence. Ali Lawrence, that is." She stood gingerly. "We'll leave as soon as you finish making your own breakfast."

Ali left the handsome mama's boy and hobbled on her crutches toward the bedroom to finish dressing. The sound of a spoon clicking against a bowl reassured her that the kid had found sustenance.

Luca drove Ali the short distance to Kitchen Bliss. He found a spot in front of the store and helped Ali and her crutches out of the pickup. He leaned against the vehicle, adjusted his sunglasses, and faced the glass window of the store's entrance.

"Welcome to Kitchen Bliss," an unwelcoming voice said coming from the area around the coffeemakers.

"A little more enthusiasm, please," Ali said to her daughter. "You sound like a funeral director."

"How's this? Good morning! Welcome to Kitchen Bliss. May I help you find the most perfect gift for whomever you are shopping for. Or is it whoever? May I be of assistance? I am here to help you, but please hurry and shop and spend tons of money and leave me alone." Kayla stopped to take a breath. "Is that better?"

Ali stood still. She scrunched up her face and tightened her lips.

"Thanks for leaving Luca home alone. What's he supposed to do all day? Why don't you consider my feelings?"

"Have you noticed how similar you are to your aunt? Everything's about you. I think you inherited the narcissistic gene."

"How'd you get here? You can't walk."

Ali pointed to the front window facing the street where Luca was standing. "I've hired him. He's my chauffeur and personal assistant."

"Wow!" She waved to Luca.

"Is the HR director here? We might have to make some adjustments. The storeroom hasn't been cleaned in a while." Ali turned her back on her daughter, left her crutches near the counter, and limped to the office where Matt was doing paperwork.

Kayla ran to catch up with her mother. "I'm sorry, Mom. I don't want to be here, but I really really don't want to work in the storeroom. Dust everywhere. Makes me sneeze and it's depressing. Thanks so much for giving Luca a job. Maybe Dad will lighten up on him now."

The bell on the front door jingled, interrupting the mother-daughter conversation. "Wait right here. Listen. You'll be impressed," Kayla said.

"Good morning, Kayla," the first customer of the day said. "I was hoping you'd be here this summer."

"Thank you, Mrs. Turnbull. I'm delighted to be here because of our faithful customers. May I pour you a cup of coffee? We're brewing an especially popular bean from Costa Rica." Kayla caught her mother's eye and nodded.

"How wonderful. Thank you, dear. And I want a young person's opinion about a wedding present for my grandniece who is a young executive."

"Please have a seat at our table for preferred customers and I'll bring you coffee and some ideas for a gift." Kayla led Mrs. Turnbull to the parlor table and chairs reserved for restless husbands while their wives shopped.

Ali stood behind the table linens display and couldn't help but giggle.

Matt joined her. "Why are you laughing?"

"Our daughter. I didn't realize she possesses excellent salesmanship skills. Listen."

Kayla's parents eavesdropped while Kayla did her sales job on Mrs. Turnbull. "My first suggestion is this totally cool Moscow Mule pitcher and copper glasses." Kayla set a tray with the items on the table while she searched for other potential gifts.

"How'd you get here?" Matt asked.

"My personal assistant."

"Excuse me?"

"I've got to run. I mean go. Can't run. Luca's waiting."

"Luca?" Matt asked.

"I've hired him. He's my chauffeur. See ya." She blew Matt a kiss.

Matt put his arms akimbo and shook his head as his wife departed.

Ali took her crutches from the counter and hobbled to the front door avoiding eye contact with Mrs. Turnbull, but she gave Kayla a thumbs-up.

Kayla approached the front window and blew Luca a kiss.

Ali joined Luca curbside where he stood next to the Green Monster like a chauffeur to a rock star. He opened the door for her. "Where to now, Mrs. Lawrence?"

"Home. I'm going to give you a few life survival tips. Your sisters will be proud."

Luca made a U-turn on Willoughby Lane and accelerated ignoring the twenty-five-mph speed limit.

"Careful. Related to the Andrettis?"

Chapter 31

Ali's cell rang before they reached home. "Better take this from my friend Olivia. Her usual mode is one of panic."

"This is totally last minute and feel free to say no even though no is not in your lexicon." Olivia, a Book Babes pal, spoke her words at rapid-fire speed. She needed help with a reception following the funeral for longtime Willoughby resident, Wallace Bigelow. "Laurie May was supposed to supply most of the food, but her dog found a stash of leftover chocolate Easter eggs and devoured every last one of them. She rushed Rocky to the vet's."

"This is Laurie May's own fault. She lets that mongrel eat anything within a paw's length." *When will I learn to say no to my friends?*

"Are you there?" Olivia asked.

"What do you need?"

"Don't want to pressure you. Are you sure you're up to it?" Olivia asked. "I mean with your ankle and your sister in town—"

"I assure you I can handle funeral food and my-suck-the-air-out-of-the-room sister simultaneously."

"We expect a good-sized turnout at the funeral and reception afterward. Mr. Bigelow had many friends in Willoughby, as you know. Other Book Babes are pitching in, too. We need the food by 1 p.m."

"I was planning to attend the funeral anyway. Tell me what you need," Ali repeated. Olivia was beginning to irritate Ali.

"We need a variety of tea sandwiches—pimento and tuna." She hesitated. "Or pimento and chicken salad. Or egg salad? What do you think? I have no idea what Laurie May planned to bring."

"I choose pimento. You can find others to do the egg and chicken salad sandwiches."

"Thank you so much. Will you do two hundred? The thought of having people coming to her house has overwhelmed Mrs. Bigelow. The neighborhood is stepping in to help since she has no children. She does have children—"

"My pleasure. Bye for now." Ali was quick to end the conversation. She hated being rude to her friend, but she didn't want to hear the saga of the dysfunctional Bigelow Family one more time. The Bigelows were a pet project of Olivia's who attempted to rescue as many people as she did animals.

Am I becoming more like Janelle? Disinterested in anyone but myself?

Ali chose the pimento cheese because she and Luca could go to Costco and buy large quantities of Ruth's Original Pimento Spread. The best. Except, here was another example of Ali's subterfuge. Ali's sprained ankle was healing.

Everyone thinks my ankle is still sprained and now everyone will think Ruth's pimento cheese is mine. I'm becoming a lying deceptive old broad. I never knew deceit could be so simple.

"Change of plans," Ali said to Luca. "Make a left at the signal. We have some shopping to do. I agreed to make two hundred sandwiches and deliver them this afternoon. And we'll shop for what I promised to make for a bridal shower tomorrow."

"Sounds like lots of work."

"With my new personal assistant, it will be easy peasy."

When they arrived at the store, Luca asked Ali if she could navigate the mammoth warehouse with her lame ankle. "You do seem to be improving though. Right?"

Good catch, Luca.

Ali chose to use an electric cart, one of several, which was waiting at the entrance. She took out the shopping list from her purse and read it to Luca: prosciutto, mozzarella balls, Kalamata olives, stone ground mustard, Brie, breadsticks, capers, wontons, mango chutney, shrimp, pimento cheese, and bread from the bakery. She maneuvered from aisle to aisle in the cart with Luca at her side filling the cart.

When they arrived home, Luca unloaded the groceries. He offered to make the sandwiches for the Bigelow reception. "Crust or crustless?" he asked.

"Crustless."

"Triangles or squares?"

"Chef's choice."

"May I make a suggestion?"

"Of course."

"Tramezzini."

"I don't understand."

"Tramezzini. Popular in Italy. Tiny sandwiches filled with egg salad or prosciutto, tuna, tomatoes. Whatever you have available. I think your friends would enjoy."

"Love the idea, but let's stick with the pimento cheese today."

Ali used her crutches to walk to the porch where her laptop awaited her. If her ankle healed, she'd feel forced to give up Luca. Maybe she could prolong her injury.

A few minutes later, Luca appeared with a glass of water with a slice of lime and a sprig of mint floating in it. "Thought you might be thirsty in this hot weather."

Aw, this is the life.

"Thank you, Luca. When you're finished we'll make our delivery."

* * *

Ali stayed in the Green Monster while Luca delivered the food. Olivia directed Luca to the kitchen inside the Bigelow home. She walked to the curb to greet Ali. "I'm so glad you decided to bring pimento cheese sandwiches. Everyone raves about your recipe. Someday you should share it with us. Don't be selfish, now."

Ali blushed, not because of the compliment, but because of embarrassment for the lie. Someday she would try her hand at making the popular item. . .or not.

"Thanks again, Ali. Hope to see you at the next book club meeting. We're reading Kristin Hannah's latest. Should be a good one." She turned to leave, but stopped and said over her shoulder, "I approve of your boy toy. Does he hire out?" She winked at Ali before waving goodbye. "He's a straight up hottie."

When Luca returned to the pickup, he said, "Your friend asked what your secret ingredient is in the pimento cheese."

"Oh, no. What did you say?"

"I said what my mother would want me to say."

"And that would be?" Ali held her breath and hoped his mother didn't adhere to a life free of deception.

"An old family recipe. I left out the relative was named Ruth."

"I like you more and more all the time, Luca."

"Wish Mr. Lawrence did." He turned on the ignition, turned up the air conditioning, and pulled away from the curb.

"Where to now?"

"Home. Don't worry about Mr. Lawrence. He's concerned Kayla might run off to Italy. If you can convince him otherwise, he'll come around."

"No worries there. I'm staying in the U.S."

"Glad to know."

"Is this typical for you, Mrs. Lawrence? Making all this food for your friends?"

"Seems as though everything happens at the same time. Several showers and parties for daughters of friends who are having weddings or expecting children. After this round of events, I'm going to learn to say no. Have to work on the book."

"They'll do the same for you when Kayla marries."

"Are you trying to tell me something?"

"No. No. Yes, I love your daughter, but we have to finish school and begin our careers."

"I'm glad Mr. Lawrence wasn't here to listen to this conversation."

"What now?" Luca asked.

"Let's get a head start on my cooking commitments for tomorrow. Here's the request list."

"Where's your pasta machine?"

"Ah, I don't make my own pasta. Too much trouble."

"Ravioli maker, cutter?"

"You're going high tech on me."

"I could go to Kitchen Bliss and purchase the items. With my own money, of course."

"No! That won't work. Matt has given me strict instructions to keep you away from the store."

"He means away from Kayla."

"Probably. Let me think. Janelle has given me gourmet appliances I never use. Check the pantry. On the floor. Dust-covered boxes."

Luca rummaged around in the pantry. "Success." He pulled out all the necessary equipment to make ravioli. He reentered the pantry and found flour. He went to the refrigerator and took out eggs, mushrooms, and cream. "We're all set."

"I'll watch and take pretend notes. You're setting me up for failure."

"I don't understand."

"Next time I'm asked to help with food, expectations will be high."

"I'm only a text away," Luca said.

"You have to give my husband a detailed report of your duties and the more duties the better. Some laundry needs washing. Can you handle that?"

"When I'm away at school I have to do my own. As you say, easy peasy."

Chapter 32

It was 5:30 p.m. Janelle and Ali had agreed to quit writing at five o'clock every day, but Ali had been on her own this afternoon. Janelle claimed she had important business to take care of. Ali couldn't complain because she had attended the Bigelow funeral.

Ali gathered the index cards from the kitchen table to make room for dinner preparation.

Matt was standing at the kitchen sink. "That looks menacing," she said, pointing to a knife in his hand. He held a seven-inch chef's knife in one hand and a stainless-steel honing tool, which resembled a Star Wars laser, in the other. "About to sharpen it," he said.

He handed her a bunch of carrots and a peeler.

The aroma of oregano and the sound of sizzling onions and garlic filled the Lawrence family's kitchen.

"Hello, hello. Just little ole me. Don't go out of your way." Virginia, with royal bearing, entered the kitchen. "Sometimes I feel invisible around here."

"I didn't hear you come in, Mother." From a seated position she hugged her mother.

"I always want to be useful, especially in the kitchen," Virginia said as she picked up a carrot and sat.

"I want to be useful," Ed said when he joined the clan in the kitchen. "I'll be at the bar in the living room."

"Where's Kayla?" Virginia asked.

"She's walking Roxie," Ali said.

"Where's Janelle?" Virginia asked.

Ali shrugged her shoulders. "Whatever her destination was required attractive attire and carefully applied makeup."

Luca entered the kitchen and greeted the family. He was holding grocery bags in both arms. "When Kayla told me you were cooking Italian tonight, I took the liberty of picking up a few things I thought you might find helpful," he said to Matt.

"That wasn't necessary. I have everything I need."

Matt put down the knife and sharpening tool. He peered into the bags and took the items out one by one. "Olive oil. I have plenty. Parmesan. Ditto." He continued to take the items out and replace them in the bag. "Too bad you spent your money on things we already have." He picked up the knife.

"But, Mr. Lawrence, these items are from Italy. I purchased them from the Italian grocery store in Dunwoody. I'd be glad to take over and finish this fine dinner you've—"

"Thank you, Luca, but I don't need your help. I've cooked many meals in this kitchen. Willoughby stores sell Italian items, by the way, including Kitchen Bliss."

"I just thought. Never mind." He turned away from Matt, but stopped and said over his shoulder, "Before I leave, I would like to do you the honor of preparing a bueno perfecto meal for you."

"Leaving? When? Is that on the horizon? Or is that news too good to be true?" Matt asked.

Ali gave the evil eye to Matt. "Hold on. I don't want to lose my assistant," she said. "You're not going any place, Luca. You're staying right here."

"Mr. Lawrence doesn't want me here. I should leave," Luca said.

"Whatever," Matt said as he grabbed peeled carrots from Ali. He returned to chopping vegetables into small pieces with machete-like strokes.

"You'll devastate Kayla if you leave," Ali said to Luca. "She'll be mad at you and Mr. Lawrence. We'll never hear the end of it."

"Who's leaving?" Ed said as he joined the family in the kitchen, cocktails in hand. He placed Virginia's gimlet on the table next to the carrots.

"It's me, Mr. Withrow."

"Hold your horses. What's going on? Who's the troublemaker? Janelle's not here so she can't be blamed," Ed said.

Luca left the kitchen and slammed the front door shut causing Roxie to whimper.

"Why did I think I could make an Italian dinner for an Italian?" Matt said to Ali. "Go tell the kid I'm having a bad day or something."

"I'm not telling him anything. You need to apologize," Ali said.

"What did you say to Luca, Mom?" Kayla said, charging into the kitchen. "He's outside and said he's going to leave." She stood in front of her mother with fury in her eyes.

Ali held up her hands as if she were complying with a police officer's demand. "I'm an innocent bystander," Ali said. "Talk to your dad."

Kayla got into her father's face. "He tried to do something for you, Dad. He spent money on Italian ingredients he thought you would appreciate. He even offered to cook dinner for you. He won't tell me what you said, but it must have been awful. Why don't you for once try to do something nice for me?"

Matt tossed the knife on the counter where it did a flutter dance before it nearly fell to the ground. "I wasn't that hard on the guy. He spent money he didn't need to. I was trying to do him a favor."

Ali snickered.

"I heard that," Matt said. "Why is everyone against me? I'm only trying to protect Kayla from developing a serious relationship before she graduates."

"Talk to him, Dad. I can't bear that he might leave," Kayla said.

Matt made eye contact with Ali and turned to meet Kayla's glare. He took a bottle of Kellerweis from the refrigerator, opened it, and handed it to Ali. "See what you can do."

Ali hobbled to the porch. "May I sit?" Without waiting for an answer, Ali squatted next to Luca. She offered him the bottle, which he accepted. "I apologize for my husband. Please don't leave. Besides, where would you go?"

"I have enough money to last till school starts, if I can find a cheap place to stay."

"What does Kayla say about this?"

"She won't be happy."

"I'll work on Mr. Lawrence on your behalf."

"Mr. Withrow seems to like me. I could stay with him and Mrs. Withrow."

"Would Kayla be okay with that?"

"As long as I don't leave Willoughby is what she said."

Ali waved away a pesky bug, which had landed on her leg. "That might work. Meanwhile, we have some hungry customers in the house. You better get back to work." She handed him an apron.

Luca took the apron but didn't move.

Kayla was standing in the foyer with the door partly opened listening to their conversation.

"Do you mind, Kayla. This is between Luca and me."

Kayla stepped away from the front door but stayed within hearing distance.

"We'd better figure out a way for you and Mr. Lawrence to develop a friendship."

"I get along fine with him. It's the other way around."

"Please don't take his attitude personally. You are a responsible young man. Matt is trying to protect his daughter, which is a father's duty. You'll understand some day."

"I understand, Mrs. Lawrence." He took a swig of beer. "I respect your daughter. She is a fine woman."

"Thank you. So, you'll be going back to school in six weeks?"

Luca nodded. He took another swig of beer.

"Let's make it a pleasant six weeks. If you think that's possible."

"Yes, ma'am."

Kayla was waiting for them when they entered the house.

"Thanks, Mom. This is absolutely, positively going to be the best summer of my life. I don't care if he moves out of our house as long as he stays close."

"Only six weeks," Ali said.

"Maybe longer than six weeks." Kayla took Luca's hand and they returned to the kitchen. She turned her head and winked at Ali.

Chapter 33

Ali sent a text to Matt asking if he wanted to picnic tonight along the river. The last thing Ali wanted was to go to the mosquito-infested Chattahoochee River. Insects survived by grazing on Ali and ignoring Matt—lucky guy. Ali hoped Matt would decline her invitation. At least she could take credit for trying to please him. Points for her side of the column, if they were keeping score, which, of course, they weren't.

No such luck. Matt texted back: **Sure, if that's what you want.**

That's not what she wanted. A candlelight dinner at a white table-cloth restaurant with no needy and/or annoying family members would be optimal. A month-long cruise in the Caribbean would be acceptable. She controlled herself and texted back a thumbs-up.

The house was empty, so Ali could walk to the kitchen without having to fake a limp. If she revealed the truth about her healed ankle, she might have to give up her boy Luca–chauffeur and chef. Matt still didn't acknowledge Luca's value to the family. Ali had observed, over the years, the way Janelle used people. She didn't want to follow in those selfish footsteps. *Or was she already doing that?*

Ali investigated the contents of the refrigerator and found a piece of creamy St. André cheese, jumbo black olives, and a bottle of sauvignon blanc. She moved to the pantry and discovered a box of sesame seed crackers and a jar of marinated mushrooms.

"What's going on?" Kayla asked as she entered the kitchen. She plopped her backpack on the floor and put her phone on the table. She observed the items on the countertop. "Going on a picnic?"

"Your Dad loves alfresco dining. I thought he'd be here by now. Don't want to miss the sunset. What time did he leave the store?"

"He's still there. We were busy, but I decided to come home and eat before I'm forced to go back so you and Dad can have a date. His word. A date. A little old, aren't you?"

Ali was flattered that Matt thought of their picnic as a date. It had been a long time since they did anything romantic, outside of their bedroom.

"Please tell me why I deserve your snippiness. I'm the one who supports your relationship with Luca, more than your dad, but still you're disrespectful." Ali put cotton napkins and a corkscrew on the countertop to add to the picnic basket, which was in the garage.

"I don't mean to be a brat, Mom. I'll work on my attitude and you can work on respecting me and my wishes. I have some rights, you know."

"Thank you and so noted," Ali said.

"I'll pack for you. Aren't you supposed to limit weight on your ankle?"

"Yeah, right. My ankle. Thanks. You can bring the picnic basket from the garage. Please." Ali reached for the Tums. If she didn't end the farce about her ankle soon, she'd have an ulcer.

When Kayla returned with the basket, Ali was sitting on a bar stool at the island. "Will you please give me the chicken salad in the refrigerator?"

Kayla removed the lid. "Passes the smell test." She handed it to her mother. "Since the store is open late tonight, I have to work for

Celeste who has a date. She wouldn't tell me who. I wonder why? Maybe he's married?"

"None of our business, so please stay out of our employee's love life."

Kayla returned to the refrigerator and eyed the contents. "Not much food in here. You used to love cooking for us, Mom."

"That was before Luca."

"You're going to miss him when we go back to school."

"I'm going to enjoy him while he's here. Like I'm enjoying you... most of the time."

"By the way, Mom. I have a complaint and a compliment."

"Okay. The bad news first."

"Why do you let Luca drive the Green Monster, but I can't? Not fair. Is it because he's a guy?"

"Perhaps your driving record has something to do with it?" She eyeballed Kayla. "So, give me the compliment."

"You're faking the injury to your ankle and I know why."

"Let me have it, Minerva, goddess of wisdom."

"You claim you hired Luca to help you, but you don't need him."

"What do you mean?"

"You could manage without him, but if Dad knew your ankle was healed, he'd make you fire Luca. I figured it all out. You're keeping Luca around to make me happy. Thanks, Mom." She embraced her mother.

Ali hesitated. She kept Luca for herself, not Kayla. Maybe it was better to keep that as her little secret.

Chapter 34

"Sorry I'm late," Matt said as he rushed in the house and met Ali in the kitchen. He kissed her on the cheek and took their insulated picnic basket and a bag of paper products to the SUV. He helped Ali into the passenger seat.

"We still have time before sunset," Ali said.

They drove to the nearby Chattahoochee River with parking lots along the river's edge. Matt found a spot near a bench. "You won't have to walk too far."

Guilt crept over Ali like the green kudzu climbing up an adjacent elm tree.

If I tell Matt about my ankle, I might lose Luca. She wasn't sure how Matt would react? Would he laugh and applaud her duplicity or accuse her of being a deceitful wife?

"I was talking to some of the guys at the gym. A physical therapist and an orthopedist. They both think you should have healed by now."

"I am improving. No doubt." If Ali could persuade Matt to let her keep Luca as her personal assistant, life would be grand. And, Kayla would be in a better mood.

They situated themselves on the bench. Ali doused her arms and legs with anti-bug spray. She removed the bottle of chilled sauvignon blanc from the basket and handed it and the corkscrew to Matt. She made a mental note to renew early evening alfresco dinners she and Matt had enjoyed but lately had stopped, for no apparent reason.

Matt uncorked the wine and filled their glasses. They were quiet while they observed the slowly meandering river and sipped the wine. Energetic runners and joggers passed in front of them. "You'll be out running before long," he observed.

With sunset less than an hour away, the number of people on standup paddleboards and in kayaks and canoes was dwindling. Others, in tubes, glided down the river laughing and drinking beer. It was a happy time on the Hooch.

"I guess I was more interested in the Peachtree Race T-shirt than running the race. Silly of me," Ali said.

"Not at all. You were never a goal-oriented person. Always trying to please others rather than yourself. Now you've achieved two objectives. You wrote a book and you trained for the Peachtree. Doesn't matter that you won't be able to run it."

This would be the ideal moment to confess about my ankle. I need more wine.

The tangerine sun was slowly descending behind the tall beech and oak trees that lined the river's shore. Like a pebble in a shoe, the irritating honks from the ubiquitous Canada geese invaded the otherwise serene setting.

"So, why are we here? What's up? You hate coming here during bug season." Matt took a sip of wine and continued watching the dwindling number of tubers bobbing along with the current.

"You love coming here. You always say we don't come often enough. It reminds you of when we were newlyweds. So happy in those days."

"Are you happy?" Matt asked.

"What kind of question is that?"

"Satisfied? Content? You know, happy with the way your life has turned out."

"A philosophical Q&A session instead of dinner by the river?" Ali asked. She nudged him with her elbow.

"Just asking. We haven't spent much time together, without distractions, I mean. Thought I'd take the temperature of our relationship."

"Sounds like you're grilling a steak."

"I'm serious."

"The ankle has set me back." Guilt grabbed Ali like a bad case of the flu. She tried to remember where a restroom was located but couldn't recall. She pressed her hands against her stomach.

"Are you okay?"

Ali couldn't confess now because she had told a humongous lie about her ankle. "I'm fine. About the state of my life," she continued. "Kayla, who has turned against me—"

"I found something on your laptop."

Matt's abruptness surprised Ali. "My laptop? Why?"

"So, you *are* hiding something."

"What's the matter with you? My laptop contains nothing confidential. My life is an open book, one boring book."

"I knew it! You think our life is boring."

"Whoops! Wrong word." Ali turned to face Matt. "What on earth did you find so upsetting?"

"A dating site—A Match to Catch."

"So?"

"Why a dating site on your computer?"

"For a character in our book. Janelle wants our pathetic protagonist to search online for a boyfriend who is a serial killer masquerading as a divorce lawyer. Pretty funny, don't you think?"

"Seriously?"

"I'm trying to embrace her suggestions. To keep the peace." Ali slapped at a mosquito on her leg and re-sprayed.

"Did you find any potential dates? Younger, more handsome men than me?"

"No one to compare with you, honey bear." She leaned over and kissed Matt on the lips. "Why are you paranoid? You know I love you. I don't want another man or another life."

He took a sip of wine. "Okay. I guess." He stared at the river.

"Something else is bothering you, Matt. Spit it out."

"What about the sexy bedroom scene? Was that us?"

"What are you talking about?"

"You or Janelle left a scene from your book on my desk. I assumed you wanted me to approve it."

"I write what I want. No approvals from husband. You sure are sensitive."

"Was it us you were describing?"

"I don't remember the scene because I leave bedroom stuff to Janelle." She looked at Matt. "Besides, our lovemaking is too hot and steamy even for a Janelle book. Don't you think?" She winked at Matt. Ali slapped at another mosquito. "There's nothing wrong with us. Unless you think there is. The dating site and the sexy scene are all for the book."

Matt smiled and took a sip of wine. "I don't want people in Willoughby to think the book is about us."

"Of course, they'll think it's about us. Don't you love it?"

Matt cut Ali a look. "Maybe I am too sensitive. You know I love you."

"And right back at you, sweetheart." Ali put her wine glass down on the bench, removed olives and cheese from the basket, and made two plates. "Let's eat."

Matt popped an olive into his mouth. "I'm glad you suggested coming here tonight."

"Confession time."

"Now what is it?" Matt asked. "The truth is coming out." He gave her a worried look.

"I didn't want to come here tonight."

"Ha! I wasn't excited about it either. I don't like leaving Kayla alone at the store. What the heck. The store will survive."

"Despite my skeeter buddies, this has turned out to be a wonderful evening."

"We should run away. At least for a few days. The new boutique hotel on the corner of Mimosa and Magnolia is offering locals a discount," Matt said.

"We can't. We shouldn't. We wouldn't," Ali said.

"But you want to, and I want to—"

"That counts for something," Ali said as she leaned into Matt.

Chapter 35

Janelle peered through the glass front of Kitchen Bliss before she entered. She hoped to find Celeste alone.

"Good morning and welcome to Kitchen Bliss." A cheerful voice greeted Janelle. "Ahh, it's you," Celeste said. She glared at Janelle as she eyed her up and down.

Janelle hesitated. "Ali was right. You certainly have changed from high school."

"We're all getting older."

"Most people think I've maintained a youthful appearance," Janelle said.

"I'm not most people. I'm one of the girls you insulted and ridiculed in high school. *Fat and Dumpy* Celeste. Isn't that what you called me?"

Janelle's face reddened. "My compliments to your plastic surgeon."

"And the reason for the visit today is to make a purchase or is it to critique my surgeon's skill? I'd be glad to give you a referral."

"I hope this isn't how you treat all Kitchen Bliss customers. I wonder what Matt would say if—"

At that moment, Matt left his backroom office and joined the women at the counter. "What would I say? What are you doing here? Shopping, or sizing up Celeste?"

"Since Kitchen Bliss is our family's business, I thought I should visit in case you need suggestions for improvements."

"Not *your* family business," Matt said. "Your business is to hurry up and finish writing a book with Ali, so you can leave Willoughby."

The bell jingling above the front door saved a flabbergasted Janelle.

Celeste turned away from Matt and Janelle and greeted the new customer.

"Wonderful. Another family member," Matt said. He waved to Virginia. "I've paperwork waiting for me."

"Oh, what a nice surprise. Celeste *and* my daughter." Virginia approached Janelle and gave her a kiss on the cheek. "Looking as pretty as a picture."

"Thanks, Mother. I have to leave. Bye bye."

"Oh, if you must," Virginia said. She joined Celeste at the counter. "Ali and Matt are glad you agreed to work here. And my, have you changed, dear. I remember sweet Celeste from your high school days. What a marvelous transformation."

Celeste smiled. "Thank you, Mrs. Withrow. May I help you find something?"

"No, no. Ignore me. I want to look at the new table linens Matt ordered." She stepped toward the linens department but glanced over her shoulder toward the new employee.

The bell above the door jingled. Ed entered and raised his hand. "You can hold the welcoming stuff. Dropping by for a drink of water. Hot out there." He approached Celeste at the counter. "Ed Withrow. You might remember me as the wrestling coach at Willoughby High," he said, as he extended his hand. "Ali and Janelle's father, too."

"Yes, of course, I remember you, Mr. Withrow."

"Forget the mister. We're not in high school anymore. Call me Ed." He walked toward the water dispenser. He turned to face her. "A heads up. You can expect a visit from my wife."

Celeste smiled and pointed to the table linens section.

"It figures," Ed said.

Janelle was outside the store when she wrote a text to Ali:

> I dropped by the store today and had a lovely conversation with Celeste. She's quite attractive. Aren't you going to be so jealous?

This is the new me. Janelle deleted the text.

* * *

The family positioned themselves around the Lawrence dining room table. Ed and Matt sat at opposite ends of the table and Ali sat on one side facing Virginia and Janelle.

Kayla entered the room and lit the candles on the table. Luca was close behind. "We need a toast," she said. "To Luca's cooking." She sat next to Janelle.

"And to my sous chef," Luca said lifting his wine glass toward Kayla with one hand and tapping his heart with his other. He took a seat next to Ali.

The doorbell interrupted the family's meal.

"I'll answer it. Please enjoy," Luca said. Curious Roxie and Alva trotted behind him. When Luca returned he said, "A guy is asking for Miss Jennings. A tall guy."

"Who is he?" Janelle asked.

"I didn't ask. I closed the door and told him to wait."

"Find out!" Janelle demanded.

"Don't be rude, dear," Virginia said.

"This situation might need some extra muscle," Matt said to Luca. "Follow me."

"What about me? I'm the former wrestling coach around here or did everyone forget that?"

Virginia pulled on Ed's shirt and said, "Sit."

Luca followed Matt to the front door. Matt opened the door and eyeballed the visitor up and down. "I remember you," Matt said.

The visitor, who stared down at Matt, wore his black hair pulled into a ponytail. His white shirt was opened at the collar revealing curly chest hair and a gold crucifix on a chain.

"You're the ex-husband who cost my sister-in-law plenty of money. What do you want, Philip?" Matt asked with a sneer.

"Blame my expensive attorney, not me. She hasn't answered my messages. Is she here?"

Janelle came flip-flopping to the front door carrying a wine glass. "I'm not here for you, you ass. Don't let him in. He's trouble." She nudged herself between Luca and Matt.

"I miss you, Janelle. Thought we could work things out. May I come in?"

"Nothing to work out. Meet my new boyfriend." She pushed Matt aside, grabbed Luca by the shirt with one hand, and planted a kiss on his lips while slopping half the contents of her wine glass on the floor. She released Luca and said, "Leave, you horrible person." She put an arm around Luca's waist and leaned into his body.

"Or what? Your teenage boyfriend will beat me up," Philip said.

"I'm not—" Luca stammered as he pushed Janelle's hand aside and lunged toward the interloper. Matt restrained him.

Virginia, Ali, Kayla, and Ed joined the potential melee.

"Deal with me or you'll regret it. I'm staying at the Willoughby Inn and will expect to see you tomorrow. We have business to discuss,"

Philip said. He turned to leave. "I've read your books, Janelle. I know how you operate and you can't fool me," he hollered over his shoulder.

The stunned family watched Philip walk to a blue metallic Ford Focus with a dent in the bumper parked in the driveway.

Kayla's eyes widened as she approached Janelle. "Aunt Janie, why did you kiss Luca? He's *my* boyfriend."

"He was conveniently close," Janelle said.

"I don't like that you kissed my aunt," Kayla said turning toward Luca.

"Not my fault. I was an innocent bystander." He reached for Kayla's hand, which she dismissed.

"You were enjoying it," Kayla said.

"Didn't look like enjoyment to me but pure fear and shock," Ed said. "Plus, Philip's a tall guy."

"But I'm younger and stronger," Luca said.

"What's going on with Philip, Janelle?" Ed asked. "Do you owe him money?"

"I don't owe him anything but a knife through his heart, a bullet to his head, and a baseball bat to his leg. Correction. Both legs."

"Take a deep breath, dear," Virginia said.

"I paid through the nose to eliminate him from my life. One lump sum of money to that hunk of lard."

"Not lardy to me. Handsome and fit," Ed observed.

"We have a lovely dinner getting cold. Let's return to the table," Virginia said. "Someone needs to clean up the spilled wine." She pointed to where Janelle had sloshed her wine.

"No need. The dogs are enjoying a pre-dinner treat." Evidently, the doggies' choice of beverage was an earthy red wine.

"Come on everyone. Luca's meal is waiting for us," Ali said.

"Who can eat after that upsetting scene?" Janelle asked.

"I can," Ed said.

The family returned to the table and everyone put their napkins in their laps. Ed and Matt picked up their forks. The others sat quietly.

Kayla glanced at Janelle then Luca and then back at Janelle.

"Janelle. You cause trouble wherever you go. What have you gotten yourself into with this ex-husband of yours?" Ed asked.

"A minor dispute. He's nothing but a lousy S.O.B," Janelle said.

"Watch your language, honey," Virginia pleaded.

"I can't eat. I'm too upset. I'm going to bed." Janelle took her wine glass, filled it from the bottle on the table, and left the dining room. She immediately returned and grabbed the bottle before walking upstairs to her bedroom. She slammed the door causing the two buddies, Roxie and Alva, to yap.

After a few minutes of silence, Ed spoke. "Tell me what I'm eating, Luca. Delicious. Your descriptions are always as fine as the food."

Luca looked relieved as he watched Janelle leave the room. His description of the meal was succinct. "I have prepared veal shanks with a gremolata and saffron risotto. Mangia bene."

Everyone began savoring Luca's luscious osso bucco.

"Excellent, Luca," was Matt's concise remark.

"Delizioso," Ed said.

The family stared at Ed.

"Don't look so surprised. I Googled it. Means delicious."

The family lifted their glasses and shouted, "Delizioso."

After the kitchen was clean, Luca approached a sullen Kayla. "Let's take a walk to the park."

"Too dark," she said.

"I'll bring a flashlight. Let's go."

They were both silent until they reached a bench in the Serenity Garden of Willoughby Park overlooking the lake and the fountain. The park was active with walkers, joggers, and people headed to the lighted tennis courts. A cool nighttime breeze whispered through the trees.

"How many times do I have to tell you, Kayla? Your aunt kissed me. I didn't kiss her back."

"Did she put her tongue in your mouth?"

"You're as demented as she is. In fact, I'm beginning to think you're all a little off. Your mother and aunt are always fighting. Your father hates me. Your grandparents—"

"What about my grandparents?"

"Nothing. They're great. I don't think I belong here. I'm glad you invited me to Willoughby and I want to always be your friend." He raked his hair away from his damp forehead. "Let's meet up at school in the fall."

"But what? You're not leaving, are you?" Kayla put her head in her hands and let the tears flow. Between sobs, she said, "If it weren't for my screwy family, you'd stay?"

"It's always so frenetic around your family. My family's loud and noisy, but yours is—"

"Don't leave Willoughby. Please. Compromise and go to Gramps and Nana's. You can't leave. You'll ruin my summer. I'll be miserable."

Luca sat still.

"I love you." Kayla put her hands around his neck and pulled him close. She kissed him hard on the lips. He returned the favor and they continued to make out on the bench ignoring the people and their dogs who passed by.

When they came up for air, Kayla noticed Logan with his tennis bag slung over his shoulder walking toward the lighted tennis courts. They made eye contact but didn't acknowledge the other. After a few steps, he turned around and gave the stink eye to the twosome. "You can forget about the concert, Kayla. I have a new girlfriend."

"What was that about?" Luca asked.

"Nothing." Luca and Kayla kissed again.

When they came up for air, Luca said, "What's your grandfather's number? Let's see what he has to say about me moving in."

Chapter 36

"Brad will be here soon. How do I look?" Janelle asked her sister who was sitting in the kitchen at the table perusing the *Art of Italian Cooking.*

"You look elegant in a casual sort of way. Not too much and not too little. Just right."

Janelle wore flowing lime green pants, a white tank, and a long-length sleeveless dark blue vest with a high-low hem and purl edges. Her dark hair was as shiny as her lip gloss.

"Matt and I had a date the other night. A picnic by the river. I should make that happen more often."

"I wouldn't call tonight a date exactly. We're just friends."

"Why do you continue this charade? You're in love with Brad and have been for many years. Equally as important, Brad loves you. Despite how you treat him. You told me he wants to marry you."

"How do you know he's in love with me?"

"Because he told me."

"When? Where? Why would he tell you? And did he use the actual marriage word?"

"He didn't actually say marriage, but he's nuts about you. He didn't want to talk to Matt about you because Matt would tell Brad to see a shrink. Brad and I had lunch, at his invitation. The poor guy is confused. If you don't make up your mind about him immediately, he's going to dump you. Willoughby is loaded with women who would jump at the chance to keep him. Some of them younger than you."

"I could have done without the age comment." Janelle stared out the bay window at the neighbors walking their dogs. "The truth is…I don't…I don't want to tarnish his reputation."

Ali chuckled. "How could you possibly do that?"

Janelle removed a mirror from her purse and checked her pearlescent teeth for non-existent lipstick. "I haven't told you my latest dilemma. Worse than a dilemma. My life's a mess." She sniffed.

"Don't start crying. You'll ruin your makeup."

Janelle ignored Ali's warning, put her head in her hands, and wailed so loud Roxie came running to investigate the frightening sound.

When Janelle lifted her head, mascara streaked down her cheeks like melted licorice. "I'm being blackmailed. I'm being freaking blackmailed."

"Sounds like something from one of your books. Are you sure about this blackmail stuff?"

"I can't face Brad. Tell him I'm sick. Tell him something."

"He won't believe you a second time and I won't lie anymore. Don't think he believed you were sick the day you arrived. Put yourself together before he arrives. We can discuss this problem of yours when you return."

Ali stood and limped to Janelle's side. She put her hand on her shoulder. "Nothing can be that bad. We'll figure it out. Together." She handed Janelle a box of tissues. "Put your big girl panties on."

Janelle raised her head and blurted, "Several years ago, while on a cruise with Philip, he took some X-rated pictures or videos or something. In fact, now that I think about it that was the reason he invited me. He plotted to take the pictures and use them against me. To top that, he used my credit card to pay for everything while we were on the ship—spa treatments, expensive wine, clothes for him. Thousands and thousands of dollars and we were only gone a week. He's a more prolific shopper than I am."

"Slow down," Ali said.

"Hi, there. Anyone home?"

"Why don't you learn to lock your door, Ali? You let in anyone who walks by."

"I heard that. I'm not just anyone," Ellen said as she entered the kitchen and headed to the refrigerator. She removed a water pitcher and filled two glasses she took from the cabinet. "Lemons?"

Ali pointed to a basket on the counter near the sink.

Ellen found the cutting board and knife and added lemon wedges to the glasses. "Drink up," she said as she handed Ali a glass.

"Make yourself at home," Janelle said. "I would put a lemon in Ali's water if she would only ask."

Ali and Ellen glared at Janelle.

"Was running in the neighborhood. Stopped by to check on the invalid. Have I walked in on a tribal meeting? Are non-tribe members allowed to stay?" She took a gulp of water. "Your mascara is running, Janelle. Not attractive."

"You *are* part of this family, El. Janelle has a problem. One of her exes is causing trouble. Philip the Third."

"I've always wanted to ask you, Janelle. How do you keep track of your ex-husbands? Do you remember their names? Or do you have nicknames like Big—"

"You are disgusting, Ellen. I have never understood why you don't seem to keep a man long term. Not partial to men?" Janelle said.

"Think whatever you want," Ellen replied. "And take a look at your record."

"Brad should be here any minute. I have to fix my makeup because Ali won't tell him I'm not feeling well, and I don't know how to wiggle out of this so-called date." She paused and faced Ellen. "Could you help me—"

"Don't expect me to cover for you," Ellen said. "Anytime you don't want Brad, let me know. I'd take him in a minute and so would most of the single female population in Willoughby and some of the dudes, too."

Ali stood and stopped her sister from leaving. "Stay. Start from the beginning. You can trust Ellen. She's a problem solver."

Janelle repeated her story about the blackmail threats Philip had been sending. His emails and texts said he wanted to meet to discuss the amount of money it would take to destroy the compromising evidence.

"Is that what he meant last night when he said you had 'business' to discuss?" Ali asked.

Janelle nodded her head.

"Is that all you're worried about? Call his bluff," Ellen said.

"Isn't that a little risky?" Ali asked.

"Blackmail is illegal. His sorry ass could go to jail," Ellen said. "Be sure to keep the texts and emails for evidence."

"The sordid details would have to come out. Wouldn't I have to testify in court? I would come across as weak and vulnerable not to mention stupid."

"Janelle!" Ellen shook a forefinger at her. "Your books are filled with women who have been wronged by their men. They overcome naiveté and lack of confidence to soar to new heights. That's more or less a quote from the jacket of one of your books. Your popularity would explode if the blackmail scam were revealed. All the TV talk shows would try to book you."

"Television," Janelle repeated. She fluffed her hair.

"Where's the damaging evidence Philip claims to have?" Ali asked. "We could decide how much harm it could inflict on your reputation if we could see what he has."

"Haven't you seen some of the stuff teenage girls post on social media? I bet whatever the scum bag has isn't nearly as bad," Ellen said.

"I'm taking sack-full-of-dog-poop's word." Janelle hung her head. "I did pose for a few pictures. It was years ago." Before I...well...never mind," she muttered.

"His word is worth donkey crap. I'm telling you, Janelle, call his bluff, and forget about the degenerate," Ellen said.

"Ask him. No, demand to see the evidence," Ali said.

"I had *most* of my clothes on when he took the pictures. . .I think. We were drinking Champagne, so my memory is a little fuzzy."

"What's your opinion, Ali?" Janelle asked.

She twirled a piece of hair. "I'll have to think about this, but I'm inclined to agree with Ellen."

With a tissue, Janelle wiped away the black streaks marring her makeup and stood.

Ali shook her head as she watched her sister walk toward the front door. Roxie followed Janelle.

"I've been helping Janelle for years, El, and it has to stop. She has to clean this mess up herself."

"Aw, come on. Janelle is not a favorite of mine, but that attitude doesn't sound like you. We have to help her."

"Anyone hungry? Food is here," Luca announced as he entered the kitchen through the garage door carrying bags of groceries in reusable totes.

"Let's resume this discussion later. We don't want to miss out on a Luca dinner," Ali said.

Chapter 37

After revealing Philip's blackmail threat to Ali and Ellen, Janelle felt the tension in her shoulders and neck loosen. If they were right, Janelle would call Philip's bluff and be rid of him forever...unless he came up with another nefarious threat.

Part of her agreed with Ellen. She should tell him to publish on social media the naked photos he took of her. It might bolster her persona—not only did she write sexy novels, but she also lived the life she depicted. Her overriding concern was that Brad would see the pictures. She couldn't live with the humiliation that would bring him.

Another concern was for her parents. Virginia would be ridiculed by her garden and bridge clubs and Ed would suffer embarrassment.

There was a solution. She could go to Ed and ask for the jewel. But, she couldn't bear admitting she was a failure, especially compared with Ali. Would he consider her the black sheep in the family? Would she no longer wear the mantel of Virginia's favorite daughter?

Janelle waited on Ali's front porch for Brad to arrive. He drove up the driveway, hopped out of the convertible, and helped her into the passenger seat. Seeing him took her mind off the evil Philip and his blackmailing threats. What she loved most about Brad was that he always seemed genuinely pleased to see her. She hoped he was

0000

being honest. Her honesty detector had failed her many times. Plus, he claimed he liked Janelle with a few more pounds on her body.

"Let's get this straight," Brad said. "You have decided to keep Phoebe's house? I don't want you to think I'm coercing you into that decision."

"My plan is to move my things from Ali's to my new house soon. Need to order furniture, etc."

"Seems quite a reversal from your initial reaction."

"You surprised me. I don't like surprises. Let's go."

Brad pulled out of the driveway, but slowed down, and stopped at the curb. He turned off the ignition. "Are you sure you want to do this? I never meant to pressure you. We can sell Mimi's house and buy one of our own. Or, we can buy a house for you. No need to live together right away, if that's what's bothering you."

"I'm sure. About living in Phoebe's house. Let's go."

"Do you know how beautiful you are?" He put his hand on her chin and turned her toward him.

"No, tell me."

"Let me show you." He leaned over and pulled her tight. They ran their hands over each other's bodies. Brad put his hungry fingers inside of Janelle's blouse.

"Not here. Not with the top down. A block from Ali's house. We're acting like hormonal teenagers."

"You have a problem with that?" He smiled and turned on the ignition.

"Let's go to *my* new home," Janelle said.

When they reached Phoebe's, now Janelle's home, Brad helped Janelle out of the car and held her hand as they approached the front door, which he opened with a key. He paused, bent down, kissed her, and carried Janelle over the threshold.

She gazed into his cognac eyes. "Isn't it premature for the threshold thing?"

"Just practicing."

They walked into the house and he closed the door.

Janelle headed to the bedroom. "I had a bed delivered."

"You know your way around, I see," Brad said.

"The important room." Janelle sat on the side of the bed and removed her shoes.

"Let me help you." He slid off her shoes and massaged her feet with slow circular motions. He pulled down her pants. He left her panties and bra on but took off the white T-shirt and sleeveless vest. "Stand up." She obeyed. He removed her bra while she was facing him. He put the sleeveless vest back on over her bare breasts. "This is a picture I'd like to take and keep."

"Picture? Are you saying you want to take a picture of me?" Janelle screamed.

"What's the matter?"

"Please leave, Brad. You don't want to be involved with me. I will only bring turmoil and heartbreak into your perfect life."

"I'm not leaving until you tell me what's wrong. What have I done? I can't take these ongoing mercurial moods. First, you want me then you don't. Make up your mind. I'll be waiting in the car to take you to Ali's."

"Never mind. I'll walk."

"Suit yourself."

Janelle sat on the king-sized bed half-clothed. She fell backward on the bed and for the second time today wailed like a teething baby.

Janelle waited until she was sure Brad had left. She found her purse and entered the bathroom to repair her tear-stained face. "What's wrong with me? He loves me. I love Brad more than anyone. Even Howard."

No, too late. I've lost him forever.

The mirror offered no solution.

* * *

Ali was watering the plants on the front porch when she saw Janelle plodding up the driveway carrying her shoes. Ali put down the watering can and rushed to Janelle. "What's the matter with you? Are you hurt? Where's Brad?"

"He's gone. Forever."

"Where? Is he moving? Is he sick? Is he dead?"

"No." She hung her head like an old woman with osteoporosis. "I mean gone from my life."

"Come inside and sit down." Ali took her sister by the arm and helped her into the kitchen. She poured two glasses of iced tea.

Janelle stared at the glass Ali had put in front of her. "A picture."

"It's a glass of tea not a picture. I should take you to the ER. I'll text Brad and find out what he did to you." Ali put her hand on Janelle's forehead. "No fever, but you're acting confused."

"He said something about taking a photo of me or a picture when we were in the bedroom and I freaked out. I thought about Philip blackmailing me and I lost it."

"Did you tell Brad why you were upset?"

Janelle shook her head.

"This is the story of your life. If you would learn honesty, you wouldn't stir up so much trouble. Where's your phone?" Without waiting for an answer, Ali fumbled through Janelle's purse. "Here, text him. Tell him to come over here right away. You can sit on the porch. I promise not to listen."

"Can't."

"But I can."

"Please, Ali. I don't have the energy to argue with you. Let's face it; I'm a failure with men." She stood to leave. "I'm going to pack. Matt wants me out. He leaves enough hints."

"Where are you going?"

"To Phoebe's. I mean my new house. I've tried unsuccessfully to imitate your life, but as you can see, I can't do it. You're you and

I'm me. I can't be you and you sure as hell don't want to be me." She trudged up the stairs.

* * *

"She's tricking you," Matt said when he returned from work. He went to the fridge and found a bottle of Modelo. "She's manipulating you because she doesn't want to move to Phoebe's and she wants to stay here. Janelle wants you to beg her to stay."

"I disagree. Something's off with her. I believe she truly loves Brad. They've been having a clandestine relationship for a while, meeting in New York, Mexico. Even Italy. We can't send her away when she's so upset."

"Give her a bottle of tequila and she'll be fine."

"I think she's off the tequila."

"Is that right? Who's been pilfering our liquor cabinet?"

Ali guessed it was Kayla and Luca but kept that to herself. "You should talk to Brad."

"About the liquor cabinet?"

Ali shot him a scowl.

"And say what? I think he should ruin his life by developing a relationship with your nutty sister. He's our friend."

"She could be happy with Brad and vice versa. Sounds preposterous but they've both had terrible romantic relationships. Surely, they know how to do it right by now. Janelle is trying to change."

"I haven't noticed."

Ali would lose any argument with Matt about Janelle. He'd seen firsthand, over the years, the misery she had caused Ali and he didn't want Ali to suffer Janelle's disrespect anymore. Ali's theory was Janelle had never found happiness. No matter how many handsome husbands or number of bestselling books, she was still miserable. Moving to Willoughby, surrounded by her family, dating Brad, and even marrying him would bring her happiness. At least it might give her a more pleasant personality.

"Go upstairs and tell her she can stay one more night. Please? With sugar on it."

"You're usually persuasive with the sugar talk." He stood and kissed her on the lips. "I'm not going to do it. I'll go upstairs and help her bring down her suitcases."

"With Janelle gone, you'll have all the hot water you need."

He ignored her snarky comment and walked upstairs.

Ali met Janelle at the front door. "I'll call you tomorrow," she said. Sure, Janelle was only going a few blocks away, but Ali didn't approve of the abrupt way Matt evicted her.

Chapter 38

Janelle thanked Matt for bringing her luggage to Phoebe's house and asked him to leave the multiple pieces in the foyer.

Before leaving, Matt hesitated at the door and turned to face his sister-in-law. "No hard feelings?"

"We're fine. I know I'm a pain in the butt." She waved him away.

Janelle hadn't decided if she was going to stay in the house or for how long. She didn't know whether she was going to stay in Willoughby.

Brad's impressive remodeling of Phoebe's old and outdated house deserved high marks. Janelle noticed the crown moldings, recessed lighting, repurposed antique mantel, and arched bookshelves. The makeover would equal anything on an HGTV show. Janelle's taste leaned toward contemporary chrome and glass, but she craved to become a different person. Why not start with the home she will create for herself, wherever that home may be.

There was something missing in this beautiful house. . .besides furniture. Perhaps it was the hectic atmosphere of the Lawrence household. Ed and Virginia, in and out. The energy of Kayla and Luca. Sweet Roxie. Despite arguments over hot water and Kayla's sometimes pissy attitude, Ali had created a home filled with love and support for each other. . . the kind of home Janelle longed for.

The house was too quiet. At least there was a large flat screen TV. She picked up the remote and searched for a rerun of *House Hunters International*. She was too antsy to sit, but the sounds of voices from the TV filled the silent void in the house.

In the kitchen, Janelle opened the door of the Sub-Zero refrigerator and found a bottle of white Burgundy. Brad was generous, not only with the bottles of wine in the refrigerator, but also with the Mercedes he claimed to loan her. She knew it was a gift. That was Bradley Patterson's way.

She'd have to return the car to Brad. Isn't that the rule? An engagement ring and/or a Mercedes convertible should be returned, if the engagement is broken. But. . .they weren't engaged. No, this was the new Janelle and she would return the car, with the dent. What would she do with a car anyway? She was a lousy driver and if she moved to New York, a car would be a burden. Of course, until she straightened out her financial crisis, she wasn't going anywhere.

Dilemmas plagued her. Staying in Willoughby would present problems. She would run into Brad and might see him dating other women. What about the strain on his friendship with Ali and Matt? Would they have to choose between Janelle and Brad? Janelle knew whom Matt would choose.

Janelle went to the kitchen and topped off her wine glass. She wandered into the living room and plopped into one of the loveseats. She stared out the French doors at the boxwood and hydrangeas, which Phoebe had tended, and Brad's gardeners had perfected. A bushy-tailed squirrel scampered by. Janelle envisioned Roxie and her dog cousin Alva playing in the yard. Luca and Kayla throwing a Frisbee, if she stayed in Willoughby.

Janelle was envious of Ali's relationship with Ellen and her other women friends. With some pleading for forgiveness, maybe Ali would invite her to join the Book Babes. *If I stay in Willoughby.* Maybe she'll meet other volunteers at the Drake Closet who could become her friends. Friends who liked Janelle for herself and not for her notoriety. *If I stay in Willoughby.* One stumbling block. There's no way she would ever make a chicken casserole.

Ali was right when she said Janelle wasn't being fair to Brad. She should tell him why she freaked out. But would he understand?

Phoebe's presence was more powerful today than when Brad first brought Janelle here. Despite the renovations to the house, Phoebe's favorite rose water scent permeated the air. Today was different. Phoebe's presence was comforting. Welcoming. Not scary. Not ghost-like.

Phoebe had been a major influence in Janelle's life and maybe she owed Phoebe and Brad respect by staying in the house.

What to do? Stay in Willoughby or leave? Live in Phoebe's house or not? Pursue Brad or give him up?

"Of course! I'll do what I've always done when trying to make decisions," she said aloud. She dashed toward the room Phoebe had used as an office and library and paused at the doorway. She stared across the room at the newly constructed bookshelf, which housed the eighteen books she wrote with Phoebe. Two vases of red tea roses flanked either side of the books filling the room with sweetness. She stifled a sneeze.

The books on the shelf were Janelle's children and it warmed her heart Brad had found a place to honor them. She would die of embarrassment and shame if Brad knew the truth—Phoebe was the mastermind behind the books. Janelle approached the shelf and ran her hands along the spines of the books, remembering the plots and the characters she loved. She knew each character as if they were her sisters, brothers, or lovers. *Speak to me, my friends.*

Loralee Livingston in *Lust and Luck in Las Vegas* might have an answer. No, she relied on her attorney father and detective brother to bail her out of jams. Kimberly Rockwell in *Burning with Desire* seemed to have all the solutions. Janelle recalled when Kimberly traveled to the North Georgia mountains to camp alone. One night when insight was not forthcoming, Kimberly yelled at the top of her lungs to the black star-filled sky, WHAT THE HELL DO I WANT?

Janelle wasn't about to go camping anywhere and especially not by herself, but she did ask the same question. What the hell *do* I want?

She recalled the notes Phoebe wrote to her after the completion of each book. Phoebe had complimented Janelle for her ideas and tenacity. Janelle's lack of sentimentality precluded her keeping the notes for which she was regretful. *What would Phoebe say to encourage me?*

Janelle took the first book she and Phoebe wrote, *The Secret of High Mountain Love,* and sat in the new black ergonomic chair Brad had purchased. She flipped through the book recalling how Phoebe urged Janelle to write the love scenes. "You know more about that than I do," Janelle recalled Phoebe saying.

Janelle caressed the book as though it were a precious jewel. *This is the only book of mine that I've re-read and re-read.*

Her eyes moistened, smearing her mascara.

A piece of rosewater-scented paper floated out of the book into Janelle's lap. She paused to wait for a sneeze. No sneeze, but rather a calming feeling overcame Janelle. She picked up the paper and saw that it was a note to her from Phoebe dated several months before Phoebe's demise. As Janelle read the note, her eyes filled with tears, which pooled down her cheeks. She wiped her face. She folded the note and put it in her pocket. As she stood to leave, she said aloud, "Thank you, Phoebe. Back to work."

Chapter 39

Janelle called Ali. "What am I'm going to do? Have you thought of anything? How can I get rid of him?"

"I suppose you're referring to Philip and not Brad," Ali said.

"I need your help with that dirty-son-of-a-gun-lying-cheating-miserable excuse for a man."

"Calm down."

"He sent me an ultimatum. Either I pay up or—"

"Ellen and I have been thinking and we have a solution. Your job is to go back to writing and don't worry. We'll meet later and finish the last chapter we were working on."

Ali disconnected before her sister could comment. Ellen was right. If Ali could help Janelle, that would be the sisterly action to take.

* * *

Ali called the family's crisis manager. She explained Janelle's situation to Ed and a possible solution. "What if we call his bluff? Confront him. But I don't want to do this alone," Ali said.

"You remember I was a champion wrestler in my day."

"That was a long time ago, Dad."

"I can take those pretty boys anytime."

Ali grinned at the phone and disconnected.

Ali called Ellen. "Meet me at the Willoughby Inn."

"Hey, wait a minute. What about your ankle?"

"Much better." She hung up.

When Ali, Ellen, and Ed arrived, Ed told his conspirators, "I'll do the talking." His assistants stood at his side. Ed asked the young, attractive female desk clerk for Philip Brulee's room number.

"We can't give you that information, sir. Security guidelines. I'll have to ring Mr. Brulee's room first and ask if he would like to join you in the lobby," she said.

"You look familiar, young lady. Did you go to Willoughby High?" Ed asked. Her name badge read *Rebecca*.

"I did, sir. Why do you ask?"

"I bet you were a cheerleader, Rebecca. You're pretty enough."

"Thank you, sir. Should I know you?"

"I was the wrestling coach. A few years ago. Ed Withrow's the name. Pleased to meet you." He extended his hand.

"I dated Toby Lee who was on the wrestling team. He was outstanding, wasn't he? At least he had loads of trophies."

"One of the best," Ed lied.

"So sad about the car accident." She leaned closer. "They say he was drinking. Better than drugs, right?"

"So right," Ed lied again.

Ali whispered in Ed's ear. "Can you skip the chitchat?"

"Now about Mr. Brulee in Room 541," Rebecca said. "Whoops. I'm not supposed to give out the room number but promise me you're not a criminal." She giggled. "Don't tell my boss." She winked at him. "You are adorable, Mr. Withrow. How may I help you?"

"I want to meet with Mr. Brulee. I have good news for him. It must be a surprise. Is he in his room?"

"Yes, he's there. He just ordered a second bottle of Grey Goose. I'm pretty sure he's alone."

"Why do you think that?"

"He asked me to come to his room when my shift was over. He said other things, too. Words that would embarrass me to repeat. If you ask me, he's a real perv."

"What did you say to him?"

"I told him I'd call the cops if he came any closer to me and I'd report him to my manager. We don't want creeps like him staying at this lovely hotel."

"Has the vodka been delivered?"

Rebecca glanced at her watch. "Doubt it."

"Can you stall the delivery for a few minutes?"

"Sure."

"Thanks so much. You have no idea." Ed patted Rebecca on her hand and rushed away to the elevator with Ali and Ellen following him.

"Room service," Ed said as he knocked on the door of Room 541.

The trio hoped their antic would save Janelle humiliation and money from the slime bag on the other side of the door...without injuring any of the parties involved.

After a minute, the door opened. "About time. Finished the bottle," Philip slurred.

Ed put his hands on Philip's chest and shoved him so hard Philip stumbled backward, and fell on the bed, barely avoiding landing on the floor.

"What the hell you doin' here?" Philip said.

"I'm going to beat the crap out of you unless you give us the blackmail evidence you're threatening my daughter with." Ed held up a pair of brass knuckles.

Ellen took a small pink cylinder out of her pocket. "One move and this pepper spray will cover you like paint."

Ali pulled a piece of rope from her jeans pocket and waved it in front of Philip. "Hand over what we want or I'm going to hog tie you."

"You have to be kidding," Philip cackled. "Janelle sent *you three* to fight her battle. Ha! Leave, you lunatics, before I call the cops."

Ed put his hand in his pocket and pulled out something wrapped in a white handkerchief. "Janelle doesn't know we're here. But this is going to protect *her* and get rid of *you*." He waved the handkerchief in front of Philip's face. "You're not the only blackmailer in this room."

"What's that, you old geezer? A handkerchief. You're gonna need it to wipe the blood from your face when I'm finished with you." He stood on unsteady feet and approached Ed with a closed fist aimed toward Ed's jaw. The vodka influenced punch landed in the air near Ed's right ear.

Cagney and Lacey approached Ed, but he called them off.

"It's a phone recording of the invitation you made to the young girl at the desk downstairs. You—"

"I merely asked her to meet me in the bar for a drink after her shift."

"Not according to what it says here." He put the evidence in his pocket. Ellen and Ali flanked him.

"Wait a minute." Philip took another unsteady step toward Ed.

Ed moved closer to his victim. "Hand over the so-called evidence and promise never to bother my daughter. Never! Do that and I'll keep the contents of this recording private. Understand, you creep?"

Philip eyed Ed up and down. "Gotta listen to it first." He reached his open palm out to Ed.

"We're not leaving until you give us what you claim to have. Janelle doesn't deserve this. Hasn't she paid you enough money?" Ali said.

"Let's all calm down," Philip said. He pointed at Ellen who was holding the can of pepper spray above her head aimed at his face. "Put that away."

"Not until you put up or shut up," Ellen said.

A knock on the door caused them all to shut up.

"Don't answer it," Ali said. "We'll be out of here soon. Won't we, mister. Because you're handing over the blackmailing evidence."

"Probably room service," Philip said. "Ordered 'nother bottle."

"Get rid of whoever it is," Ellen said.

"Room service," an odd sounding voice said as the knocking continued.

"Damn. Go away," Philip yelled.

"Room service," the voice repeated. The knocking escalated to pounding.

"Changed my mind. Go away."

"Need your signature to cancel the order," the voice on the other side of the door said.

"Better open the door, but keep your mouth shut," Ellen said. She followed him to the door with the nozzle of the pepper spray pressed against his neck.

Philip sidestepped Ali and Ed. "Hold your horses. I'm coming," he mumbled.

He opened the door wide enough for Rebecca to push the door so hard he stumbled and fell backward into the wall. "Had to check on you, Mr. Withrow. I was afraid this jerk might hurt you." She shoved Philip and the lady detectives aside and rushed to Ed. "You okay, Mr. Withrow?"

"Thank you, sweetie. I appreciate your concern."

Philip raised his arms in the air. "I give up. You're all a bunch of crazies. The truth is. . .I have no evidence. Yes, I was trying to blackmail Janelle, but if you all forget about that and get the hell out of this room, you'll never see me again and I won't call the cops."

"I have to hurry to the front desk before my boss sees I'm gone," Rebecca said. She opened the door and motioned to Ed, Ellen, and Ali to leave. "We better get out of here. If Mr. Withrow weren't here, I would use a bad word to describe him." She pointed at Philip.

"Old man. Wait," Philip yelled. "What about the recording? The conversation was innocent."

Ed patted his pocket. "Insurance, buster, insurance."

When the trio returned to the lobby, Ali asked, "Do we believe him?"

"Doesn't matter. If Janelle saved all the texts and emails, that's damaging evidence against him. Besides, he's about as smart as a stick," Ed said.

"I hope you're right," Ellen said.

Ed pulled out his handkerchief, unfolded it, and said, "Anyone want some gum?"

Chapter 40

Ali was in the kitchen sitting on a stool at the island peeling cucumbers. The Beach Boys were serenading her and Roxie via the Bose sound system.

"Knock, knock. I'm coming in, ready or not," Ellen hollered as she entered through the front door and joined Ali in the kitchen. "I thought Luca was doing the cooking around here?" She popped a cuke into her mouth.

Ali lowered the volume on the Beach Boys. "Luca has plenty to do besides cooking. I'm giving him a head start on chilled cucumber soup. My friend Deb had oral surgery yesterday and I thought soup would be easy on the gums."

"Where is the Italian lover?"

"Running my errands. Delivering food, which he helped me make for Brenda's daughter's shower. The dry cleaners. The library. He suggested my pantry needs organizing, so I let him loose. He claims I have lots of *use before the date* items, which have expired."

"Is he gay?"

"What difference does it make?"

"I never had a man in my life who was interested or capable of doing what he's doing for you."

"He's a keeper," Ali said. "Don't hold me in suspense, Agatha Christie. Did you find out where Janelle goes on her mysterious errands?"

"You won't believe this."

"Let me have it." Ali put the vegetable peeler down and waited for Ellen's news.

"She's volunteering at the Drake Closet."

Ali shook her head. "How reliable is your information?"

"I was jogging on Mimosa Street on the opposite side of the Drake Closet when I saw her enter. I called my friend who works there and asked if she could tell me what Janelle was up to."

"An odd place for Janelle to shop," Ali said.

"My friend confirmed Janelle's name was on the orientation schedule for new volunteers."

"Are we talking about the same person? Janelle Jennings? Could your friend be confused?"

"The one and only Janelle."

"She does loves clothes and shoes." Ali picked up the peeler and attacked the cucumbers.

"She's donating all her designer clothes, shoes, and bags. Names like Jimmy Choo, Stuart Weitzman, and Michael Kors. My friend says they might cordon off a portion of the store dedicated only to Janelle's items...with a life-size cutout of Janelle and a stack of her books. Think about the reaction. Customers will be lining up at the door."

Ali returned to skinning her victims.

"She volunteered to take your Tuesday shift until your ankle heals. So altruistic, don't you think?" Ellen said with a smirk. "Slow down with the peeling. You want carpal tunnel?"

"My shift?"

"There's more. She has grand ideas for a gala and fundraiser. Something similar to the Willoughby Book Banquet you chaired. She's going to make a presentation to the decision makers."

"Is there more?"

"A fashion show. She's going to ask other well-known authors to model the donated clothes. Janelle volunteered to be the stylist."

Ali threw a mangled cuke and the peeler onto the counter. "Sounds like she wants my life. . .but it's not up for grabs."

* * *

Too many people had raised doubts to Ali about her injury. Ellen and Luca were suspicious and surely, Matt was, too. She couldn't decide whether to confess outright or to gradually heal. Ali's Google search revealed she should be improved by now. Matt made the decision for her.

"Time to confess," Matt said when he brought Ali a cup of morning coffee and placed it on the bedside table.

"What's *your* confession?" she asked.

"Not me. You." He pointed to her ankle.

She bit her lower lip. "You are right. Fully healed." She swung her legs over the side of the bed, stood, and did a jumping jack. "Aw. That wasn't a good idea, but I can walk."

"Sneaky, aren't you. How long has this charade been going on?" He sat in the bentwood rocker in the corner of the room and sent a smile her way.

"Not long."

"Does that mean you'll fire Luca?"

"I wish you didn't feel that way about him. He's a fine young man. You should let him work in the store."

"No way. Not when Kayla's there. They wouldn't get any work done."

"You might be surprised. His work ethic is better than your daughter's."

"*Our* daughter."

"If not in the store, we have to keep him on as my personal assistant."

"Aren't you the clever one," Matt said. "I say no to him working in the store, so how can I say no to keeping him around for you."

"Isn't that a fair deal?"

Matt patted his stomach. "The guy can cook."

"By the way, we haven't paid him. Why don't you discuss it with him? I asked him to keep an accounting of his time."

"What do we pay him? Minimum wage?" Matt asked.

"Sure."

"You talk to him. I'll choose the wrong words and you and Kayla will be on my case," Matt said.

"Aren't you mad at me, for tricking you and everyone else about my ankle?"

"You weren't tricking many people other than your mother." He turned to leave and crumpled to the floor. "Not my Achilles' heel. I'll never run again."

"One faker in the family is enough. Leave," Ali said with a smile.

* * *

Later in the morning, Luca joined Ali on the back porch where she was typing on her laptop.

"As you requested, here is an accounting of my time and duties," Mrs. Lawrence. "Mr. Lawrence gave me the news about your ankle. He didn't say if I'm fired."

"Don't you even think about another job. I think Brad Patterson wants to hire you at his restaurant, but you're mine. You belong to the Lawrence family. You're happy, aren't you?"

"Yes, but I want to spend more time with Kayla."

"We can arrange that."

"What do you have planned for me today?" he asked.

"I left a grocery list and money on the kitchen counter."

"Okay. I'll leave now." Luca hesitated at the doorway.

"Something else?"

"I read the book you wrote with your sister. Broken Bats? Broken something. Anyway, I couldn't sleep one night, and it helped me fall asleep."

"Great to know our book put you to sleep."

"I'm not your usual reader. I did like the historical aspects of the story." He paused. "I don't think your male characters are strong enough. Yes, they are evil and conniving, but in the end, they cave. Not manly. Just thought I'd throw that out."

"Thank you, Luca. I'll certainly consider your observation."

Ali smiled as Luca made his exit. She made a mental note to add book critic to his résumé.

Chapter 41

"Coming, Dad," Kayla hollered from her bedroom. She rummaged through a pile of clothes she had dumped on the floor and pulled out a pair of ripped jeans and a wrinkled, faded red T-shirt. She shuffled down the stairs carrying Roxie, kissed the dog goodbye, and put her on the floor.

Father and daughter left home under an overcast sky for the short walk to Kitchen Bliss. The weather report guaranteed late afternoon thunderstorms, which would wash away the saffron-colored pollen assaulting Willoughby. The cloud cover was a soothing respite from recent hot temperatures.

The duo waved to neighbors who were walking their dogs to take advantage of the cool air.

"I've been looking forward to this," Matt said.

"Walking to work?"

He chuckled. "Walking to work with my daughter so we can have time alone. So, how's it going?"

"Great. Mom's given up the inquisition and now it's your turn."

"And you're okay with working at the store?"

"I suck at customer service, which is so important to you. I apologize for that, Dad. I try, but all I can think about is—"

"Luca?"

"Yes. If you would let him work in the store that would be perfect."

"Your mother would have something to say about that. She doesn't want to give up her personal assistant."

"Everyone likes Luca. Mom, Gramps, Nana. How come you don't?"

A young skateboarder whizzed by. "Slow down," Matt shouted.

"Asshole," Kayla yelled.

"Excuse me, young lady?"

"Sorry, Dad. Sometimes I forget I'm home. College language is pretty rough these days." She gave her dad a gentle elbow to the ribs and smiled. "By the way, I need to leave early today, but I called Celeste and she's going to fill in for me."

"Seems like you would consult me first before asking Celeste."

"At least I found a sub. Give me credit for something."

"Celeste's new and isn't as familiar with the merchandise as you are."

"She's super smart and anyone can do my dumb job."

"Are you and that Luca of yours planning something?"

Kayla stopped walking and turned to face Matt. She put her hands on her hips. "Why do you hate Luca so much? Tell me, right now, Dad."

"Whoa, there. If I hated him he wouldn't be living in my house, eating my food, using up all my hot water—"

"He's trying. You'll see tonight…never mind. You don't get it." Kayla sprinted ahead of Matt. She met him at the front door of the store with a scowl on her face.

As Matt unlocked the door, another merchant opening her adjacent store greeted Matt and Kayla. "Hey you two! How's it going?"

"Another lousy day," Kayla said as she stomped to the back of the store. She put on her Kitchen Bliss apron before she prepared the store for business and avoided conversation with her father.

Around noon, she asked her dad if she could have a lunch break.

"I'll buy if you want to pick up food from the Fickle Pickle. You love their roasted vegetable sandwich. I'll have one, too."

Kayla put out her hand and took money from her dad. She wasn't hungry, but the lure of the Fickle Pickle food was appealing. Maybe if she were nicer to her dad, he would do the same to Luca. It was worth a try.

* * *

"Let's go, Roxie." Ali hooked the leash to her dog's collar. "Freedom," she said as she bounded out of the house with Roxie struggling to keep up. "No jogging, just a nice long walk around Willoughby to see what's going on. I can't believe it's been over two weeks since I sprained my ankle."

They headed toward Willoughby Lane and made a stop at the Books in the Nook. When they entered the store, Diane said, "Shouldn't the Willoughby Reads book have been announced by now?"

"I'm not holding my breath."

"Your co-author has a few enemies on the selection committee."

"Shouldn't their feelings for me outweigh bad feelings from years ago?"

"Write the next one on your own. In fact, I thought that was what you had planned."

"Things change," Ali said. She shrugged her shoulders.

"Glad to see you out and about."

"How's business?"

"Could be better. Look over there." Diane pointed to a display in the center of the book store. "I thought I'd make a more prominent display of *Broken Bones* after hearing what Janelle's doing at the Drake Closet."

"So, you've heard," Ali said with a forlorn expression.

"Don't look so sad. Janelle's a whiz at marketing. If she promotes the book, more money for you. She's creating buzz for your next book."

Before Ali had a chance to answer, a customer entering the store was Ali's cue to leave. She waved to Diane and left with Roxie.

"What's the matter with me, Roxie? Am I still in high school? Jealous of my big sister?"

Chapter 42

"I like the boy, but I don't understand why he's moving in with us," Virginia said to her husband. "He's been in Willoughby over a week. Why now?" The couple was sitting on their front porch enjoying twilight cocktails underneath a whirling fan.

"I didn't tell you something. Luca called and asked if he could stay with us and I agreed without consulting you. I was afraid you'd say no."

"You're right. I do not approve. Now there's not much I can do since the boy's on his way here." She frowned at her husband.

"You know, Virginia, sometimes you are a good sport."

"My only goal in life is for family harmony. However, I still don't understand."

"Matt doesn't want Kayla and Luca living in close quarters. Although how's that different from college life where they all live together, share bathrooms, and beds?"

"Not Kayla. She's not that way."

"Wise up, Virginia. This isn't the Neanderthal times." With his finger he swirled the ice cubes in his gin and tonic. "Coming here was Kayla's idea. . .and Luca's, too. Better to keep Matt and Luca apart."

"We won't see him much since Ali's hired him."

"I'm glad her ankle has healed. I've missed her help transporting my antiques."

"I've offered to help."

"And I appreciate your offer, dear husband. You don't have the patience Ali has and her driving is better than yours."

"So be it. Gives me more time to work on my inventions." Ed stood and watched Matt pull his SUV into the driveway. "Here's Matt and our houseguest."

Luca stepped out of the car and removed his duffle bag from the rear seat.

Matt rolled down the window. "He's all yours, folks."

Luca watched Matt drive away with his back to his new hosts. He turned around to face Virginia and Ed and took a few steps forward.

Ed put his drink down on the wicker table and stood to greet Luca. "Don't be shy. We're glad to have you, son." He looked over his shoulder and glowered at Virginia. "We have a ranch style house so everything's on one floor."

"Yes, yes. We're happy to have you." Virginia remained seated. "How long do you plan to stay?"

"For Pete's sake, Virginia. The poor kid hasn't walked in the door."

"Won't be long, Mrs. Withrow. I promise not to trouble you. Mrs. Lawrence keeps me busy."

An out of breath Kayla arrived while everyone was still on the porch. "Please be good to him, Nana. I like him so much. Thanks for taking him in. Otherwise, I was afraid Dad would make him leave Willoughby." Kayla grabbed Luca's hand. "At least you're not going far." She turned to address her grandparents. "How about if I move in here, too?"

"Wait one second, missy. Under no circumstances are you moving into our house with Luca here. What would people think? That would be disgraceful," Virginia said.

"I don't see why not—"

"Better not argue with your grandmother. She usually wins." Ed put his arm around Kayla and whispered in her ear. "I'll keep the front door unlocked. Just be quiet."

Luca stood on the edge of the porch with a dazed expression looking back and forth from Ed to Virginia to Kayla.

"This humidity is making a mess of my makeup," Virginia said as she blotted her forehead with a white lacy handkerchief and opened the screen door to the house.

"Follow me," Ed said to Luca. Kayla trailed behind. Ed showed Luca his bedroom and bathroom and joined Virginia in the living room. The door to Luca's bedroom closed with Kayla inside.

"Let's give up. No way we can keep those two lovebirds apart. I'm going to my workshop," Ed said. "I have an idea for an invention every dog owner will covet." His cell rang while he walked to his workshop. "Hello."

"Congratulations, Dad. You answered your phone," Ali said.

"Never any good news when the damn thing rings. What's going on with you, Gingersnap? Is Matt happy that your interloper is interloping here?"

"How did it go? Kayla left here in a hurry. I'm guessing she followed Luca to your house."

"She's fine. Holed up in Luca's bedroom," Ed said.

"Whatever."

"You sure have changed."

"What do you mean?" Ali asked.

"You've gone from an overly protective helicopter mom to one who doesn't care."

"Of course, I care. Kayla's going to do what she's going to do. Will you put Mom on the phone, please?"

Ed walked back to the house and handed his phone to Virginia.

"Yes, dear?" Virginia said.

"Is there an antique show tomorrow?"

"Yes, and I'm meeting Pete, my picker, to see what he's found for me."

"I have an idea. We must keep Luca busy to appease Matt. Why not let him take you to meet Pete? You can pay him a little. I don't have anything for him to do tomorrow."

"Can we use your truck?"

"Sure. But you better arrive early before all the desirable items are gone."

"You're sounding like me. Thanks, honey."

Virginia walked down the hallway and knocked on Luca's bedroom door. She entered without waiting for a response. Luca was sitting in a flowered club chair in the corner and Kayla was sitting on the side of the double bed facing him. Luca stood at attention.

"Luca. Alicia's given me a great idea. She's letting me use you tomorrow. To go to an antique sale."

"Mom's not loaning a lawnmower. He's a person. You don't 'use' a person," Kayla said.

"No offense taken, Mrs. Withrow."

"Use, borrow, hire, whatever. We'll leave early. Go back to Ali's and bring her pickup here so we'll have it handy in the morning."

"I'll go with you tomorrow," Kayla suggested.

"You have to work at the store," Virginia said.

Kayla stood and took Luca's hand. "Bad enough Mom and Dad are ordering me around. And now my grandmother." She dragged him out of the bedroom, down the hall, and out the front door.

When they were halfway down the driveway, Luca turned around to face the porch. He and Virginia exchanged waves.

* * *

"So how did it go today?" Ed asked Virginia when she and Luca returned home the next afternoon.

"We had a lovely time, didn't we, Luca? Pete found some real treasures."

"Yes, ma'am. But it was a long day. Why aren't you tired?"

"She's not tired because she gets high on all that old junk she buys."

"I'm no expert, but some of the pieces are beautiful," Luca said.

"Thank you for your help. Now run along. Kayla's probably waiting for you," Virginia said.

"Thank you, Mrs. Withrow."

"Call me Nana. Everyone does. And we'll have a key made for you, so you can come and go as you please."

After Luca left, Ed said, "*Everyone* calls you Nana? Where did that come from? Only Kayla calls you Nana. You hardly know the kid."

"He's delightful. So polite and intelligent. He wants us to go to Italy to meet his parents, Francesca and Giovanni, and his grandparents, too. Helpful to have a strong young man to transport my antiques."

"This family. I swear. A bunch of nuts."

"Excuse me?" Virginia asked.

"Nothing. I'm so happy you're in love with Luca. That makes three. You, Ali, and Kayla. I'm not in love with him, but he's pleasant enough."

"He's molto bella."

"Glad he's teaching you Italian. I'll be in my workshop working on my latest invention."

* * *

Ali knocked on the door of Janelle's new home. She looked at her cell phone. One o'clock, just as they had agreed to meet every day. No answer, so she walked to the backyard.

"Good afternoon, Big Sis," Ali said, causing the Carolina chicka-dees at the feeder to flutter away. "This pergola will be gorgeous when the vine grows around it. Will give you some shade."

"It's star jasmine. Should flower through the summer. Hope it doesn't make me sneeze."

"When did you become knowledgeable about flowers?"

"I was talking to the gardener this morning."

"Mother will be impressed." Ali appraised her sister whose white French terry robe had red wine stains down the front and she was barefoot.

"You didn't answer my text this morning. Did you sleep last night?"

Without responding to Ali's remarks, Janelle spoke. "How do I make him understand I'm remorseful for all the pain I've inflicted and that I want to start over?" She reached for a box of tissues she had placed on a side table and removed a handful.

"This is about Brad? Thus, the bags under your eyes have bags, your hair's a mess, you won't answer your phone, and you're drinking wine before five?"

Janelle nodded.

"I'm fond of Brad, but he's not the only man in the world. Move on," Ali said. "This relationship, whatever it is, isn't working for either one of you."

Janelle took a piece of paper from her robe's pocket and showed it to Ali. "We're meant to be together. Read this."

Ali unfolded the paper with a rose water scent and read:

Dear Janelle: I regret I waited too long to marry. Joe brought me untold happiness. An eligible man lives right here in Willoughby. Under your nose. Someone who has loved you from afar and near. For once, choose the right husband! Put away your passport and settle down. That is why I gave you this house. Of course, you may sell it, that's your

*choice. I hope you don't. Take off your blinders and toss your
haughty, demanding attitude and only then will you find
happiness. Yours, PP*

"I guess she's talking about Brad?" Ali asked.

Janelle cut Ali a look. "The only way I can change Brad's mind
is if Phoebe wrote the same note to Brad," Janelle said.

"Let's write a fake note supposedly from Phoebe," Ali suggested.

"We can say 'Dear Brad, I regret that I...this won't work. He's
already been married once and the...what a stupid idea."

"Sorry," Ali said.

"Do you have another suggestion?"

"Not at the present. Let's work on it."

Janelle neglected to read Phoebe's p.s. on her letter: "P.S. Write
with your sister. She should and could take my place."

Chapter 43

Kayla was standing next to Luca in the Withrow's kitchen. Luca handed her a spoon to taste the sauce he was making. "Tastes and smells so good," she said. "When Dad continues to see what a talented cook you are, you'll win him over. He loves your food. Plus, Mom raves about the help you give her. Nana, too."

"It's going to take more than food to get on your dad's good side because so far that's not working."

"How's it going living here with Gramps and Nana?"

"Good. Your grandmother waits on me, just like my mother and grandmother."

"Don't get used to it, Mister Mammoni."

Alva, barking at the front door, announced the arrival of the Green Monster and Ali, Matt, and Roxie.

"The parents have arrived," Kayla said. "At least Mom. Hope Dad shows up."

"Hello, everyone," Ali chirped when she entered the house.

"Out here, on the porch," Virginia said. "Don't go to the kitchen. Off limits. The younger generation is in charge tonight."

Ali and Matt joined Virginia and Ed. Ali was surprised to see Janelle. "Glad you decided to come, Janelle."

"Glad to be here," Janelle said.

"Well, look at you. No limp. No crutches," Virginia said.

"All healed," Ali announced.

"Oh goody," Virginia said. "Of course, if Luca's here, I won't need you as much, dear."

Ali smiled. "He's handy to have around."

Kayla popped onto the porch carrying a red and green enameled tray with two glasses filled with a carmine-colored drink. "You're in for something special. Luca and I are cooking dinner tonight. Here's an aperitif."

Ed and Virginia accepted the drinks served in clear glasses. "Looks like strawberry soda," Ed said.

"It's a Negroni. The Italian way. No manhattan or gimlet tonight, Gramps," Kayla said.

"Whenever I send my characters to Italy, I make sure they enjoy a Negroni or two," Janelle said. "Be sure to tell Luca I said that, Kayla."

"I don't much like the looks of it, but anything our granddaughter suggests I have to try." Ed took a sip, wrinkled his nose, and set the glass aside.

"I saw that, Gramps. It's an acquired taste. Give it a try. Don't want to hurt Luca's feelings," Kayla said before returning to the kitchen.

"If your characters like this so much, you must too." He placed the drink in front of Janelle and headed to the bar in the living room.

"Why are we not allowed in the kitchen?" Virginia asked. "I would be happy to help." She continued holding the drink but didn't taste it.

"They don't need any help," Ali said. "Luca knows his way around the kitchen."

Virginia placed the colorful beverage in front of Janelle.

When Ed returned, Virginia gestured to him that she wanted whatever he was drinking.

"We're ready to serve," Kayla called out from the dining room. She approached her dad and said, "Please be nice."

"I'm always nice. Perhaps nicer to some people than others." He escorted Virginia to her seat at the dining room table. "Looking as lovely as always, Virginia. How do you stay so cool and refreshed in this 90-degree weather?"

"Air conditioning," Virginia replied.

Placed lengthwise on the dining room table sat a checkered red and white runner. Opened bottles of Chianti and miniature clay pots holding aromatic basil and oregano served as centerpieces. A stack of small white plates, a decanter of olive oil, and a basket of ciabatta completed the tablescape. An Andre Bocelli CD enhanced the Italian atmosphere.

"Reminds me of the restaurants we visited in Italy," Virginia said as Luca entered the room with a tray of glasses. He set the tray down and filled the glasses with the red wine.

"For the first course. The appetizer is an antipasto salad to be shared," Kayla said. After the family took their seats, she placed a large white platter on the end of the table. She pointed out roasted red peppers, marinated olives topped with lemon zest, an assortment of vegetables, salami, and bocconcini. Kayla distributed a plate to everyone. "Buon appetito. Please enjoy." She directed her comment to her dad.

"Too pretty to eat," Virginia said.

Ali took out her phone and snapped a picture of the colorful platter. "This will make a great Facebook post."

Kayla and Luca disappeared into the kitchen. Kayla stuck her head around the corner a couple of times to gauge her guests' eating progress. "They love the food," she said to Luca.

"What about your dad?"

"He ate everything."

Kayla returned to gather the empty platter and plates.

"That was lovely, Kayla," Virginia said. "And Luca, too, of course."

Janelle and Ali contributed their compliments.

"Much better than that negroanee drink. What's next?" Ed asked.

Luca arrived carrying bowls of spaghetti and meatballs on a tray, which he placed on the table. "Family style," he said. As the diners filled their plates, he moved from person to person grinding fresh Parmesan on top of the pasta. The two servers, wearing Kitchen Bliss aprons, stood back to observe. No one raised a fork or opened a mouth. They all stared at Kayla and Luca.

"Sit," Ed commanded to the servers.

"Not tonight. We are here to serve you," Kayla said.

"Don't want to eat cold food. Let's dig in," Ed said.

The family was quiet as they ate. Between bites, except for Matt, the family praised the food.

"This meal is excellent, Luca. Family recipes?" Ali asked the chef who was standing in a corner of the dining room.

"No recipes, Mrs. Lawrence. A handful of this and a pinch of that. However, this is not a typical Italian meal. We don't serve meatballs and spaghetti together as you do here." He paused. "Not that there's anything wrong, not one thing wrong, I don't mean to say there's anything wrong with spaghetti and—"

"Understood. Calm down," Matt said.

"That's exactly how I cook, Luca. No recipe—a pinch here and a sprinkle there. I suppose that's typical of many talented cooks," Virginia said.

"Don't say a word, Dad," Ali whispered to her father who ignored her plea.

"You should try using a recipe for a change, Virginia. You might be surprised," Ed said.

"Please excuse my husband, Luca. He thinks he's a comedian."

"Who wants more wine?" Matt asked.

The usual suspect raised her hand. Matt filled Janelle's glass.

Ed said to Kayla and Luca, "Sit down. You're hovering in the corner like Secret Service agents."

They complied and joined the group. Kayla took two glasses from the china cabinet and filled them with wine. "Everyone drinks wine in Italy," she said as she made eye contact with her parents who said nothing.

"What do you all think of Celeste, our new employee?" Ali said after their servers took places at the table and there was a lull in the conversation.

"Isn't she cool?" Kayla said. "She's been to Italy. She thought my idea of going to Italy for the summer was awesome. She said I should apply for a study abroad grant." Kayla took a bite of a meatball. "Isn't this the best meatball you've ever had?" she asked the family.

Most everyone agreed. Matt still said nothing except, "More wine?"

"Celeste also told me about this new consignment shop where I can buy some excellent clothes."

"Are you going shopping with Celeste? What about our shopping sprees? And, don't I always pay for whatever you want?"

"Not to hurt your feelings, Aunt Janelle, but you didn't pick a date. I'm on Celeste's calendar."

Janelle swept her bangs off her forehead. "I have a calendar, too. Try to fit me in."

"She's full of ideas." Ali stared at a meatball on her plate but opted for a sip of wine.

"Celeste added slices of cucumbers to the water dispenser at the store. Nice touch," Ed said.

"She does seem perfect for the job," Matt said.

Ali cut Matt a look.

"Ali made the right choice," Matt conceded.

Until now, Janelle had been too busy eating and drinking to join the conversation.

"I don't recall that she dated much," Janelle said.

"So?" Ali asked.

"Janelle certainly had her share of male admirers," Virginia noted.

"Celeste's recovering from a bad divorce. She's wants to be useful," Matt said. "She knows most everyone who comes in the store. She'll help us increase sales."

Kayla beamed. "I work great with her. We're changing the shelving and making many improvements. She wants to serve wine at the Alive in Willoughby events."

"I didn't know Kitchen Bliss needed any improvements," Ali said.

"Don't be jealous, Mom. Just be glad *you* don't have to work there anymore."

"Excuse me," Matt said to Kayla "The store pays for our house, your tuition, your clothes—"

"Okay, okay. Sorry. Come on, Luca, let's clean up." She put her napkin in her lap and pushed away from the table.

Ali looked at Matt. "Do I sound jealous? Don't mean to. Or do I have a reason to?"

Chapter 44

Ali took Roxie and arrived at Janelle's house. She and everyone else were trying to remember to call it Janelle's and not Phoebe's house.

The sisters took their places at the kitchen table with their laptops facing each other.

"Okay. Where did we leave off yesterday?" Ali asked Janelle.

"Something's off with you," Janelle said.

Ali fiddled with a pencil. "No, nothing." She pulled out a water bottle from her tote bag. "I saw Monica Livingston and she told me you wanted a volunteer opportunity. And then El told me—"

"What did that nosy Ellen tell you?"

"The ideas you have for the Drake Closet."

"A problem for you?"

"Why would it be?"

"You could be a little jealous because I'm going to increase sales and everyone there will love me."

"I heard you donated some of your clothes. Your designer clothes."

"Why not? I've gained a little weight. A few pounds only. Can't stay a size two forever."

Ali gave Janelle a look that said more than a few pounds. But she couldn't criticize. She had fallen off the diet wagon and was trying to scramble back on. Hard to do with an Italian cook as an employee.

"Congrats for doing something good for the community."

"You're not jealous or mad?"

"A little jealous but mostly proud. I'm healed and will take my shift back soon."

"We could work together at the Drake Closet. Wouldn't that be a hoot?"

"We already work together."

"Take your time about coming back. You need to keep writing."

"You mean *we* need to keep writing."

Janelle's eyebrows pinched together forming a crease between her eyes. "I'm coming to a life-altering decision. I should turn over the writing to you. You can become me, and I'll become you. Don't you think we're sort of moving in that direction? Sister reversal?"

All Ali's life she wanted to become more like Janelle and if she stopped to think about her life, she *was* becoming more like Janelle. "I couldn't be you if I tried for a million years."

"Yes, you could. Try."

"I don't plan to divorce Matt. One marriage is plenty for me."

"I didn't mean you should dump Matt."

"I'm glad you're finding things to do in Willoughby. Sounds as though you are putting down roots. You have to develop your own interests though, Janelle."

Every time Ali turned around Janelle was joining something Ali was involved in: Friends of the Willoughby Library, the Drake Closet, she even asked to join Ali's beloved Book Babes, despite Janelle's unwelcoming intrusion.

"I want to be useful. Like you."

"Let's finish the book. Then we'll talk," Ali said.

* * *

The sisters were taking a break from their writing. Ali was making lunch. Janelle was reading her email. "Look at this. Willoughby Reads has chosen the book for their banquet. I thought you were on the committee."

"I resigned. Conflict of interest. Want to get the book done. Pronto. ASAP," Ali said.

"Guess you don't have much pull on the committee," Janelle said.

"They didn't choose our book?"

"Afraid not."

Ali put down the jar of mayo she was using to make turkey and Havarti sandwiches and joined Janelle at her laptop reading over her shoulder.

Janelle read: "'Willoughby Reads Chooses Book,'" and look at this. My competitor Laurel Atwood is the honoree and speaker. C'est la vie."

"Your books have never been chosen. I thought the book we wrote together was a shoo-in, especially since I'm a local author."

"I'm a local author, too, since I have a permanent address here."

"You can finish making lunch. It's your house. Why am I making lunch in your house? I don't feel much like eating."

"Knock, knock. Can I come in?" Ellen appeared at the screen door.

"Close the door behind you. You follow me wherever I live. Invited or not," Janelle said.

Ellen entered the kitchen. She pointed to the sandwich. "Bread. You should give up bread. Too bloating, but I'll have water." She filled her YETI tumbler from the faucet. "I came to offer my condolences. Not the book choice you wanted."

"I don't care. Ali's the one who's down in the dumps."

"I'm going home for a while. See you later," Ali said.

When Ali was out of hearing range, Ellen said, "She sure has changed. She acts more like you every day."

"And I act more like her, don't you think?"

"Ha! Whatever," Ellen said.

* * *

Ali and Roxie headed to Willoughby Lane and made a stop at the Sugar Shack. "Iced coffee, today," she said to the clerk. "No cream." Ali took her coffee and sat outside on a bench on the street, watching the traffic, pedestrian and vehicle, going up and down. Someone honked his horn at her and waved. Roxie barked a greeting. Ali adjusted her hat to shield her eyes from the late afternoon sun.

When she finished the coffee, she walked to the Flower Mill where she was greeted by Jill. "Glad to see you're out and about. No more crutches."

"I might have dragged my injury out too long," Ali said.

"You didn't want to give up your handsome chauffeur."

Ali smiled.

"To what do I owe the pleasure of your company? I know you won't buy flowers. What would your mother say if she knew you bought flowers when she has a garden full?"

Before Ali could answer, Monica Livingston strode in. After perfunctory greetings, Ali said, "I heard you had a great lunch with my sister."

"Well, it was entertaining. I think I made her cry. Hard to read her sincerity meter. Let's give her the benefit of the doubt. Maybe she's trying to make amends ala Alcoholics Anonymous. Isn't that one of the twelve steps? But frankly, I don't trust her, Ali, and you shouldn't either."

"I know all about my sister. I don't need anyone—"

Monica put up her hands. "Don't get defensive. I'm on your side. It just bugs me that she waltzes into town wearing that same superior attitude she had in high school."

Jill stopped snipping the stems of a bunch of red roses resting on the counter. "Someone should topple her off her high heels," she said.

"Forget about Janelle. How's the new book coming along?" Monica asked.

"It's coming along."

"How's it working with Janelle?" Jill said.

"Hasn't been too bad."

"Liar."

"No, it hasn't. She's changed."

"Or you have," Monica said.

Chapter 45

"Where have you been?" Ali called out from the sunroom when she heard the garage door open.

When Kayla joined her mother she said, "Don't worry, Mom. I'm not truant from Dad's precious store. He gave me permission to leave."

"I didn't mean—"

"Luca and I made a trip to the grocery store. He's going to cook dinner again tonight. He told me about learning to do laundry and helping you with the shopping and making little tea sandwiches. Now he wants to show you he has real talents. He doesn't want to be a mammomi anymore."

"Laundry is no easy task. Ask your father about the time he put his madras Bermuda shorts in the washing machine with my white underwear."

"What happened?"

"Guess I didn't teach you much about laundry."

Luca entered the kitchen carrying bags of groceries.

"Who paid for all this?" Ali asked.

"Mom. You sound as cynical as Dad. Luca paid."

"If you hadn't interrupted, Kayla, I was going to ask Luca how much we owed him."

"Oh."

"This is on me," Luca said.

"You relax and keep writing. I'd give you a glass of the wine you love so much, but Prosecco is more Italiano. We'll have wine with dinner," Kayla said.

"Si, signorita," Ali said.

Kayla took a bottle of Prosecco from the fridge and popped the cork.

Ali returned to the sunroom with a glass of the sparkling beverage in hand.

The horn on Ed's SUV announced his arrival.

"The grandparents have arrived," Kayla said.

"Hello, lovely ones. We're here," chirped Virginia as she and Ed entered the Lawrence home. Where is everyone?" White capri pants and a lavender long-sleeved tunic enhanced her fresh appearance despite the lingering evening heat.

In contrast to Virginia's pristine appearance, Ed wore a Georgia Bulldog's T-shirt and baggy paint-stained cargo shorts. "What's for dinner? I'm good and hungry," he said. He tapped a finger on his watch. "A little late for dinner, isn't it? Seven on the dot."

"Where's Matt? He wouldn't leave me here with this harem," Ed said.

Roxie ran to the bay window in the kitchen and barked a greeting to Matt who entered from the front door.

"Here he is," Ed said. "Come join the group, but don't go into the kitchen," Ed called out to Matt.

"I'm sweaty. See you in a minute." Matt waved to his father-in-law and the others and retreated to the bedroom.

"What's going on? I thought I was grilling tonight?" Matt asked when he joined the group. A few wayward drops of water trickled down his neck onto the collar of his Jimmy Buffet type shirt.

"Everyone. To the dining room," Kayla ordered. "Luca's made a porcini mushroom soup." She and Luca distributed the bowls and then sat.

"Awful hot for soup, but sure smells good," Ed said.

The family continued the feast with spaghetti alla carbonara followed by grilled marinated swordfish with Luca and Kayla serving.

"I'm impressed, Luca. You are an excellent chef. More wine, please," Janelle said.

"Time for a toast. To our own Rocco Dispirito," Ali said.

"Our chef is more handsome," Kayla said. She gave her Italian chef a kiss on the lips.

Everyone heaped compliments on Luca who graciously said, "Il piacere é tutto mio. My pleasure."

"Too bad Celeste couldn't join us, but she was busy at a homeless shelter where she volunteers," Kayla said.

"You invited her?" Janelle said.

"I thought everyone would like to hear her ideas she's been giving me about school, and how to shop for cool bargains. And whenever we have a taste testing of a product, we sell out."

Finally, Matt participated in the conversation. "Speaking of invitations, I invited someone, too—Brad. He couldn't make it either. I thought Brad and Celeste would make a good couple."

"I like Celeste, but Aunt Janelle and Mr. Brad are a better couple. Wish I knew why you broke up with him?" Kayla said.

Janelle had a mouthful of pasta, which she nearly choked on when Kayla mentioned Brad. She took a sip of water and then blotted her lips. "Wasn't meant to be." She and Ali shared a look.

Janelle took a sip of wine. "I'm going to try volunteering, too. Seems so popular in Willoughby."

"Volunteer?" Virginia asked. "You could join my garden club. They would love to have you."

"Where will you volunteer?" Kayla asked.

"Maybe something at the Drake Closet," Janelle said.

"I thought it was a sure thing," Ali said.

"Whoever, whatever, all I can say is good luck," Ed whispered to Matt.

"Something else. I'm changing my name. Not legally. Only here in Willoughby. Janelle seems too formal."

"Please refer to me as Jay Jay. Seems more down to earth."

"Initials J and J or spelled out J-A-Y space J-A-Y?" Ed asked.

"Doesn't matter. Won't be written anywhere. Just spoken aloud. Will give me an approachable demeanor. Opinions please, dear family."

No one spoke.

"You don't seem like a Jay Jay to me," Luca said. "Not sophisticated enough."

Everyone agreed. "Better keep Janelle, Janelle," Matt said.

"I disagree. This is the new me. New name, new volunteerism, new home, new life. I want a second chance to be a part of my loving and caring family."

* * *

Later that night while in bed, Matt said to Ali, "What do you think about Celeste and Brad as a couple?"

"Janelle almost choked on her food when that was brought up."

"She might be jealous," Matt said.

"Sometimes I think I sound jealous? Maybe I am."

"Nothing to be jealous about. Remember, you're St. Ali in this town. But in our bedroom, I expect a devil, not an angel." Matt turned out the light.

Chapter 46

Ed: I'm in my workshop. Need to see you both.
Janelle: OK
Kayla: omw

E d was wearing his brown leather carpenter's apron. His unsuccessful patent applications covered the walls. He pointed to
two stools. "You two. Sit. Listen up."

Kayla's and Janelle's eyes widened.

"I received a call from my friend Jim at the pawnshop."

Kayla gulped.

"Here's what I figured out. Kayla takes a gift from her aunt, a very
pricey gift, and tries to pawn it to pay for a trip to Italy to see a boy
who comes here so she doesn't need the money and tries to retrieve the
gift but can't." He paused and took a breath. "So far, how am I doing?"

"But—" Kayla said.

"No, 'buts,'" he said.

"You're right, Gramps. Guess I was selfish."

"Yes, you were. And foolish. Did you have any idea of the value
of the jewel?"

Kayla blushed and shook her head.

Janelle turned to face Kayla. "Plus, you tried to tell me you were going on some kind of humanitarian trip," Janelle said.

"That's not exactly what I said, but that's what you heard." Kayla dropped her head and avoided eye contact with her aunt.

"What's *your* story, Janelle?" Ed asked.

"I don't want Kayla to hear any of this."

"She's old enough. Might help her when she chooses men to marry. Make that singular. One man."

"My ex—"

"Philip, who caused all the trouble the other night at dinner?" Kayla asked. She moved the stool closer to Janelle and put her hand on Janelle's arm.

"Yes. I foolishly spent a week with him on a cruise. Several years ago. He took some pictures, er, some video. Private pictures. I'm not sure what he has."

"Ha! I bet I've seen worse on the internet, Aunt Janelle. You wouldn't believe—"

"Never mind. Go on, Janelle," Ed said.

"To make a long story short he's blackmailing me. I haven't been prudent with my finances and needed the money from the sale of the gem to pay him off. I decided...er...Ellen and Ali helped me decide to call his bluff and take the consequences. They reasoned my readers would identify with my predicament and the scandal might increase my book sales. The more I thought about their advice, the more I thought, yes, let him do what he wants, the evil bastard." She examined her cuticles.

"It's not as if you're applying for a job and a potential employer checks you out on Facebook," social-media expert Kayla said. "Mom and Ellen are right. Call his bluff."

"If I don't pay him off and he posts something, what would other people think or say? I don't want to tarnish the family's reputation. Mother would be devastated."

"But Mom said to call his bluff?"

Janelle nodded. "There's someone else who might be hurt. Someone I care about so much I'm willing to give him up to spare him embarrassment."

Kayla and Ed stared at Janelle.

"A new man in your life?" Kayla asked.

"Perhaps," Janelle said.

"Take it from me. You don't have to worry about Philip. With the help of Ellen and your sister and a sweet desk clerk at the Willoughby Inn, he's no longer a problem," Ed said.

"How can you be sure? He's one tenacious S.O.B.," Janelle said.

"Don't you trust your father?" He raised his right hand. "I'm telling you on my mother's grave, you don't have a problem with him anymore. You should have come to me at other times in your life, daughter. I couldn't have helped you with fashion and that girly stuff your mother loves. But, I could have taken some of your exes and kicked the crap out of them."

Janelle closed her eyes, dropped her head, and sagged her shoulders. "How in the world—"

"It doesn't matter how. Problem taken care of."

"Thank you so much, Dad." She stood and approached Ed but tripped on a piece of wood and fell into his arms.

"No, you don't. No more sprained ankles around here."

"I'll have a good night's sleep not worrying about him anymore. Tell me how you did it."

"Later. It's not important. What matters is you are rid of him forever."

"Kayla doesn't have to worry either because our guardian angel has stepped in to help us," Janelle said.

"What? Do you have the gem, Gramps? Do you?"

Ed turned his back on Janelle and Kayla and walked to a cabinet on the wall. He opened a drawer and took out a small white box. "I have a problem." He opened the box and showed it to them. "Does it belong to the original owner or does it belong to the recipient of the gift from the original owner? I sound confused. Does it belong to my daughter or my granddaughter?"

"It belongs to Kayla because it was a gift."

"It belongs to Aunt Janelle because I tried to sell it and lied about it."

"I don't need the money now that Philip's taken care of and even if I did I was wrong to ask for Kayla to return it," Janelle said.

"It belongs to Kayla, but I suggest, young lady, you put it in a safe place. You must promise never to sell it. This will become a family heirloom you can pass along to your daughter one day," Ed advised.

"Thank you, Gramps." She jumped off the stool and hugged him.

"Let me put it on you," Janelle said. She stood back and admired the necklace. Aunt and niece hugged.

"Tell us about this so-called new man in your life? I sure hope he's Mr. Brad."

"Doesn't matter who he is. He's gone, and I'm doomed to be alone forever just like my character Angelica Austin in *Love Secrets of Luxemburg*." Janelle heard the words she was speaking but was hoping more than anything, they weren't true, that a miracle would occur, and Brad would beg for Janelle's love. *Fat chance.*

"You're doomed to whatever you decide to be doomed at," Ed said. "Change your attitude and happiness will come your way."

"I should not have tried to pawn the emerald, Aunt Janelle. Did it have a particular memory for you?"

"You might say that. Enough about the emerald. I don't need money to pay off Philip and you, Kayla, have the gem, thanks to Dad."

"Everyone happy?" Ed asked.

Kayla and Janelle smothered Ed with hugs and kisses.

"Let's discuss the important question of the day," Kayla said. "Tell us about your new man."

"I misspoke. The new man is another in my long list of romantic exes. He won't have anything to do with me. I'm a lost cause. I'm a freaking mess."

"We can help," Kayla said. "Right, Gramps?"

"Speak for yourself, honey. I've done enough problem solving for my lifetime. I'm staying out of my daughter's love life."

Chapter 47

Ali read a text from her daughter who said they had to talk. "Oh dear, Roxie. This can't be good."

"It's about Aunt Janelle," Kayla said when she joined her mother in the kitchen.

"That's a relief." Kayla and Ali hadn't had a real conversation since Kayla returned from school.

Kayla explained that despite a few misunderstandings with her aunt, Kayla was proud of Janelle for not becoming upset over Kayla's mistake to pawn the gem. Janelle's desire to do volunteer work also impressed Kayla. Her aunt was truly changing. However, Janelle did something to upset Brad. Kayla thought she could remedy that relationship. In fact, she was convinced she could.

"I'm going to have to fix this. We all have to fix it."

Ali was touched by Kayla's concern for the Brad and Janelle relationship. "I'll talk to him, but I don't hold out much hope."

"Just try, Mom. Try." Kayla left for work but sent a text to Brad while she was walking.

Kayla: need to talk
Brad: Sounds important. An emergency?

Kayla: yes
Brad: I'm at the restaurant
Kayla: c u in 10

Brad greeted Kayla and ushered her into his office. Always the perfect host, a bottle of sparkling water and two glasses on a silver tray sat on his desk. He filled one and offered it to Kayla.

Kayla didn't waste any time on small talk. "You've got to hear what I have to say about Aunt Janelle."

Brad listened, ignoring several text message alerts and an employee who stuck his head into the office. Brad waved him away.

Kayla detailed the meeting in Ed's workshop where Janelle professed her love for him. "She didn't actually say your name. Who else could it be?"

"You're a loving niece and a loyal friend. I'm grateful for your visit today. Janelle doesn't want to commit to me or to anyone for that matter."

"My aunt has changed."

"Only one person can prove to me she's changed." He poured a glass of water and took a sip. "You're brave to come to me and I'll always love you for it."

"You won't change your mind and go to her, and kneel and propose, Mr. Brad?"

He laughed. "A man can only take so much abuse. Janelle is persona non grata as far as I'm concerned."

"What about us? You and Mom and Dad and me? Are we going to be personas non grata or whatever the plural is? What about the holiday parties and birthday celebrations we always share with you."

"Don't worry about my friendship with you and your family. We'll figure it out as we go. I promise you, Janelle and I will behave like adults. She likes to travel. She won't be around much. Book tours and whatever goes along with being a best-selling author."

He stood to indicate this meeting was over. "Give me a hug and run along."

Meeting with Brad did not go the way she had planned, but she was not deterred. She was determined to get Janelle and Brad together.

* * *

"Life has calmed down, don't you think?" Ali asked Matt as they were lacing up their shoes to take an early evening stroll.

"You were foolhardy to confront Philip at the hotel. At least you met him in a public space, and didn't go to his room, so he couldn't physically harm you. He's an unscrupulous guy."

Matt doesn't need to know everything.

"Glad you came home early today. Love to take our evening walks together," Ali said. "I needed a chance to shake off my disappointment about Willoughby Reads."

"You have no reason for disappointment. Don't you think the fact that your sister's name as co-author could have influenced the choice? She's not as popular in Willoughby as she is in other parts of the country. Besides, you're my favorite author and that should count for something. Right?"

"Thank you."

"Someday you'll write a book by yourself, a best seller."

"That's a thought."

"For now, I'm just happy Celeste and Kayla can handle the store without me. It's a relief not to have to be there all the time. Leaves more time for us."

"This might be ominous," Ali said pointing to Kayla who was sprinting up the driveway, panting, and out of breath. Her face was as red as the Knockout roses lining the driveway.

Ali and Matt stood and approached their daughter. They guided her to the porch where she sat.

"This is awful. Absolutely awful."

"What?" they both said.

"Aunt Janelle loves Brad and Brad loves her, but she's been mean to him or something I don't understand and now he won't have anything to do with her and I bet she'll leave town and not come back."

"Lots of facts in one long sentence. The only part I understood was that Janelle might leave town," Matt said with a smile.

Kayla retold the conversation she and Ed had with Janelle when they were in his workshop.

"Nothing we can do about it. Brad's not an adolescent. And he's not—" Matt said.

"I know what you think about Brad and my sister as a couple, but maybe they do belong together. Kayla was right going to Brad. We should all go to Brad and try to convince him to hang in there with Janelle."

"I absolutely forbid anyone in this family from harassing Brad. He's our friend. He was my friend first," Matt said. "And why did you leave the store, Kayla?"

"You can't forbid us. You're being silly," Ali said. She scrunched up her lips.

"Celeste can handle the store. What are we going to do? We have to do something," Kayla said.

"For now, we do nothing. Sometimes things work out...with time," Ali said.

* * *

Later the next day, Brad made a visit to Kitchen Bliss. "Is he here?" he asked Celeste who was with a customer. She pointed to the office.

"Hey, man. You don't come by often. Something wrong?" Matt stood and let Brad sit in his chair. Matt took a seat on the nearby stool.

"Your family."

"Tell me about it."

"They mean well. I've heard from or had visits from your in-laws and Ali and even Kayla. Roxie will be the next in line. Can you call them off? Janelle and I are finished. I should have listened to you."

Matt was quiet. "Ali's been working on me. She thinks you two might be able to have a relationship. I disagree. You're better off without her. Lots of women in Georgia. I'll try to straighten them out."

"Thanks for your help. I don't want my non-relationship with Janelle to interfere with the time we spend together."

"Never. I'm on your side. Believe me."

As Brad left Matt's office, he stopped at the counter. "We haven't had a chance to talk lately. Dinner tonight?"

"Sounds like a plan. This time, I'll cook," Celeste said.

Chapter 48

Ali and Janelle were in Ali's kitchen reviewing the previous day's work on their novel. Ali stood and limped to the coffee pot. "I thought it was your right ankle. But, you're limping on your left."

"I fake limped so much I think I hurt the other side of my body."

"You know, I knew all along that you were faking," Janelle said.

"I wasn't faking. . .not at first. You saw how swollen my ankle was. I just stretched the recovery time a bit." Ali bit her upper lip and scrunched her eyebrows together. "How come you didn't squeal on me?"

"I owed you since you've kept my secret about Phoebe. . .you know, the books," Janelle said. "You owe me a big freaking apology. Making me feel guilty for your injury or non-injury. Forcing me to wait on you."

"I don't think you went out of your way to help me," Ali said.

"You're right about that. I'm not much of a caretaker."

"I was trying to milk it as long as possible."

"Now we both have a secret. You are becoming more like me and I'm becoming more like you."

"I wouldn't go that far. Let's get back to work," Ali said. "Besides your secret is a bigger deal than my ankle."

After Kayla and Matt returned home, the writers decided it was too noisy in the Lawrence home to accomplish serious work.

"Tomorrow we'll go to Phoebe's house. I mean my house. Unlike your house, I never have visitors and we can crank this out—"

"Pronto. Fast. ASAP. Immediately."

The sisters laughed.

* * *

"Sounds great. Read it once more," Ali said. The sisters were sitting in Janelle's house at the kitchen table overlooking the garden.

"You liked something *I* wrote?"

"Read it! I've never been to Lake Tahoe so I'm relying on your description, which seems to mirror what I've seen on the internet."

"Howard and I visited that part of the country when we were first married. Didn't have as much money then. We toured California. Yosemite, on to Highway 1, Big Sur." Janelle drifted off staring out the window into the flower garden.

Ali snapped her fingers. "Wake up, Janelle. What's the matter with you?"

She put her hand to the base of her throat. "The emerald."

"The one you gave Kayla, tried to take back, and then gave it to her?"

"Howard bought it for me after he made his first million. Said it reminded him of Lake Tahoe and the fun we had when we were newly-weds." She gazed out the window again. "What were we talking about?"

"Howard."

"Ah yes. Howard promised we would return to California someday and stay at the fancy places we couldn't afford during our first trip. He was a man of his word. He did take me back. Too bad I didn't stay with. . .he wanted children." She returned to observing the garden.

"Tell me about Howard. I didn't have a chance to know him."

"He's the character in my first book, *The Secret of High Mountain Love.* Don't you remember?"

"Sort of," Ali lied. She vaguely recalled a handsome character who was decent and kind, unlike most of Janelle and Phoebe's male characters. "I've often wondered. Why did you keep Howard's name?"

"I don't know. Alliteration maybe." She paused. "Brad reminds me so much of Howard. They even resemble each other. Howard was older though. Enough reminiscing, let's get back to work."

"You had your chance," Ali said.

Janelle shrugged her shoulders.

The sisters resumed writing: Ali at the keyboard and Janelle standing behind her reading from their index cards where they had written ideas for chapters.

After about forty-five minutes, Ali paused. She turned to face her sister. "Look at the time."

"So?"

"We haven't said an unkind word to each other," Ali said.

"Calls for a toast."

They clinked their coffee cups.

"We need more than coffee." Janelle headed to the bar and returned with two glasses of sparkling wine. Her phone rang. "It's *him.* It's Philip. What am I going to do?"

"Don't you trust Dad? He took care of Philip."

"Dad's old—"

"Remember, he was a wrestling champ." Ali tried to hide the smile, which was growing on her face. "Listen to what Philip has to say."

Janelle let Philip's call go to voicemail and put his message on speaker. "You win. I'm outta here. Enjoy your life with your crazy family."

"What's that all about?" Janelle asked Ali.

"Good advice. Take it. Let's get back to work."

Chapter 49

Ali received a text from Janelle asking her to meet at Anna Lee's on Market Place for lunch.

After the sisters were seated, Ali spoke. "This is a first."

"What? Coming here?" Janelle asked.

"No. *You* asking *me* to meet for lunch."

"Perhaps another time you'll invite me," Janelle said. "That would be the sisterly thing to do and it does seem as though we are becoming more sisterly. Don't you agree?"

Ali nodded her head. "I'm also surprised you chose a restaurant that doesn't serve wine at lunch."

"I'm a changed woman. Besides the iced tea here is so fresh. They use limes instead of lemons. No seeds."

"This is where I had our book launch, which you didn't attend. You disappointed many people. Sort of the same way you didn't agree to be my matron of honor and crashed my wedding."

Janelle took the mint from her tea and placed it on a napkin. "If I tell you the truth, will you believe me?"

"If you are convincing enough."

"See. Why waste my time trying to explain?" She took a sip of tea. "Does the name Alexandra Ryane ring a bell?"

Ali turned away from Janelle to read the daily specials printed on a chalkboard hanging on the opposite wall. "Maybe."

"I think it's more than maybe. Here." Janelle handed her sister a white envelope.

"What's this?"

"Open it."

Ali felt her neck redden. Of course, she recognized the name of Alexandra Ryane. She was Howard's stepdaughter who told Janelle if she wrote a book with her sister she would receive a generous amount of money. Ali opened the envelope and a check fluttered out. No note of explanation.

Ali stared at the check. "I'm dumbounded. This is an enormous amount. Why are you giving this to me?"

"To pay for Kayla's remaining three years of college and enough for graduate school, if that's what she wants." She tapped a finger on the envelope. "And, a trip to Italy for the family. This time I'm coming with you."

"I don't understand."

"Of course, you do."

"But we were supposed to finish the novel—"

"Gotcha! St. Ali's a sneak. You read a letter to me marked personal and confidential."

Ali twisted the napkin in her lap. "Guilty as charged."

"Ken Luzi and I convinced Howard's attorney that we would finish the novel. He considers this an advance. Promise not to die on me."

"Janelle, I can explain."

"The gazpacho soup is refreshing on a hot day. You seem to need refreshing."

"Let me explain." She twirled the stem of her water glass. "I have no explanation except pure nosiness. It wasn't any of my business."

"And you are repentant?"

"You want me to grovel? I made a mistake, but didn't I make it up to you by agreeing to write the damn book?"

"Is that all you're going to say?"

"Thank you, Janelle. You don't have to share this money with me. We'll make enough from the sale of our book." She handed Janelle the check. "I can't accept this."

"If you can't, Kayla will."

"Give it back." Ali snatched the check from Janelle. "Matt won't like this one bit. He'll feel indebted to you."

Janelle smiled. "Sounds good to me."

Chapter 50

Ali took her jacket and gloves off as she entered Janelle's home. "Brrr. It's cold out there," she said.

"Coffee brewing. There's a bottle of Bailey's next to the coffee pot," Janelle hollered from the kitchen.

"Remember our rule. No drinking until five p.m."

"I think that was your rule," Janelle said.

Ali met Janelle in the den/library where they did most of their work on their novel. She unpacked her laptop, and sat down, ready to work. "I'm glad you decided to stay here in Phoebe's house and in Willoughby. Although I never in a million years thought I'd say that."

"About the house or Willoughby?"

"Both, I guess." Ali winked at her sister.

"I'm glad, too. For many reasons. Which reminds me. I haven't heard too much from Kayla since she returned to school. An occasional text. It's been around three months."

"She's striving for good grades. . .if studying doesn't interfere with her social life."

"What about Thanksgiving? Will she be home? Only three weeks away."

"She and Luca will be here. He's going to cook Thanksgiving dinner."

"Let's come here, to Phoebe's, er, my house."

"Okay. Then we'll have Christmas at my house," Ali said.

"This house will always be Phoebe's. . .Phoebe's Writers' Retreat," Janelle said.

"The Sisters' Writing Retreat."

The sound of leaves crushing under tires caused the sisters to look out the window.

"You have company," Ali said.

"It's Brad."

Ali stood. "I should leave."

"Sit down. He comes by every week to supervise the gardeners. Although there's not much going on in the yard this time of year. We don't speak." She stared out the window. "Last week we did. I invited him in for coffee."

"How was it?"

"The coffee?"

Ali laughed. "You know what I mean."

"We *might* go out tonight."

"Hmm."

"Just out of curiosity, are Celeste and Brad still dating?" Janelle asked.

"No. Celeste and Logan's father are an item. They seem well suited for each other. I haven't seen Brad with anyone in particular. Actually, haven't seen much of him lately."

"What a waste," Janelle said.

"You had your chance."

"That I did. Let's get to work," Janelle said.

* * *

When Brad invited Janelle out to dinner, he suggested they meet at his townhome on Goulding Place. She preferred to meet in a public place where she could easily retreat in case their conversation was uncomfortable. She chose a popular Cajun restaurant on Woodstock Street.

"Do you believe in communications from the dead?" he asked Janelle after the server had filled their wine glasses and left.

"One of my characters did, but Phoebe, I mean, I decided against it."

"Funny you would mention Mimi."

Janelle took a sip of wine. "Hard to separate you from your grandmother."

"What do you think about this?" Brad asked as he took out a piece of crumbled paper from his pants pocket.

Janelle detected a faint rose water scent. "Where did this come from?"

"Mimi left it in one of the neglected birdhouses swinging from the trees in the front yard."

"Those birdhouses needed sprucing up."

"I decided to paint them and, in the process, found this note. My grandmother's trying to communicate from up there." He glanced toward the ceiling and smiled.

She read the note silently.

"Why are you laughing?" Brad asked.

"She left something similar for me. Not in the birdhouse. In one of our, I mean, my books."

"My grandmother was a smart lady."

"That she was. In fact, you'll never know how smart she was."

Chapter 51

Ali checked her phone for the outdoor temperature before she decided what to wear. A high of fifty-five degrees only required a light jacket. She called out to Matt who was eating breakfast. "Going to Janelle's."

Matt called out to her. "What's the progress report on the book?"

"We're going to send our first hundred pages to Ken today. Another six months and we'll be finished."

"How about taking a break before Thanksgiving? The fall colors in the mountains are at their peak. Should be spectacular."

"I'll check with Janelle. She's become quite the taskmaster. No time off. Even for good behavior."

"We can stay in a yurt," Matt said.

"As long as there's a bathroom, I'm okay." She zipped up her jacket. "What's a yurt?"

Like a little kid, Ali jumped on the leaves overloading the driveway crunching and crushing them. "The sound of fall," she said aloud.

* * *

The sisters were meeting at Janelle's house writing a wedding invitation for their character Sidney Weaverton whose family life was complicated.

"You've been married four times. You should write the wedding invitation," Ali said.

"I eloped every time. You write it."

Ali opened her laptop. "Let's recap. We've given Sidney two biological parents and two step-parents."

"The exes despise each other, and the steps are jealous and want to stick their noses into every aspect of the wedding. As a result, poor Sidney is seeking psychological counseling and suffering migraine headaches. Maybe we should add bulimia."

"Add to the hysteria are Sidney's overbearing sets of grandparents who are picking up the tab on everything wedding related including the honeymoon," Ali said.

"You were wise to orphan her fiancé."

"Search the internet for suggestions for how to write a wedding invitation when the sets of parents despise each other," Ali said.

"Sure." Janelle stared at the computer screen and sat motionless. "'Search'? Like in research? Phoebe did the research for me."

"Forget it. I'll do it."

While Ali was searching and typing, Janelle refilled their coffee mugs.

"How does this sound? The parents of Janelle. I mean Sidney Weaverton, request the pleasure of your company at the marriage of Bradley—," Ali said.

"You're doing that on purpose. You think you're so funny," Janelle said, smiling.

"Promise me one thing," Ali said. "When and if—and I'm not saying you and Brad are planning an event, but you've been pretty chummy lately. Some people in Willoughby consider you and Brad an item. If you take the plunge, please don't elope to Las Vegas. Promise me? Don't cheat us from a grand party with lots of Champagne. Music and flowers, too. Not too many flowers since you seem to be allergic."

"You mean a wedding like yours at Primrose Cottage? The perfect wedding, which I always wanted?"

"Exactly."

"Don't you think I'm too old for a fancy wedding? What would Mother's garden club friends say, especially if I wore white?"

Ali laughed. "Mother would be delighted. Not so much about the white. She'd take any opportunity to show off her beauty queen daughter—no matter how old you are. Do this while Dad can still walk down the aisle. He's been shaky on his feet."

"I'd need a matron of honor."

"You're looking at her, Big Sis."

"It's something to consider. No promises." Janelle's attention drifted as she watched Roxie from the window strolling around the garden sniffing the heliotropes.

"Now, what to do about Sidney and her maniacal family?" Ali asked.

"Elopement! We'll write a marriage announcement instead of a wedding invitation," Janelle said.

"Solves *our* problem, but poor Sidney won't have the wedding of her dreams."

"We're writing fiction. Remember? Sidney does not exist. You're sounding like me when I think of our characters as real people." Janelle began typing. "Let's see what I can do. How does this sound?"

Mr. and Mrs. Preston Weaverton
are pleased to announce
the marriage of their daughter Sidney
to Mr. Roger Bentley on December 24
at Paradise Island Hotel and Casino
in Las Vegas, Nevada

"Could you pick a venue without the word casino in it? Sidney's grandmother doesn't approve of gambling."

Janelle returned to her laptop and let her fingers fly on the keyboard. She stopped typing and turned her laptop to face Ali. "Here's another version." Ali read aloud:

In the spirit of joy and peace this Christmas season
Mr. and Mrs. Edward Withrow
request the pleasure of your company
at the marriage of their daughter Janelle
to Mr. Bradley Patterson
grandson of the late Mr. and Mrs. Joseph Patterson
Saturday, December 23
six o'clock in the evening
Primrose Cottage
Willoughby, Georgia
Dinner and dancing will follow…and the Champagne will flow

"Now who's the funny one?" Ali asked. She read the wedding invitation again with her brow furrowed. "Hmm," she said.

Janelle took something from her pocket and put it on the third finger of her left hand. "Not a joke. Brad gave this to me last night. I wanted to tell you first."

Ali took her sister's outstretched hand. "Wow! It's gorgeous. One humungous rock." Ali grabbed her sister and hugged her. "I'm not totally shocked. You've seemed so happy and—"

"Not as bitchy. Is that what you wanted to say? Be honest, Little Sis."

"Everyone has noticed your personality change since you and Brad have been together."

"He makes me happy and I'm trying to do the same for him. I hope I'm capable."

"I have all the confidence in the world in you."

The teary-eyed sisters hugged.

"Kayla will be over the top. Send her a text right away! Mom and Dad. . .they love Brad."

"What about Matt?"

"He'll come around. He always does."

As usual, Janelle's mascara ran down her cheeks.

"You have to buy waterproof mascara, at least for the wedding," Ali said.

"Look who's giving *me* makeup tips." Janelle wiped the black streaks from her face with the back of her hand. "What about *my* wedding invitation?" Janelle asked. "How does it sound?"

"I like the wording. Let 'er rip."

"Wait one sec," Janelle said. She returned with a bottle of Dom Perignon and three flutes. The sisters lifted their glasses.

"Here's to you Phoebe Patterson. May you *finally* rest in peace," Janelle said.

The End

Acknowledgments

I owe a great big thanks to many people including:

My first readers—Jill Weisenberger (my prom queen sister who sets a high standard for sisterhood, unlike my character Janelle); Debbie Gsell who somehow found the time to read and advise; Pat Armgard who gave me the idea for a mammoni...

My talented writing group—Mary Helen Witten, Beth Carey, and Jason van Gumster. Couldn't do it without you three...

Leah Carey (Beth's daughter) who gave me valuable advice...

Jennifer Steinwart Graham, smart and supportive...

Editor Wayne South Smith, talented writing coach...

My final reader, eagle-eyed Dianne Gillman...

Everyone at Jera Publishing...

To my sweet husband of over thirty years, Roland Steinwart, who honored the *do not disturb* sign on my writing room door. I love you.

Meet Sue Horner

Sue was born in San Francisco and stayed in California for forty years before moving to North Carolina and finally Roswell, GA. *Second Chance Sister* is the continuing story of sisters Ali and Janelle who readers met in *Second Place Sister*. Both novels are set in fictional Willoughby, Georgia. Sue's inspiration for Willoughby is based on the hours she has walked and jogged the streets and parks of charming Roswell. When not writing, Sue can be found on the tennis courts where she participates in ALTA (Atlanta Lawn Tennis Association). When she volunteers at the Roswell Library's used book store, she never leaves without buying a book. Someday, she'll read all the books stacked around her house. Sue has been married to Roland Steinwart for a long time. She is a member of the Atlanta Writers Club, Roswell Historical Society, and the Book Babes. Sue has a degree in American studies from Cal State-L.A.

Dear Reader: Thank you so much for reading my latest story about sisters Ali and Janelle, my follow-up novel to *Second Place Sister*. Will you consider submitting a review to Amazon.com? Amazon requires a minimum number of reviews (no matter how brief) before it will promote or recommend a book. Ali, Janelle, and I will be most grateful. . .and Roxie, too!

Best regards,
Sue

suehorner@bellsouth.net
www.suehornerauthor.com
facebook.com/suehornerauthor

CPSIA information can be obtained
at www.ICGtesting.com
Printed in the USA
FFOW02n1857070718
47289700-50235FF